PF
GILDIN
BY JU

"*GILDING THE LILY by Justir* debut thriller, with twists a.... ..... that you will never see coming." Books Of All Kinds

"*Wow, this book was one of those books that just had me say wow at the end. It is steady to develop. It spans over two years but it pulled me in. I couldn't put it down.*" NovelKicks

"*The author has done a superb job of creating a suspenseful atmosphere, with surprising twists and peopled with complex characters.*" The Library of Clean Reads

"*I thought I had it worked out and although in part I did I just did not see the final twist coming and was left nodding my head in appreciation to the author.*" The Very Pink Notebook

"*I was pulled completely into the lives of Amelia, Jack, Roger and Evelyn, and couldn't wait to see where the story would take me.*" Whispering Stories

"*This fast-paced debut novel, a psychological thriller, captured me from the introductory words and held my attention to the end.*" Goodreads

"*What a brilliant opening to a book...a super suspense thriller that manages to throw in a brilliant couple of curve balls when you least expect them.*" Books From Dusk Til Dawn

"*The author clearly has a talent for writing, I really did want to know where the story would go.*" TripFiction.com

GILDING

THE

LILY

JUSTINE JOHN

Our lives are like the course of the sun,
At the darkest moment, there is a promise of daylight.
Anon

Therefore, to be possess'd with double pomp,
To guard a title that was rich before,
To gild refined gold, to paint the lily,
To throw a perfume on the violet,
To smooth the ice, or add another hue
Unto the rainbow, or with taper-light
To seek the beauteous eye of heaven to garnish,
Is wasteful and ridiculous excess.

Shakespeare: *King John* (1595)

Contents

PROLOGUE

She stood solemnly at the graveside. A single tear ran down her cheek. A man and a woman stood either side of her, and a younger man opposite. They all looked down at the expensive coffin being lowered into their family plot. A few other mourners were scattered around; they formed a small, sad crowd, as the priest said the familiar burial prayer. But she barely heard the words as the coffin settled with an audible thump.

"... commit her body to the earth, for we are dust and unto dust we shall return..."

She looked around her. It was a warm, bright day in September, but there was an unusual wind – a hurricane was forecast. There were many headstones here, and a few statues. Of angels mainly. Different colours but somehow, the same hue. A few trees lined the perimeter fence, some bare, some evergreen. Beyond them, the city buzzed – it went on with its day and didn't notice anyone missing.

The woman next to her was wearing a hat that didn't suit her. It kept catching the breeze, and the woman's gloved hand caught it each time. It was annoying. She should have pinned it or something. She shivered as a gust blew by them and then smiled inwardly. How was it she came to be here? How was it that it all went so well? Was it her own cleverness, or was it luck?

"... the Lord lift up his countenance upon her and give her peace. We ask this through Christ our Lord. Amen."

"Amen," she joined in.

Amen indeed, she thought to herself. The relief was immense. The day after it happened, it flooded through her. How was it she had become capable of such a thing? And now, it was a huge secret. But she had always been good at keeping secrets. It was over now. She could get on with her life.

"The Lord be with you."

"And with your spirit," everyone replied together.

Another gust. She felt it curl around her stockings. The woman next to her snatched at her hat.

"God of the living and the dead, accept our prayers for those who have died in Christ."

She wiped away the tear. The young man opposite caught her eye and sympathetically smiled. She smiled back in a way that said, "Yes, I'm ok, thanks."

And she was ok.

"Let us pray."

They bowed their head; some held hands and some sniffed as they all solemnly recited the Lord's Prayer.

Her mouth moved as she mumbled the words, but her thoughts were still elsewhere.

It was thrilling what had happened. And justifiable. She wondered if she could do it again. But the need would never arise, of course. She now understood how others could do it. This criminal act. How other people could get away with it. If she could do it, anyone could. How many people could be getting away with it right now? Thousands, millions? Was the city beleaguered with people crawling around, getting away with their sins?

"Gracious Lord, forgive the sins of those who have died in Christ."

And, it was easier than she thought. That's what surprised her the most. It was just a matter of thinking it through carefully. Planning well. Did this make her a bad person? She was still the same inside. She was still capable of love, big love, and still wanted to be loved in return. Isn't that what life is all about – what everyone wants? And she felt more... worthy... or worldly, perhaps that was a more appropriate word. She felt more "something" anyway, and that could only be a good thing. To feel more. To be more understanding of other people, and why they do things. Yes, she was still a good person – in fact, a better person. It's not as if she didn't know the difference between right and wrong. What she did was wrong, but also right. She had righted the wrong. It felt good.

"Kindle in our hearts a longing for heaven."

There was a sudden movement from the woman next to her as her hat actually blew off. The woman made a quiet apology as she ran gracefully to the point where it had landed. The wind allowed it to stay there, and she picked it up, before returning to her place in time for the next Amen.

"Amen."

"Lord, have mercy."

Would anyone else forgive her if they found out? Or just God?

She looked for the words in her booklet and joined in again: "... raise us from the death of sin unto the life of righteousness..."

Righteousness? What is righteousness, really? A state of mind? A quality? A knowledge that one is morally correct? What she'd done was morally correct, even though it could be termed bad. So it was righteous. She stood a little straighter. A small movement. Yes, it was righteous. She was righteous.

"May the love of God and the peace of the Lord Jesus Christ console you and gently wipe every tear from your eyes. Amen."

"Amen," she repeated. Amen indeed.

CHAPTER 1 (AMELIA)

I looked down over Ground Zero from 35 floors up. It was early, around 7a.m. one April morning, a few years after the fateful 9/11 when the Twin Towers came crashing down. I took in the aroma of the freshly-made coffee in my hand. It wasn't the jet lag that woke me, but the rainstorm at dawn, an hour ago. It surprised me that there seemed to be no sign of it now, with the sun glaring in the bright, blue sky and flashing off cars lining up at the traffic lights below. Above me, the buildings soared and shined all around and I felt thrillingly small. I loved New York.

Last night had been fun. After our seven-hour flight, and queuing for ages at JFK, we'd begun our visit with Manhattan-style cocktails in the hotel bar, and followed them with dinner in a downtown restaurant, just a couple of blocks away. The wine had soon gone to our heads. Jack had made a joke about petty criminals – it had made me laugh so loud, the other diners had all looked.

I was naked now. I usually try to cover up at all times, as I'm rather plump – and tall. A big girl, my mum would say. I suppose I should be grateful that she didn't say fat. "You take after your father, Amelia, with your height and big bones." I make the best of my good features now – my thick, dark-blonde hair, my smooth, unblemished skin – far less troublesome than worrying about the rest.

I heard Jack snore behind me. I am lucky to have him. He loves my body – relishes me in heels when he has to reach up to kiss me. When I met him, in my late 30s, I said to myself, "Oh I see, that's what everyone means about 'the one'." And he was being brilliant about all the stuff with Evelyn and my dad.

It was a good choice my father made when he moved here in the '70s, after he divorced my mother. Life was better here. But I wasn't allowed to visit then because Helen, his new wife, and I didn't get along. She was so... pretty and well spoken, her accent clipped. So neat and sophisticated. So unfriendly and cold. Like a Disney villainess – beautifully terrible.

But things were different now. We were all grown up. Dad had retired from a wildly successful career in a busy financial office, a few years before this trip. His office had thrown so many parties – it even made the industry news. I had kept the cutting.

The industry legend, Roger Kavanagh, finally retires, aged 72. International CEO of The National Bank is stepping down after 42 years. 'I am leaving the bank in the safest hands,' he stated, at one of the many events to honour his career.

And his handsomely-chiselled, younger face beamed out professionally from the black and white photograph.

With one of his final 1990s' bonuses, when the economy, and he, were still rich, he had bought outright an old Dutch barn-style house with three and half acres, in a beautiful part of Long Island's North Shore, near Glen Cove, called Oyster Bay. Here, Helen and he would live their life perfectly in their understated, affluent way, surrounded by friends, family and any pets or strays that came their way. After various renovations, including landscaping, putting in a pool and adding a new kitchen, it was a true haven for them and every visitor. They were both elated with their new project – their new home. But after only eight months, just before the final completions, Helen met her sudden death in her Honda Civic, at the crossroads at the top of their road, on the way to the grocery store. It was hit, sideways on, by a speeding Mercedes, driven by a local teenage girl, who had run the red light. Helen had died instantly on impact. It was so close to the house that Dad heard the sirens. Two days later, I was on a plane to New York. It was the first of many regular trips. Now that Helen wasn't there, I was finally free to visit.

And visit I did. Frequently. This was the chance I had searched for; to bond with my father at last.

Back in the view from the room, the tiny diggers, and some ant-like men below, worked harder than ever – all moving surely and silently, as if in a slow, choreographed play. Some stood around doing nothing, and there was a crowd of three, leaning over the front of a red pick-up truck, studying a map or plan. Maybe they were discussing whatever the area was going to be – a park, waterfalls, another building – no one seemed sure yet. The window was not quite floor to ceiling and there was a ledge about a half a metre high from the floor. The blind was up (we hadn't bothered to close it last night, enjoying the thought of allowing in the early morning light), and the long, white drapes curtained each side completely. I thought suddenly about standing on the ledge, pressing myself against the cool glass, spread-eagled, and imagined what it would look like from far below, if anyone would see. But I decided it would leave marks.

I looked behind at Jack in the bed, his short, dark curls all mussed, his tanned arms stark against the white sheets. He looked sexy. Good for his age – he'd be 50 soon. That would often surprise people. He looked more like 40. He would have been up ages ago at home. Jack was such a straightforward, hard-working person. Organised. It always took me just a bit longer in the mornings. I wanted to be more like him. As if he heard my thoughts, his eyes opened.

"Nice arse," came his sleepy, Bow Bells accent.

"Thought you were having a lie in," I said, giggling, walking back to the bed. I put the coffee on the side table and slipped under the warm, white linen, allowing him to wrap me in his arms. "Mm. I love it here. I'd like to work here someday. Maybe I can get some contract work out here some time, or even better, open an office."

"You can do anything that you want to do, you're good at that."

I yawned, widely.

"You ok, baby? Feeling jet-lagged?"

"Yeah, I'm ok – nervous about tonight, but we'll handle it, won't we?" I gave him a friendly dig in the ribs.

"Sure. And it will be fun," he said confidently, before kissing me deeply on the mouth.

A little while later, we were lying on our backs, holding hands – his big, green eyes open, my blue ones closed; I was adrift.

"So, what's the plan, Stan?" he said, happily. I felt so sleepy, I could only mutter my reply.

"... go wherever you go..."

"Come on, wake up, its 9a.m. Breakfast – NOW! Or I'll go without you."

"Ok, ok, shower first, me then you!" I was laughing.

"Or together?" he suggested.

We enjoyed a huge American breakfast with crispy bacon, waffles and too much coffee, before heading out into the brightness to find a taxi to take us to the more affordable hotel. The warmth of the day surprised me and I worried I'd be too hot in my jeans. Once our luggage was stored in the trunk ("... it's a boot where I come from, mate," Jack told the driver with a friendly smile and a wink), we climbed onto the tired back seat. Once in the midst of the now less excessive traffic, we headed downtown, asking the driver to take the slightly longer route, giving us the chance to experience the Brooklyn Bridge, rather than the tunnel to Route 27. By the time we reached the Holiday Inn, Brooklyn, I was distracted. This trip was unlike all others because my father did not know we were here. Tonight, there was to be a big surprise party. And he didn't like surprises.

"It's going to be a wondrous event," Evelyn, my father's glamorous new partner, had said a few months previously. He'd met her only a year after Helen's death. I'd thought it too soon. But, of course, I said nothing. He was not one to be told, my father. He was a stoic and professional person, as much outside as in. For me to waltz in say "Don't you think you should grieve a little longer, father, before you throw yourself into another relationship?" just wouldn't be right, and would be met with a severe rebuff. No, Dad knew what he was doing. It was no place of mine to counsel him.

It was clear that Evelyn had once been truly beautiful. I guessed her age to be mid-70s. She was tall, slim and swished around the place like a woman half her age. She also seemed very well connected – either that or she was a relentless name-dropper. But I liked her because she seemed to take me seriously. She approached me as an adult, not my father's little girl, as Helen had always done. The second time I met her though, something strange happened. She was partial to a Martini cocktail or two, and I can't remember her drinking that much that night, but she progressively got more and more inebriated over dinner. When she began to eat her vegetables with her fingers, we decided to leave the restaurant early, and by the time we got home, she couldn't even stand. We helped her up the stairs and into my father's bed (weird), and I stayed with her for a while, just talking to her, making sure she sipped some water. At one stage, she began to cry. I stroked her hair like a child and soothed her to sleep. My father had been furious, and embarrassed. He couldn't bear to even look at her. He loathed drunkenness. The next morning, she was weary and mellow. She didn't bother getting dressed. I was leaving that day, but did suggest my father take her to the doctor – those symptoms seemed odd – she wasn't just sloshed; it could possibly be something more worrying. He rather disregarded the idea to my face, but took her anyway. Turned out she had a small bleed on her brain. They fixed it quickly and painlessly, as I understand it, and I was told not to bring it up again, due to Evelyn's embarrassment.

"I'm not sure it's the right thing to do," I had tried to warn her. I thought it would help. "He hates surprises. He says it's because he can't prepare for them. And I don't think he's that fond of parties either – too much small talk, he says."

"Nonsense." she'd said, determined to ignore me. "Absolute nonsense." I had noticed a few wild, grey hairs falling loose over her eyes as she'd shot a look in my direction.

A sharp sense of annoyance had cut through me at this point, because I remembered Dad's words: "Always be as prepared as you can be – know your audience, your guests, your surroundings." I couldn't recall quite when he'd said that, but it was probably advice he gave me when I was speaking or presenting for the first time after I set up my recruitment agency. He'd been so supportive.

On the other hand, I thought, maybe Dad had changed his mind over the years. He had also told me lately that he thought he'd been "far too sensible for far too long; it was time to have some fun". I had laughed encouragingly. From Evelyn's description, the whole thing did sound fun – perhaps we could really make an occasion of it. I could only try – and I *really* wanted to try.

CHAPTER 2 (JACK)

Jack Jones lay in the bed, smiling to himself, sleepily watching his wife at the window. He liked how things had turned out – working from home, making his own money. There wasn't much of it coming in right now, but he was confident that would change soon. It hadn't been long since he'd retired from the force, after his 30 years, and started his consultancy. Amelia had helped him get going – she knew the ropes, after setting up her own business. He didn't think he could have done it without her. A big swell of love, or lust (he couldn't be sure which), physically moved him as he stared at her bum. He thought about when he first met her. He knew as soon as she walked through his office door, in that black skirt, after he selected her recruitment agency for the volunteers' project, that he loved her. He remembered how he had noticed those legs immediately – his eyes had followed them all the way up from her ankles to that awe-inspiring arse, which was right in front of him now. The way her knees looked pretty as she crossed her legs in front of his desk. That project had bored him with its daily, mundane, paper-pushing exercises. But she had fascinated him. By the time their work was done, they were secretly engaged. He had to marry her. He knew she wouldn't stand for anything less than total commitment. He'd been married before, but he couldn't remember his first wife making him feel like this. And he'd been desperate to get away when she demanded children. Kids were most definitely not part of his plan.

He hoped no one could see her there, standing naked in front of the open curtains. How long had she been there anyway? Was the glass the kind where you could see out but not in? He'd never been a jealous person before. He found it curious that at the same time, he *wanted* other men to look at her. Loved how he had what other men wanted. But they weren't to look for long – that would be like a red rag

to a bull. Before, he'd always played the field; even when he
was married the first time. For him, it was an easy field to
play, and some games were irresistible. As soon as he told
a lady what he did, she seemed to trust him, all of them did.
A policeman wouldn't rape you, a policeman wouldn't steal
from you or hit you. It never occurred to him, the first time
around, that other men might fancy his wife. Amelia was
different. People *always* noticed her.

"Nice arse" said Jack, as Amelia turned away from the
window and walked back towards him in the bed. He held
back the covers for her as she climbed in and curled her
long legs around his. He grabbed her bum and squeezed it,
which made her giggle, and he was reminded of how she
had laughed out loud last night.

"You ok?" he said. She nodded and said she was. He
tried to reassure her about the party later on. He knew she
was worried about it. "It will be fun," he said, confidently.
"There'll be lots of good people there, nice people, and they
will make it fun."

He wondered if Evelyn was a good person. She didn't
seem to be like Roger's other good friends – he couldn't
quite say why – maybe she was shallow. He had only met
her once and found it difficult to relax. She'd annoyed him.
She seemed a bit... thick. He'd pointed out to Amelia that
she hadn't offered any help or advice with accommodation
for the party – of course, they couldn't stay at the house,
that would ruin everything, but wouldn't it be natural to
suggest something – a good hotel, a B&B close by? "Oh she's
probably just wrapped up in organising everything else,"
Amelia had responded, and he'd been impressed that she'd
defended the woman. Evelyn just didn't seem to have a clue
what was going on in the world – if she talked about current
affairs, it would be sound-bites from *CNN* or something. Like
she didn't really understand the complexities of modern
economics, so she had to learn what to say from the media.
He'd tried to test her by asking her view about Afghanistan's
Kunar Province, where a helicopter had crashed recently,

but she'd had no idea where it was – Afghanistan, not the Kunar Province. Most of the criminals he'd known were like that. Very knowledgeable on their own subject, but about any other matters, nothing, *nadda*. They'd pick up opinions from smutty tabloids, without fact-finding any further.

Drug squad days. When his undercover look was hip – messy hair, scuffed baseball boots, ripped denims, a stained t-shirt and a roguish earring. When his only aim was to wipe dealers off the planet (and pull women, sometimes... much of the time. Ok, all of the time.). Those grimy and smoky pubs, with their sticky, dark carpets, stale beer smells, and exhaled marijuana. Black Sabbath or Deep Purple would scream from jukeboxes and the loutish punters would slur their orders noisily across the wet bar. He would sit and watch for hours, like a raptor. Invariably, his prey would be watching too, with his back to a wall for a better viewpoint. The dealer.

"The professional dealer never converses directly with a buyer," he once explained to Amelia, not long after they first met, as if letting her into his secrets. Pleasingly, she was very impressed, even though those days were behind him. "That's the runner's job. Protects him from being identified, you see."

Jack's game, then, was slick – no dealer was safe on his turf. He was particularly proud of how he got Gerry Larkin. They'd been after him for years. Jack had stalked him for a while, watched a deal or two go down, and then set up his team outside the pub. First, they arrested the buyer and the runner as they swapped money for drugs. Then, they brutally busted the pub, which led them to Gerry, the dealer. Easy peasy. All that forensic evidence matching up – three people involved, a conspiracy to supply was in place – bish-bash-bosh. But it wasn't always that easy. To get the buyers to inform – that was the key. Cultivating informants was a hobby – so much more than a job. He could offer freedom in return for information. And lots, interestingly enough, were women on the path of revenge. Yes, those were the best days. Later, he moved onto international surveillance. To say those criminals made a rich living was putting it mildly. It was disgusting. Clever – bloody clever – but obscene. He made a lot of contacts back then – good connections. Knew a lot of people. Could probably still count on some of them.

He respected Amelia's position where Evelyn was concerned. She was trying hard to like her – or at least ignore her irritating traits. She felt a desire to support her father, and he, in turn, wanted to support that. "She's nice. She's... slightly odd. And very rich. But harmless. And I think we can be friends," she had told him after she had met Evelyn the first time. "I think she will make my father happy, and that's what's important."

He sighed and pulled Amelia in closer, taking in the scent of her hair, her skin. It was not his place to judge. He kissed her head and then on the mouth, remembering her words earlier. "Promise you'll help me stay calm at the party," she'd pleaded with him at the airport. She needed him. That turned him on. He kissed her again, harder this time. As the sheet bobbed over his manhood, and she pressed herself against him, he was reminded of just how much.

After breakfast, they checked out and got a cab to Brooklyn. The journey took them over the famous bridge, and when they arrived at the hotel, he paid the driver, uncomfortably, because he wasn't sure how much the tip should be. By the lack of a smile or a thank you, and the screech of the wheel spin, he deduced that he'd got it wrong. As they wheeled their luggage into the lobby of the hotel, he saw a sidewalk florist a few metres down the road.

"You check in, baby, I'm just gonna look for the gents."

"Ok."

But instead, he ran to buy her some flowers – they could only afford one night in the posh hotel in downtown Manhattan, and he wanted to try to make this one lovely for her too. Maybe the flowers would brighten things up and lighten her mood at the same time.

"I love you, Jack," she said quietly when he handed them to her, her smile lighting up the lobby, and then turned to the receptionist. "Can I have a vase for these?"

"A vay-ze? Shoo-re," the receptionist responded, before the porter arrived to show them the way. Jack fumbled in his pocket again for more dollars.

CHAPTER 3 (AMELIA)

Evelyn's invitation had arrived by mail in February. It had baffled us both as we had assumed, after a variety of descriptive conversations, the party would be held in the middle of glamorous Manhattan. But, as a New Yorker, we thought perhaps she'd know something we didn't, and were swept up in her excitement.

> *Please come and help me celebrate with my Roger at his*
> *SURPRISE 75th Birthday Celebration*
> *at an exquisite extravaganza*
> *in a beautiful period Russian nightclub*
> *with chandeliers and the very best cuisine.*
> *7.30p.m. ~ Babushka's, 3650 Coney Island Avenue, New York.*
> *Dress to impress.*
> *RSVP to Evelyn DeGrawe, Apt 1892 Huffington Plaza, NY 10017*

The website for Babushka's, however, diminished the vision. It was described as "New York's answer to Moscow in Las Vegas", with show dancers and pop music until 3a.m. "Everything here is over the top," it promised. This was not my father's cup of tea at all. Not only that, but he'd told me years ago how he'd felt about Coney Island. In the 1970s, not long after he'd emigrated, I had glimpses of the place from films and TV shows, with the magical Luna Park, thrilling fairground rides and candy floss. As a child, it had seemed a guilelessly awesome place and I begged for a visit, but he'd said, "Sweetheart, Coney Island is just a tacky seaside resort. Everything is faded and used up; it's a ghost town now – it's not like it's made out to be on the TV – it's shabby and run down – you'd hate it there." I believed him completely, as I always did.

As we entered the room at the hotel in Brooklyn, we realised how we'd been spoiled the previous evening. It offered the bare essentials in furniture. The sheets on the bed were thin, the blanket old. I imagined that many seedy, illicit sexual encounters had taken place right there, and shuddered inwardly.

"It's only for a night," said Jack, as he hung up his suit, and I arranged the sweet-smelling flowers that he'd so thoughtfully rushed to buy for me, like the man on the Impulse commercial. I inwardly smiled.

***

We arrived at Babushka's on time, as the spring light was fading. On the sidewalk, we gawked at the neon italics above the glass door, and the dozens of tacky fairy lights that hung in the window, in front of a closed, red velvet curtain. A burly doorman, wearing a black bomber jacket and no tie, beckoned us earnestly behind the red rope barrier.

"I busted better-looking joints than this back when I was on drug squad," said Jack, bluntly. I giggled as I pulled out the invite.

"Evelyn DeGrawe's party please." My smile was not returned.

"Downstairs, to the left, table 46," the doorman said, as he looked me up and down. I was wearing an elegant, dark-blue dress that finished above the ankle. I'd been delighted that I'd found it on sale at John Lewis, and it matched Jack's suit so well, but now I wondered if it was too tight around my bum, or too low-cut, or worse – both.

We entered a massive, wood-floored dance hall with a huge, darkened stage at the back. Tables and chairs surrounded the main floor in a ring, going up in levels all around, like a circus, and set so that each table had a good view of the stage. The music was quiet and there was an air of expectant excitement, as other guests filed in and looked for their seats, murmuring enthusiastically.

Everyone, except for Dad and Evelyn, was already there. We saw straightaway that the table was too small – it was set for 12 but only meant for 10. We already knew two of the couples: Ali and Raymond Schilling and David and Elizabeth Reynolds, and their welcome was warm, and inspired with "ohh mi Gaawds" and "how ARE yews". Then we shook hands with two other couples and sat down between them, squeezing in and trying hard not to knock the table's cargo of various beverages.

"Hi, I'm Laura," said the younger lady loudly, over the music, her blonde hair trailing neatly over her shoulders, and her teeth a little too white. "Evelyn is my step-grandmother."

"Oh Laura, yes, I've heard very good things about you." It was true, even though Evelyn had showed me a very flattering picture of her (which stood in a frame on a sideboard in her huge apartment in the City), and described her as "spoiled". "The up and coming lawyer, right?"

Laura blushed and shook her hair with a shy-looking smile.

"That's me – and right now, I'm still looking for an internship, so I guess I won't be up-and-coming until then."

The wine was already on the table, and after checking everyone else's glass was full of something, Jack poured himself a shot of white. He put the glass to his nose, sniffed, and squinted in disgust.

"Don't think you'll like that," he said in my ear and squeezed my knee with his spare hand, while he poured a glass of red.

"Thanks," I said, looking into his eyes, loving his attentiveness. He winked and went off to find a beer.

I looked around the huge space, as it continued to fill, and took in the crowd. Whilst there were many young people, there was also a generous helping of grans and granddads celebrating.

"Have you seen what we're in for?" called Laura, over the now louder music, as she handed me the menu, which also displayed the itinerary for the evening. It was clear that a party in typical Russian style was coming our way.

The feast offered four courses to gorge ourselves with, followed by a lavish performance of cabaret, so glittery and glamorous that it would "make a personal appearance from Liberace appear dull".

"How exciting." I bellowed. Her smile was so big, and her eyes so wide, I couldn't work out if she was serious or not.

Then Ali was sitting down next to me. I was very fond of Ali. She had been very close to Helen – they had been like sisters. It was her who had reassured me that the mistakes with Helen weren't all mine. "She wasn't completely blameless, honey," she had said once. She cupped my face with her hands and kissed each cheek like a clucky mother hen.

"How I miss you, you goygeous darling goil," she said now, with her slanting New York accent. "What about this place?" Ali raised her eyebrows so high, I thought they would break through her hairline. "I mean, it's a little trashy, right? I'm surprised that Evelyn chose it. I'm not sure your father will like it."

"Me too, Ali," I replied, relieved that someone thought the same. "But I couldn't interfere."

"Of course you couldn't, darrling. It will all be just fine and we'll all have a BAWL. She makes your father so happy; she must have a reason for bringing him here."

I turned into the room to look for Jack, and immediately, Evelyn's form emerged in front of me, silhouetted, walking towards us, trailed by my father. Her cracked smile was wide, as she prepared to embrace her guests. I thought she looked absurd in a rich, red velvet dress that fell straight to the floor, black lace covering her bare, skinny shoulders, and a long, black feather stuck precariously, and ridiculously, into her pinned-up hair. Like a Wild West barmaid, I thought. She dropped my dad's hand and left him behind her, open-mouthed, as she welcomed us, one by one, with stiff air kisses. I looked at Dad. He'd gone as pale as Evelyn's face powder, and I felt a stab of sadness. But it was quickly lifted with the cacophony of "hooray" and "surprise" and "happy birthdays" – he finally pulled himself together and smiled with a little chuckle. He greeted everyone with a strong handshake or a gentle kiss. He said no words to me, as he brushed my cheek with his, but he squeezed my hand, which abundantly let me know he was pleased to see me. Then he sat down with a struggle, between Ali and I, and asked the waiter, who had suddenly appeared, for a "very large gin and tonic please, my good man". Evelyn placed herself opposite us and next to her friends. Jack was by my side again, grinning widely, having already bear-hugged my father.

Once everyone was seated, Dad leaned over and said, "How long have you known about this?" The music pounded in the background and everyone chatted excitedly in the dismal light. A sudden sense of panic gripped me because I realised he could be thinking it had something to do with me, or even that it could have been my idea.

"Well, *Evelyn* has been planning it for months, so I understand. She invited us before Christmas, although we didn't know where it would be until a few weeks ago."

"Mm – and what do you think of this place?"

"It seems ok, I guess," I lied. "Everyone seems to be enjoying it." I consciously beamed a huge smile at him.

"Well, I'm not sure I agree. But I think I'm still in shock." And then his voice raised. "Aha, here's my G&T, that's more like it, thank you, thank you!" he said to the waiter, as the drink was passed across the table into his waiting hands. Two large gulps then he leaned across me to Jack. There was laughter but their words were lost in the din. "She loves it here." He was leaning my way again. "Warren, the guy sitting next to her there, that's her step-son..."

"Laura's father?"

"Yes... his sister owns a huge mansion house around here somewhere... have their own private security, who turns away anyone unauthorised. There's a high fence all around it. She's somewhat of a recluse. It's beautiful apparently – backs onto the ocean with its own they used to spend a lot of time there, so I hear never been; can't stand Coney Island. Can't understand why anyone does."

A short while later, whilst I was chatting to David and Elizabeth, who were impressing me with enthusiasm on the benefits of having a house in Grenada, there was a sudden grand arrival of three smartly-dressed waiters. We were all instructed to clear the table to make room for the feast. Noisy rearrangements of glasses and cutlery were made, and the food was passed into the middle. And a feast it was. There was suckling piglet, complete with a small apple in its mouth – it looked guilty, as if it had thieved it from Eden. Beef on a silver tray – sliced, showing a pink middle – and half a roast turkey, which looked dry and crumbly. The food was steaming and its mixed aromas reminded me of school dinners. Perhaps that was the gravy. After the meat was laid out, a few salads were placed precariously near the edge of the table, and then, a seafood medley – Atlantic salmon, peppered prawns and chunky scallops, all laid beautifully on a bed of lettuce and decorated with zesty-looking citrus fruits. Evelyn had booked enough food for twice as many people. It was nice of her to remember that the pork was a favourite of my father's, but it was unfortunate, and obviously overlooked, that half the guests were Jewish. What shocked me more was the presence of the shellfish, to which Dad was dangerously allergic. There wasn't enough room for it all and an extra table was placed beside us. By the time the waiters found a starched cloth to cover it, moved the salads and the seafood, and rearranged the main table again so we all had room to eat, the food was near cold.

Nevertheless, we all feigned delight and tucked in with rapture. More wine was ordered and it flowed like there was no tomorrow. Laughter was loud and the table became a little noisier with celebration. The music was pumping out onto the dance floor. A few party poppers popped and

glasses clinked. But my father was aloof the whole time –
he continued to ensure his glass was full, and gulped each
new refill with a desert thirst. Before dessert was served,
the stage lit up. Badly-dressed performers sang cheesy
songs in Eastern European accents, and did their best to
encourage the audience, whilst behind them, a PowerPoint
presentation of birthday-themed pictures flickered. A child
could have done better, I thought, as I wondered what
was going through his mind. The dancers reminded me of
amateur cheerleaders; out of time and turning the wrong
way. When they did the can-can, we all cringed, and my
father drank more wine.

Once the show was over and the raucous, but
questionable, applause had died down, Evelyn took the
chance to stand and tap her glass, bringing us all to quiet
expectation. We turned to look at her.

"Welcome, everyone," she said, looking back with her
watery eyes, her smile wavering. I noticed her crimson
lipstick had bled into the creases above her lips. Jack
nudged me in the side. "Thank you all for coming to
celebrate wonderful Rogey's 75th birthday." She clapped
and we all followed suit. Dad looked down, embarrassed.
He hiccupped. "Happy birthday, darling, I hope you enjoy
the evening. And now, speeches! Amelia! You first, say some
words?"

I jumped as she said my name. I stared at her and she
stared right back, unwavering. I was completely unprepared.
But I stood anyway.

"Happy Birthday, Daddy, and many happy returns – Jack
and I are so happy to be able to celebrate with you tonight."
I bent and kissed him fondly on the cheek and he blushed.

"Now, Warren" Evelyn said, and looked at her step-
son. Laura had explained that he was a highly-respected
Californian lawyer, as was his own father, Laura's
grandfather. "Grandpa Thomas DeGrawe" had passed away
some time ago, devastating Laura, and leaving Evelyn (his
third wife) to carry on alone in New York. Laura's mother

(Warren's wife) was an artist, and was too busy to join the party, deciding to remain at home in California. Warren duly stood, and waffled on confidently and loudly about how he hadn't known Roger for long but what a great person he was, and how he had made Evelyn happy, and then he thanked her for organising such a wonderful event and for being his friend, and for being so good to his late father, and a great influence on the kids, and introducing him to Roger. On and on and on. About 10 minutes later, he finally sat down. If there had been a glimmer of a hope for a good atmosphere, this had killed it.

Then my father stood up boldly. Aside from having to use the back of the chair to balance, it was a definite movement – one that said: *now listen to me*.

"Thank you all for coming tonight" he said, slightly slurred. "I don't know what Evelyn wants from this. It's not exactly what I would have chosen." He began a smile, but opened his mouth to take an audible breath before it became complete. "Perhaps she thinks I will leave her my fortune in my will, mm?" and he looked pointedly at her. She looked down and giggled in a Scarlett O'Hara kind of way. "But I suppose I should say thank you for remembering my milestone." He raised his glass to everyone before slumping back into his seat, his eyes down toward his scraped-out dessert bowl. There was a short hush from the group – Jack started clapping in an attempt to appease the embarrassed silence. Thankfully, the rest followed. Raymond said, "Happy Birthday Roger," his glass still up in the air. I stole a glance at Evelyn – she had stopped smiling and looked very hurt. I felt quite sorry for her and was compelled to console her. I thought it unnecessarily rude, what my father had said. Once the crockery and cutlery was cleared, I stood and walked over to her side.

"Great food, wasn't it?" I began, bending down to her ear, as the disco had started now.

"Yes, they're known for their culinary skills here." She dabbed elegantly at her cheek with a ladies handkerchief.

I spotted an embroidered "E". "... but," she paused "... it's not quite what it used to be somehow." She glanced at me quickly, meeting my eyes, and then away again, like a bird.

Still stooping, I said, "Don't worry about Dad. He's a bit drunk. He'll come around. You did a great job." I smiled, but she just looked at me blankly and I felt awkward. A tap on my shoulder relieved me of the need to find something else to say.

"Amelia, how lovely to see you. Are you in town for long?" It was Raymond, coming back from the bar, more wine in hand. I allowed myself to be rescued.

"Not this time, we fly back tomorrow night."

"Hey, that *is* a flying visit," he said, "Well, we won't let you go without chewing the fat a little," and led me by the elbow over to Ali's empty seat (she was flirting playfully with Jack across the table). After placing two bottles in the ice-cooler, he leaned in close to whisper, "Watch that Laura DeGrawe. From what I hear, she's not to be trusted."

"Really? What do you mean... she does seem ambitious, but in a good way. When I was chatting to her, she was telling me she wants to be an even better attorney than her father and her grandfather, but was struggling without their help. I did wonder why they weren't supportive, but didn't ask – I don't know her well enough."

"Well, I don't know..." he said, "just don't believe everything she tells you. Evelyn informed us that she'll stop at nothing to get what she wants. Apparently, there was a big thing at the school when she was accused of cheating in some way in her examinations..." I looked around for Laura, but her chair was empty.

"What?" I said, disbelievingly.

"That's what Evelyn told us. It's why she and Thomas fell out and she stopped coming to New York so much."

"Oh – well, I'll try to remember that." It just didn't seem believable. But then again, I'd only met the girl that night.

A little later, when the music was booming, and the remains of the feast (dessert bowls and nearly all the pig

– I questioned why they hadn't taken the meat earlier) had been quickly cleared, I led my drunk father uneasily to the packed, throbbing dance floor, where we joined Elizabeth and David. They waved welcomingly and over-exaggerated their swaying hips. Teenagers wearing grungy, wide jeans and baggy t-shirts, or squeezed into skin-tight, brightly-coloured dresses, body-popped and swaggered. A 90-year-old man, who was gyrating with reckless abandon in a shiny suit two sizes too big for him, made me laugh, and I discreetly pointed him out, along with his geriatric partner in a sequined mini-dress and knee-high boots – they both looked so happy. But my father could only stomach a few seconds of what he probably thought was humiliating, and announced to my ear "I can't do this", before staggering away to the men's toilets, leaving the three of us staring after him. David followed, and Elizabeth and I returned to the table. Fifteen or twenty minutes passed before David returned alone, looking rather dishevelled.

"Roger's not well – he was practically passed out, sitting on the floor against the wall – we need to get him home. I've got a car waiting. He's ok now, and Lizzy and I can go with him."

In what seemed like a flash, most of us were outside, in the fresh night air, clucking over Dad, whilst Evelyn looked on from the side, morosely. David helped him into the roomy back seat of a black sedan, strapped him in, and got in the other side. He lolled slightly. Then I heard Evelyn in my ear and her long nails dug into my upper arm.

"Your father does not want me to accompany him home tonight, he doesn't seem to appreciate anything I've done for him. I'm very displeased. You organise everything from here because I'm leaving for Manhattan now!" And before I had the chance to reply, she whirled off to the blue Mercedes behind and elegantly slid into it, pulling the door closed behind her. It swerved slowly out into the empty street, blinding us momentarily with its headlights, and was gone.

Elizabeth had now squeezed into the back seat of the sedan. Dad was looking out of the open window, gulping like a goldfish, and finishing a stilted, but amusing, conversation with Raymond. They tried to shake hands but my father missed and grabbed a handful of warm night air instead, making Ali laugh affectionately. Laura, her father, or the other couple, who we hadn't even spoken to, were nowhere to be seen. I kissed my father on the cheek.

"See you tomorrow, Dad. Sleep well."

He nodded, and when he spoke, he sounded surprisingly sober. "Just make sure you're on time – noon, ok? Because I'm not sure I will be punctual!" His chuckle reassured me.

"Look after him," I mouthed to David, and blew them all a kiss as I stepped back. The tinted window rose up and the cars pulled away, leaving us alone on the pavement with Ali and Raymond, our four shadows flicking on and off with the flashing, neon light behind us.

"I knew it was all a mistake, I absolutely knew it," I said sullenly, and sighed deeply.

"Aw, don't blame yourself, honey, everyone will think it's funny in a week or two, just you wait and see," said Ali.

"Yes", Jack agreed, "and there's nothing more we can do tonight." He put his hand on my shoulder, and turned me back to toward the building and the party to join the others.

CHAPTER 4 (EVELYN)

Deep down, I know there could have been no other way. I breathe deeply the scent of sweet protection and pray to the Lord that I never lose it. Because, without my strength, I would be nothing. Dead as well.

These days, my thoughts are all over the place. That's why I have to take a deep breath and compose myself. Like this. Sit on a chair, slow things down. Put them in order. Just talk to myself and go through things one by one by one. Roger will stay with me. He will love me and marry me. He will take care of everything.

I saw something in her eyes that reminded me. That girl. She terrified me in the middle of the night. Woke me up by whispering evil things in my ear. *You goodfanothing wetsmack. You no' but a dingy crumb. You'll grow up to be a ho, just like your mama.* How I wanted to hurt her. More. I only managed a slap once. A few kicks. And a stab in the leg with a pencil, which broke in two. But the reprimands were too painful. She was bigger than me and knew my weak point. I was so young. So unhappy. Breathe deep the scent. Slow it down.

The Home was the old Forrester farm, outside the city limits in Indiana County. There was a long dirt road from the highway that led there. It went on and on. In the summer, there was so much dust that sometimes, I found it hard to breathe. I used to get a stick and write in the sand. Daisy. Is. Mean. *Her* eyes remind me of Daisy's. Her *eyes*. Breathe deep.

We were mostly orphans. But there were some old people there too. Old people with no family or money. A lady with no husband. Daisy had family. A mother. But her mother couldn't control her. I was there because my father was dead and my mother was sick in the head and was taken away. I don't remember either of them very much. I had pictures of them both once. Whatever happened to that old photo? I learned to swallow the missing feeling. Swallow it down like a little pill. All gone.

When I was old enough, I worked in the fields. All those rows of golden corn. Blood-red tomatoes. Ugly, old potatoes. Hate potatoes. Roger loves potatoes. And tea. He loves his tea. Clothes and hands were always dirty. And sore. My knees too. I remember the schoolhouse because I liked it there. It was in the big barn and it smelled of oil from the tractor. I enjoyed the learning. I could sit far away from Daisy. Daisy shut me in the linen closet once – where the shirts and pants were kept. No kid owned their own clothes. We just picked from the closet. Sometimes they fit, sometimes they didn't. It was so dark in there. It smelt funny – acrid, like rat shit. The panic grew and I screamed until my voice was harsh and my throat sore, the snot dried crisply, and the tears stained my face in clean tracks down my dust-caked cheeks. I was in there for hours. I thought I might stop breathing. I don't like small spaces now. Small spaces and Daisy's eyes.

I have to swallow down that fact that Amelia's eyes remind me of Daisy's. Swallow it down. That's in the past. All gone. Breathe the scent. It's something about the colour. The slant. But I must be nice to her. She is Roger's daughter, after all. He loves her. She won't get in the way. And she lives too far to be a nuisance. Maybe I will learn to like her. She IS nice, isn't she? It was Daisy who wasn't nice. This isn't Daisy. Swallow the pill. Breathe. Breathe the scent. Look how far I've come. I've controlled this. I can do it again.

Maybe we could be friends. She was good to me, that time when she helped me up the stairs. That time I was ill.

And how I'd love to have a friend.

As I grew, so did the desire to leave, and one dark night, I ran. I think I was 15, maybe a year younger. I remember the hard ground through the hole in my shoe, and my breath, loud in my head. The thrill of the first couple of hours – scared of every shadow, frightened of each turn. I took some money from the jar in the kitchen, some clothes from the closet, and some pie from cupboard. I thought everyone would wake at the sound of my beating heart. It was summer, and warm enough to sleep out under the long bridge. No one saw me and the next day, it wasn't hard to get to town. The shop owner caught me stealing apples. But she ended up allowing me to stay for a while. Mrs Cullimore, I think, but I don't quite remember. I told her a different name and I cut my hair short, like a boys, so even if they did look for me, which I don't think they did, they wouldn't recognise me. I cleaned in return for board and lodging. I did my very best. She sent me to her sister's farm in Connecticut, and I worked there for actual money. I must have stayed there for two years. They were good women. I should have stayed in contact.

I was 16 when I met Daniel. He was 18. He worked on the farm next door. I only knew I was pregnant when my body began to bloat. He ran. He would be whipped if they found out. I would too, and thrown out, I was sure, so somehow, I managed to conceal it. It came early anyway. I remember the pain in my stomach, my legs, my heart, my back – the force of it doubling me over, paralysing me. I took off to the woods and the stream there. I remember the smell of the peaty moss, and the dead leaves and the blood, turning my aching stomach, as I buried my face so no one would hear the wailing. I used the leaves and moss to mop up the mess, before I plunged it in the water, watching the globs ebb and separate. I had the sense to take another dress with me, and buried the blood-stained one. I swallowed the anger and the hurt. Swallowed it down like a little pill. All gone. No one ever knew. They thought I had a fever from the lily of the valley, which was crushed into my hand, and they gave me medicine. But they never knew.

After the war ended, I went to my first dance. I met a European boy, Ernie. His family were all due to go home the following year. But their city in Austria had been bombed and devastated. They would stay a few more years. He enrolled into school in Boston and we married while he was still a student. I looked beautiful, of course, and his whole family were there. We lived with his parents at first, but I think they hated me. They sent me off to school so I could learn to be a secretary. I kinda liked it and they told me I would be able to earn a good wage with the skills. They eventually went back to Europe, and we stayed so he could finish his studies, and I did get a job, but as a waitress. It didn't go down very well, but they gave us enough money to rent an apartment anyway. He did well, graduated, and went straight into a highly-paid job. He worked hard. One night, he got drunk. I wouldn't put out and he grabbed me by the arms and bruised them badly. I wore long sleeves for an age. It became more frequent and he ended up using my body like a punch-bag about once a month. Around that time, I came across some lily of the valley in the woods. I recognised its beautiful scent – like citrus, honey, and jasmine all mixed, curiously reminding me of spring and happy times. It was May. It comforted me.

Ernie died after we'd been married for only two and a half years – a fatal case of food poisoning. It was 1953 and I moved to New York City. It was humming, hectic, *alive*. Marilyn Monroe and Elvis dominated the theatres and gossip columns. Eisenhower was just in. TVs, poodle cuts, big skirts and Jackson Pollock. Oh, what a time. I was so happy then – free from guilt and rules. I was thankful for the secretary's course that Ernie's family had paid for. He had saved a good amount of money, which he kept under the mattress. It was enough to get me started. I never saw his family again – went back to my maiden name and never told anyone that I had even been married. I was 21, the world was my oyster and, well, no one needed to know that, did they?

I start to shake, so I breathe deep the scent of the lily of the valley in the jar on the table, and I relax. It's trivial to get upset at how childish Roger's daughter is, how *insipid*, because I can control it. Control her. See how I've controlled my life? I am strong. The scent makes me stronger. Look how well I deal with problems. But how he seems to dote on her. He said they got closer to her after his wife died. He distanced himself from her after he left her mother, and she resented him for a long time. But now, he said she was truly there for him. He felt bad for not always being there for her. Wants to make up for it somehow, some way. But he should dote on me like that too – I am there for him now. Me. Not her. She can't look after him. Pah! Listen to me... she lives on the other side of the ocean. She is no threat. Breathe. Swallow. Breathe the scent of sweet protection.

CHAPTER 5 (JACK)

The dark clouds matched Jack's mood. Amelia had been right all along – it had been the disaster she had predicted, and he had been unable to fix it.

He sighed and squeezed Amelia's hand, then smiled at her quietly and she mirrored him. His arm crept around her shoulders gently as they bounced over a bump in the road. They were in yet another cab on the way back to Manhattan, and Evelyn's apartment. He shifted uncomfortably – his back was sore from the lumpy, old mattress. One day, he'd be able to afford five-star all the way. He was not looking forward to the night flight home later. They'd stayed up most of last night, berating Evelyn's blundering arrangements, and agonising over Roger's reactions. They were to leave their luggage there then go together to the Yale Club for lunch. She had instructed them not to be late because she and Roger had plans for that evening. The "gift giving" was to take place back at the apartment over coffee, before they left for the airport. This was the only part of the trip that Amelia had been looking forward to.

"Please, please let it be good," he said to himself.

"The Yale Club is unique and exclusive," Evelyn had told him last night. This had irritated him – it's what she'd said about the bloody Russian club too. And anyway, what did he know about Yale? Something to do with law degrees? This "club" was probably full of tossers. A "club" for stuck-up, rich Americans who put themselves above others, just because they had a law degree, *from a special school*. He could see that Evelyn enjoyed associating herself with those sorts. He didn't like school and had left as soon as he could to join the cadets. He remembered his East London comprehensive, where there was regular fighting – and how, aged 11, he had beaten up the school bully, smashing his nose to bits, the blood smearing the boy's face and his own hands. He'd come close to being expelled after that, and his mother had proverbially rubbed salt in the wound by beating him hard with a wooden spoon. He'd only been protecting his little brother, Kevin, who was autistic. They'd called him a "stupid spastic".

At 11.55a.m., they arrived at Huffington Plaza, a 39-storey office and apartment building on the east end of 52nd Street, near the river. Evelyn lived on the 17th floor. After taking care of their luggage, the friendly, uniformed doorman ushered them over the thick carpet to the elevators. Jack quickly shoved some dollars into his hands, as he'd done with the cabbie, this time, not caring about the reaction.

Their gift for Amelia's father was tucked securely under her arm, encased in protective polythene bubbles, carefully wrapped in soft, brown tissue paper, and tied gently with a black ribbon. Roger was not an easy man to buy for and Amelia had always struggled with presents. She cherished the idea of delighting him with something wonderful, to see his face light up with joy at the fact that she, his daughter, had chosen so well. But this had eluded her always. Perhaps until now.

It was a small, square, specially commissioned oil painting of Roger's beloved Cotswold cottage, where he had lived after he and Amelia's mother had separated, and where he stayed now, if a visit to the UK allowed the time – usually for a week at Easter and two weeks over summer. His Christmas stays at the cottage had ceased after Helen was killed. Amelia had found several old and slightly faded photographs of it on a blue sky, sunny day, and carefully researched and chosen a painter whose expertise was in old buildings. The detail was vital – pink and red roses around the door, the honey colour of the 200- year-old bricks, the steepness of the gables, and the deepness of the terracotta roof. It had wide, stone-framed windows and nestled comfortably in its own little garden, which was crowded in the summer with colourful wild flowers. Over the back fence was a charming wood, where bluebells would grow tall and thick each spring. Amelia had told Jack that, as a child, she spent precious moments sitting on the grass and watching the bees and the butterflies that flew frantically between the blooms, buzzing and flip-flapping. Even in the winter when frost coated the lawn and the icy air chilled the glass panes, the walls seemed warm with a glow, as if they had secretly collected the sun's rays months earlier. The painting was stunningly accurate.

"It's beautiful," Amelia had said when they picked it up from the studio. "You can almost smell the honeysuckle when you look at it. Oh Jack, he will adore it – I can't wait to give it to him. This painting will be the gift of all gifts, the one that touches his heart. Finally, I've done it – at least, I hope I have."

When Evelyn had first told them about the party last year, Amelia had tried to be supportive. When they'd got back to London, she'd even asked Evelyn's advice, by email, on what to buy Roger for his big birthday. But the reply had been disconcerting and, Amelia thought, insulting.

Amelia

It is clear to me that you are very different from your father. Your gifts to him don't ever seem to be quite to his taste, or he already has something similar. But he would never tell you this. We prefer not to clutter the house, so we usually put your gifts in the garage or the little guest apartment above, so they can still be enjoyed. I'm only saying this to try to help you. Since you asked for suggestions, it would be great if you could contribute to the cost of an original antique ship painting that I am purchasing from Christie's for him, by one of his favorite artists. It cost $6,000 – or, if you cannot afford that, then some help with the drinks at the party would suffice.

Evelyn

It gave Amelia the whole idea of the commissioned piece, and the irony was not lost on Jack.

Evelyn opened the door and stood aside, indicating that they should enter. She was stony-faced and didn't smile. Perhaps she was hung-over too, Jack thought. He had watched her down at least three Martinis, as well as wine.

"Hello Jack, Amelia. Your father is in the drawing room."

They returned the greeting, but they didn't embrace her. It was Jack's first visit to the apartment and Amelia's second. Evelyn led the way, through the hall, where there was a musty smell, a bit like a vintage clothes shop, past a couple of doors, and into the L-shaped lounge.

Jack opened his eyes wide and then whistled softly. The huge floor to ceiling windows allowed in a glorious sight of the impressive, celebrated skyline. He could see skyscrapers all around, some shorter, some taller, and a small section of the Queensboro Bridge was visible through the structures. This view is probably worth a million alone, he mused. He tore his eyes away to see Roger, sitting in a leather Regency armchair and Amelia, who was crossing the room towards him. He looked around quickly – the furniture was an odd mix of antiques and modern items that didn't quite match. Even though the decor had an unmistakable '70s feel to it, it was voguish and elegant – Evelyn's expensive taste was clear. Two long, sky-blue sofas placed opposite each other beckoned visitors to relax. But something was missing – it was warmth.

Amelia had put the painting down on one of the sofas while she embraced her father, who was standing now. Their hug made Jack smile.

"Hi Dad," Amelia said over her father's shoulder, "happy birthday, again."

"Hello Amelia. And thank you," and he did a quiet, little chuckle, before letting her go and sweeping his hand out toward Jack.

"Jack." He looked tired but much happier than the night before. Perhaps they had kissed and made up.

"Lovely flowers," Amelia said to no one in particular. She was referring to a glass vase, filled with a stunning arrangement of lily of the valley, its long, green leaves cradling an abundance of tiny, white flowers, which was set on the sideboard behind one of the sofas. "They smell divine – oh, and roses too. So, did you sleep in, Dad, or were you up with the lark as usual?"

"Well, I did get up late, but I felt it was well deserved." He gave her a knowing look and smiled.

Jack laughed. "All that celebrating, you see, not good for your health."

Evelyn cut in. "The flowers are from your father's garden. I'm a very keen gardener, you know, always have been. I've been replanting some things there, helping it along a little as it's been a tad neglected, you see."

Roger cleared his throat loudly. "So, now that we are all here, we can go," he suggested, changing the subject and making it clear that questions about last night were most certainly not allowed. "Laura is meeting us there."

"Great – I'm looking forward to seeing her again, and to this lunch," said Amelia. "Lead the way, Evelyn." Evelyn didn't look at her, but put her arm through Jack's.

"Jack, you will love the food there, it's divine. I have been a member for years, and after Thomas died, bless him in heaven, they let me remain so. It's delightful to have the opportunity to share it with guests." He caught a waft of her perfume and allowed her to lead him away from the sunny city view.

***

"Good afternoon and welcome to the Yale Club. It is forecast rain today; I hope you have your bumbershoots?"

Amelia and Jack looked quizzically at each other while Roger leaned in. "Colloquialism for umbrellas," he explained.

Evelyn smiled daintily at the man and said, "Why, yes of course," and tapped the side of her designer handbag.

The man led them to the restaurant, which was on the first floor. Jack thought the place had an air of self-placed aristocracy. It was a huge, bright space. Red leather chairs set at square tables, draped in white. High above, thick beams were exposed. Several bold archways lined one side of the room, behind which was a fully-stocked bar, where an aproned cocktail waiter was shaking a shiny mixer. Laura sat on one of the high stools. As soon as she saw them, she waved, picked up her clutch, along with a glass with a straw sticking out, and came towards them.

"Hi everyone, how's it all going?"

"Hello Laura," said Amelia, kissing the air to the side of Laura's face.

"Lovely to see you again," said Jack.

"Hello dear, you look very nice," said Roger, and kissed her on the cheek. Evelyn said nothing.

Another waiter took them to a table where they sat and unfolded stiffly-starched napkins. Everyone remained quiet, except for Evelyn, who was beginning to explain the history of the venue, as if she were a tour guide and it were the most significant building in the world. Amelia leaned to her right where her father sat.

"Is it really as good as she says?" But he just raised his eyebrows in a "see for yourself" kind of way.

They quickly chose their meal from the oversized menus, and the wine, which Evelyn had chosen without consulting anyone, was generously poured. In a kind of protest, but also wanting to avoid the certain drowsiness she knew would follow, Amelia refused and stuck to water, as did Laura. Evelyn continued to inform Jack about the Library and the wedding of one of her friends' daughters that took place there. Laura was quiet but she agreed enthusiastically with everything that Evelyn said. The starters were served, and everyone relaxed and fell into enjoyable chatter.

Laura was impressing on Jack how determined she was to be a good lawyer. "Eventually, I'd like to end up dealing with human rights. And Amelia said last night she would introduce me to one of her work contacts, who is high up in a big American law firm in London."

Jack encouraged her. "Ah well, you're in luck then – Amelia knows some bigwigs – she'll help you fill your little black book, that's for sure." He managed a glance over and was happy to see that Amelia was proudly telling her father about the award her company had recently won.

"There was a big gala dinner at the Grosvenor House Hotel on Park Lane, and we invited our best clients to join the celebration..." He knew she had been dying to tell Roger. The little girl inside her wanted so much for him to be proud of her. She was explaining every detail and Roger was listening intently. Because of this, Amelia was last to finish her first course. The other empty plates where whisked away and the space they left was filled with main courses. So it surprised them all to see that, even though Amelia's plate was not empty, and her knife and fork was still in her hands, a waiter abruptly pushed it to one side and plonked down her main course too. She looked up to protest, her mouth still full, but the waiter was walking away. She swallowed and looked with dismay at Jack, who laughed, for want of anything better to do. Her gaze moved to her father, who was watching the waiter and trying to get his attention. Across the table though, Evelyn was waiting like a hawk. When their eyes met, she lashed out.

"What's wrong, Amelia? From the look on your face, you despise the food, the wine, as well as the waiter."

Jack took a deep breath, as if willing Amelia to remain calm. He could see she was shocked by the maliciousness of the elder woman's tone.

"I don't despise anything," Amelia said, her voice hushed. "I'm just a bit surprised that they brought the main course before I'd finished the starter – I thought the service was supposed to be second to none here. That wouldn't happen in London."

"You spoiled little bitch – you wouldn't know good service if it hit you in the face." it was a slow hiss, and they all looked at Evelyn.

"Evelyn!" Roger muttered and his glare silenced her.

"I'm sorry," she said, visibly upset and suddenly searching for something in her clutch bag. "Please excuse me, I am... very sorry." she said, a pinkness rising in her cheeks as she pulled out a tissue. She stood and left the table quickly.

Roger tried to cover for her. "Evelyn had a lot to drink last night – I don't think she's feeling on form."

Jack thought it would be good to get out of the firing line as soon as possible. "Shall we go right back to the apartment after this then?" he said politely "Avoid too much hanging around?"

"I agree," said Amelia and Laura together.

Roger rolled his eyes, but nodded and drew in his cheeks. "It probably would be best," he agreed, and began tucking into his duck.

***

An hour later, they were back in Evelyn's apartment, sitting on the blue sofas. The rain had begun, leaving wet, silvery streaks on the huge windows – the room was dark and Evelyn had switched on a couple of lamps. Gift giving time.

"Amelia, why not go first."

Jack looked at his wife. He recognised that this was the most important moment of their trip – why they had gone along with the idea of the party, travelled the night flight, stayed in the cheap, grotty hotel. For Amelia, her father's happiness was paramount, and he could see it in her eyes.

"Yes, ok," and she picked up the carefully-wrapped painting and handed it to Roger. All of a sudden, he looked somewhat brighter as he took the parcel from her and began to slowly unwrap the ribbon she had so carefully tied. The bubble-wrap proved a bit tricky, but once it was off, the pure pleasure shone from him like an aura. Amelia almost visibly swelled with happiness, the smile about to stretch out of her cheeks. Jack could almost touch the sense of joy that had formed around her and her father.

When Roger looked up, he said, "Well, I'm almost speechless. Its very pleasing, Amelia, thank you. Thank you very much." In a moment of joy, the sun suddenly came out from behind a cloud and shined into the apartment, as Roger embraced his daughter lovingly. Jack thought Amelia might burst into to tears, but if she wanted to, she hid it well.

"Show it to me," said Evelyn. Her eyes scanned the canvas. "Oh. It's nice. What is it?" she asked, unmoved.

"Dad's cottage in England. It's in the Cotswolds."

"How thoughtful."

Roger was now carefully unwrapping the next surprise. The other painting, from Evelyn – presumably the one from Christie's that she'd described in her email. It was a dark and dismal representation of a stormy sea scene, with a troubled tall ship being battered by high waves and white foam, its beautiful sails billowing. It was a dramatic, attractive piece that told the story of bravery and stamina.

"How marvellous," was Roger's simple reaction.

"Yes, it's by a British painter, darling, Alfred Vickers, who lived in the 19th century." Evelyn looked across at Amelia with a little, triumphant glint.

"Very nice. Thank you, Evelyn," Roger said genuinely, before he handed it back to Evelyn to put safely away. She leant it against the wall so that it commanded the room. Jack noticed that she had quickly re-wrapped the smaller painting and laid it flat on the table next to the flowers. He knew Amelia would have noticed too. He moved a little closer to her so their knees touched.

"My gift is smaller, and *not* a painting," smiled Laura, who handed him a little, white box. It contained a silver pocket watch with a short chain.

CHAPTER 5 (JACK)

Roger leaned back and sighed. "I'm a very lucky man to have such wonderful family and friends," he said platonically, but with meaning. Amelia took Jack's hand and squeezed it. All of last night and lunchtime's upset disappeared through the tall windows and into the cool air outside.

CHAPTER 6 (EVELYN)

I will never love Roger but he is so nice and I'm very lonely. It's taking ages to persuade him into marriage. He says he doesn't want to wed again. But I think he will eventually. It's so important, I believe. And maybe one day, we can grow the lily of the valley, here in Oyster Bay. It won't grow there in New York. I need to be there too because I don't want pesky Laura going through my stuff. It is my private place. Thomas' possessions are still there. I don't want to let go of them. I don't, I won't. But how will I afford to stay, if Roger doesn't... Oh, there is a tear in my eye now, I can't catch my breath. I must breathe deep. Deeply the scent. Breathe it in. Control it. I can control it.

Roger is lovely. We go to nice places, fancy restaurants, and he has taken me to Bermuda twice now. The daughter is a pain though. God, those eyes. They appear to me in dreams. Daisy's eyes. The dreams started again after I met her. And that husband of hers. Well, he's so arrogant. And I can't understand his accent. I want to like them both, but I don't seem able. She doesn't know her father. Not like I do. I don't want her here. So I have to pretend. Otherwise... there would be consequences. And I don't want him to pay her attention. *I* need him more than she does. And he needs me. Not her. Breathe. Breathe. The scent of the lily.

In my first job, I had a relationship with my boss. It just lasted a few months. He was married already. I didn't love him, but sleeping with him helped me get promoted. Only then, I ended things with him. But he wanted me back, and when he said he'd rent me an apartment of my own, I decided not to leave. He'd give me pocket money to spend on clothes. We continued for a few years. I was ever fastidious with my "wages". I travelled around a lot – even to Europe once with my friend, Joan. Then I fell in love with Richard, who was an up-and-coming executive in a big insurance firm. Richard was the only man I ever really loved. He was handsome and funny, and he took care of me like no one else in my life had ever done. We were married in May 1961. I tried to give him children but I couldn't. I won't think of that time as it's too upsetting. But Richard was good to me. He had a place in Coney Island, which I adored, and could afford a small apartment in the city too. We just lived the best life. Oh, the parties! And we used to go to Babushka's every Friday night and dance and dance and dance. It was beautiful there with all the glitter balls, the fancy decorations and the music. And Betty and Donald would throw the best parties. It really was the finest time. I miss Richard still. I miss those times. I am sad that he died. But it turned out that he was almost bankrupt. I hadn't known. I lost everything when I lost him. I stayed with Betty for a while – it must have been 1970 by then. Coney Island was at its peak. That's when I met Thomas DeGrawe – he was Betty's brother. A Yale man.

He was nice-looking, smartly dressed and fit. He played tennis, but not well. He was a little overweight, but he was so charming. He was a bigwig at that famous law firm that represents all the film stars, and was very wealthy. He owned a fabulous apartment in New York, and was having a place built up in Cornwall, Connecticut. We married in 1981 – in May – almost exactly 20 years after I married Richard. He showed me the world, Thomas did. He took me sailing, and hiking, and to the most beautiful beaches. We went to Europe and the Far East. I didn't love him like I loved my first husband... no, my second - oh, what was his name? Was I married before that? But I liked him a lot. Thomas. Yes, Thomas. He had two kids with his first wife and the daughter had kids of her own. They would all come to Cornwall with us occasionally. They didn't like Coney Island. We were like a family, sometimes. Until they moved to California. Then we hardly saw them, which was a good thing. But Laura, the granddaughter, was always a spoilt brat. She always came back – each summer. It was so inconvenient, having her all that time. Goodness knows why she wanted to come every year. Anyway, she soon had to work harder at high school and once she was at college, we saw less of her. Thomas was so disappointed when she... she dropped out.

Thomas was much older than me, and soon, I began to notice his bald patch and his paunch. By the time we were married 10 years, he had slowed up and needed "rest" time often because his heart was getting weak. Our age difference showed. My dislike turned to disgust. When he was 71, he had a heart attack. He didn't die though. He wouldn't die. Life went on. I had the lily of the valley all around the house. It made me strong. We were married 22 years by the time he finally passed away. It was another heart attack. Poor Thomas. Poor, poor Thomas. Deep down, I know there could have been no other way. How else would I survive myself? I am strong. And the scent makes me stronger. But he left me cashless and I'm angry about that. I have a small retirement plan and yes, the apartment, of course. But it's not enough.

Roger is here now. He knows it's sensible not to trust his daughter. I am his faithful companion now. I can be with him daily. She can't. I told him, he needs to embrace that sense of distance, because she'll never be there for him truly. She has her own life, over the ocean – he shouldn't expect anything from her. I proved it to him when I showed him how much she uses him. Doesn't even know his likes and dislikes. Doesn't know his favourite food. Or his favourite colour. He knows now that his doting is wasted. I am his future. Me. Just me. All I have to do is kiss him and he knows it.

CHAPTER 7 (AMELIA)

"Amelia, leave your father alone now. Can't you see he's tired? He's 76, for pity's sake." Evelyn had rudely (so I thought) picked up an extension somewhere else in the house, whilst Dad and I discussed various candidates for a new role that had opened at work. His advice was always invaluable. We'd been on the phone for half an hour.

"Oh..." was all I could muster, and the second handset clacked down. There was a brief pause.

"Sorry about that, Amelia." On the end of the line, my father sounded embarrassed. "We have been talking for a while, I think we're due at friends for drinks soon, so I had better go."

"I'm so sorry, Dad, I hadn't realised the time..." I said, worried now that I could have worn him out, or worse, made him late! "I'll let you go then... sorry."

"No need to apologise. We'll talk next week, bye-bye Amelia."

"I think you should just forget it," was Jack's suggestion, when I mentioned it to him over dinner. "She's just like that – there's nothing you can do – remember the party? That was over a year ago now and you're still worrying about it. You want him to be happy and he is. Personally, I can't stand the woman, but, she makes him happy. It's his choice who he goes out with, Amelia – if he wants our help, I'm sure he'll ask."

Jack was right. I should just put up and shut up. "I know. It's just annoying, that's all."

On an infrequent day off, I had already cleaned the house and was now working on the ironing. The radio blared eighties music and after a round of adverts, announced the eight-week countdown until Christmas. Time flying again, I mused. Laura would be arriving this evening. Despite the warning from Raymond at Dad's party, both Jack and I had taken to her and we had kept in touch regularly over the past 18 months, sending emails, cards, even letters sometimes. When she'd said she was visiting London to see a friend who was working in the city, it seemed only fitting to invite her to stay with us, in our little Wimbledon townhouse. I had proudly made up the spare room, plumping up the pillows and cushions in readiness, and placed some fresh flowers on the bedside table. I liked our little house – it had always felt like home and I enjoyed any opportunity to welcome guests and show it off. We had rare off-street parking at the front, for my run-of-the-mill Mazda, but we were also lucky enough to have a garage, which was big enough to provide shelter for one Jack's prize possessions – his C reg Porsche Carrera in Prussian blue.

Later, as we sped through the dark evening in the sports car towards Heathrow, I mused quietly over Raymond's suggestion that Laura couldn't be trusted. He'd hinted that she'd lied or cheated at college somehow, but she seemed so sweet, and such a determined character that maybe he must have got the wrong end of the stick. It was Evelyn that had told them about what happened, but I thought it would be nice to hear the other side of the story at some point, before making a decision on whether or not to trust her.

"I hope she won't find the room too small," I said to Jack. "All the rooms in America seemed huge – she'll probably think this one is a walk-in wardrobe!"

"Well, tough if she does," he replied. "We can't stretch the walls out for her. She should be thankful she's got somewhere free to stay, and career advice to boot."

"You're right, she'll be delighted." We both chuckled.

Laura's CV was impressive and I had arranged a lunch on Wednesday with a business friend – Catriona Lewis – who was a senior partner in a law firm called Brown & Burton, with offices in London, Paris and New York. They often took on interns and she was interested in chatting to Laura informally, before setting up an interview with her US counterpart. I was really hoping it would work out – not only for my business credibility, but to help smooth down any differences that could be growing between Evelyn and I.

My mobile came alive in my lap, its brightness lighting up the car. Assuming it was Laura, I picked it up quickly.

"Hello," I said with a smile, "are you here?" We were, as expected, stuck in traffic on the A4. It was cold and windy outside.

"Who am I speaking to please?" asked a male voice.

"Oh sorry, I thought you were going to be someone else." I laughed but there was no response.

"May I have your name, please?" the voice repeated. Cheeky, I thought, and was a little offended.

"Well, who are you? You're calling me…"

"My name is Mr David Webb from HM Revenue & Customs. Can I have *your* name please?"

"Oh. Right. It's Amelia Jones. How can I help?" I gripped Jack's knee while the car moved forward slowly. He looked at me with concern, then immediately focused back on the road ahead.

"Thank you Mrs Jones. Can you please confirm you're picking someone up from an airport this evening?"

"Oh yes, it's Laura, Laura DeGrawe. From Heathrow – is she ok?"

"Yes, she is fine. There is no problem; we're just carrying out some routine checks. Can you confirm where she has flown from?" I put my thumb up to Jack to let him know Laura was ok.

"New York, JFK, I think."

"And how long is she staying with you?"

"Um, well, she's staying with us for three nights then going on to someone else, but I don't know their name or where they live, I'm afraid."

"That's fine. And do you know the nature of her visit - is it business or pleasure?"

"Oh pleasure, I hope. Or leisure, whatever... I don't think its business..." I was trying to keep it light because I wasn't sure if I should tell him about the lunch, but decided it was only informal.

"Ok, that's fine, are you here at Heathrow now?"

"No, not yet. Unfortunately, we're stuck in traffic on the A4. We'll be there shortly though, probably another 20 minutes."

"Ok, well I will let Laura know you're running late and she'll be out by then. Thank you very much for your co-operation. Good evening."

"Wow, Jack – Laura got stopped and searched! They're letting her go though, thank goodness. I wonder why."

"We'll soon find out," Jack replied confidently, as the traffic began to move a little faster. "At last..." he said, "we're moving."

Fifteen minutes later, we'd parked and were marching toward the arrivals lounge. We saw Laura waiting forlornly, sitting on an otherwise empty bench, with a huge suitcase, one other bag, and a very large handbag.

"Probably enough clothes for a month, let alone a week... you women," remarked Jack quietly, with a smile. I smiled too, looked directly at Laura, and opened my arms wide as we approached.

"Laura... how are you? We hear you've been through the mill – what a welcome!"

"Oh. My. Gawd!" said Laura. She was almost in tears. "It was so upsetting, they took all my clothes out and messed them all up, and now they're all creased and dirty and there was absolutely no need for any of it. I don't know why they picked me, out of all the people they could have chosen on the flight... I kept asking 'why, why', but he didn't want to tell me a thing, just kept asking personal questions, and randomly looking in my bag..."

"Ok, ok, you're here now, we'll take care of you..." Amelia put her arms around Laura, as she burst into tears in relief.

"I'm sorry. It's just that it was sooo traumatic."

"What did they ask you when they first came up to you?" Jack asked.

"Oh that... they wanted to know why I'd taken the labels off my luggage..." She sniffed, her tears gone as quickly as they came. "... well they'd put a *sticker* on it... it's brand new Calvin Klein, from Saks Fifth Avenue! I just ripped them all off as I took the luggage from the conveyor." She smiled guiltily and I noticed a glint in her blue eyes.

"That's why," Jack told her, as he took the large suitcase and they walked back towards the car park. Laura looked quizzical. "Look, people who smuggle things try to conceal where they have flown in from, and ripping luggage tags off is a way to do that. It would have been clocked."

"Gotcha! As if *I* would be smuggling anything." She giggled girlishly. "How would *that* look on my CV, huh?"

"Well," replied Jack, "you'd be surprised at the sorts who do."

"Traffic should have died down by now," I interjected, trying to change the subject. "We should be home in 45 minutes. Just in time for a nice glass of wine and some supper."

"Wow, nice car," beamed Laura, as Jack hauled her designer bag into the front boot and she squeezed into the tiny back seat. He smiled with pride, but it was the only compliment she paid it.

When we finally arrived home, we were all exhausted, but the delicious smell of a homemade stew in the slow cooker enlivened us. Firstly though, we showed Laura upstairs to the spare room.

"How... quaint," she said, looking around. She thought it was tiny, I knew it.

"I hope you don't think it's too small."

"Are you kidding? I love it."

49

"Well, I'll leave you to settle in for a while, freshen up; the bathroom is just next door. About half an hour for something to eat, but just come on down when you're ready."

"No problem, thank you so much."

There was something about the way she pronounced the "you" in "thank you" that irritated me. But I couldn't put my finger on why.

It was about 9p.m., and I had just pulled out the cork from a bottle of red wine with a pop, when Laura came into the kitchen, freshly showered and dressed in a pair of leggings, thick socks and a baggy jumper.

"I hope you weren't expecting me to dress for dinner?" she smiled

"Oh no! You look very comfortable – have a seat – red wine?"

"Sure... thank you."

The incident with Laura's luggage was forgotten and we all tucked into the delicious stew.

"It will be so much better when I can live in New York full time. I just stayed one night on my way through from California."

"Did you stay with Evelyn?" I asked.

"No, I stayed in a hotel. Evelyn likes her privacy."

"So why you are so keen to be there – is it because the job scene is better for grads?"

"Oh, I just LOVE New York – I HATE California – it's too hot and nothing changes. And the people are sort of shallow. In New York, there's a buzz like no other. Somehow, I just wanna be there all the time." She took a second to put a dumpling in her mouth and carried on regardless. "I used to visit every summer for two months and stay with Granddaddy and Gramma." She swallowed. "We'd picnic in Central Park and they took me to the theatre and the zoo. I loved it and I was so close to Granddaddy. I miss him so much – he was such a nice man – like another father to me. He married Evelyn when I was in my early teens. A couple of years after that, halfway through school, the summer trips came to an end. Just like that. I wasn't invited anymore. It was like they didn't want me there. I sort of know why... but I'll tell you another time."

"Oh, that's sad," I said, remembering the cheating rumour.

"Yeah, really sad. When he passed away in 2003, he left me that apartment, the one that Evelyn is living in. He gave her the right to live there for the rest of her life. It would be good if I could live there so I can find work... but Evelyn won't even let me stay over. Even if I do get work, I won't be able to afford a rental." She looked pensive for a moment. "I guess he thought she'd be more generous – I think we all did."

***

Three days flew by. The pre-arranged lunch with Catriona was a complete success. We took Laura to see a musical on the London stage. The three of us strolling by the river afterwards, the dim, old-fashioned streetlights, illuminating our way along the blackness of the lapping Thames. We took her to the Tower of London to see the Crown Jewels (neither of us had been since we were kids) – the story of the two Princes fascinated her. We pored over paintings at the National Gallery, and after Jack went back to work, she and I shopped until we dropped in Kensington and Knightsbridge. In Harvey Nichols, we eventually finished off in the cocktail bar on the fifth floor.

"It's been amazing staying with you guys. I am so glad we have become friends," Laura said, her eyes sparkling with emotion as she clinked a champagne flute against mine.

"Me too, Laura," I said honestly. "Me too."

CHAPTER 8 (JACK)

Jack and Amelia's kitchen was small, with Shaker-style mod cons and just enough room for a pine table and four matching chairs. As there were only three of them, there was room for the pink roses that Laura had bought, from the stall by the station, as a thank you. Jack had made pizza and they were all tucking in greedily.

"How was the lawyer's lunch?" Jack asked Laura.

"Totally awesome. They're going to try to set up my interview during Thanksgiving week, when I'm back in New York. Hey... why don't you guys try to come out too – we can all be together and celebrate."

"That's a great idea. Jack?" Jack's wife looked at him with such hopefulness that he couldn't help but agree.

They chatted into the night. Amelia poured the last of the wine. She had been talking about the '70s, when Laura was born.

Amelia laughed. "I remember one summer – it was long and very hot. Ban the Bomb, the Queen's Jubilee, the hosepipe ban... and that's the year Dad married Helen. I think I was nine – I thought she had stolen him away, and I would never see him again."

She looked wistful, but she had Laura's avid attention. "How was that? I can't imagine my parents ever being with different people. It must have been so hard."

"It was for a while. My mother didn't handle the divorce, or his remarrying, well. She blamed everyone but herself. But I only knew how to be loyal to her, you see, because I stayed with her after they split. To see her anguish in watching my father marry someone else was awful, and I wanted to be unkind to my new stepmother, as a sort of punishment for hurting my mum's feelings so much. Helen didn't respond well to that, of course. She didn't have kids of her own and it was clear that she was uncomfortable around them, unsure about how to approach them, as if they were scruffy, stray dogs. The first time we met, when she held out her hand, I felt intimidated. My whole body stiffened and I looked wide-eyed at my dad for instruction. He just looked at me expectantly and nodded – his eyebrows high. I took her hand, gingerly, because it seemed big and had rings on it, and I thought it would crush my own; but it was soft and plump. Still, my whole arm moved with the force of her handshake and I was immediately startled. It must have come across as rude, because Helen dropped my hand abruptly and glared. It wasn't a good start. But, as adults, Helen and I had both made the effort and tried to be friends – it never got deeper than a shared cigarette or sneaky last glass of wine, But we sort of bonded, a little... you know? I wished I'd known how to try harder earlier – it was all too late by the time she was killed."

"Wow," said Laura with sympathy. "Do you miss her?"

"You know, I never felt grief for Helen because she wasn't part of my life – I never really knew her – not properly. Eventually, Dad had stopped including Helen when he saw me. He'd even make trips to the UK without her. I was relieved, but it was problematic for him. Of course, I never realised that. When she died, I felt ashamed – I could have done so much more to help him be happy. I could have befriended Helen if I'd tried. I'd never understood how much he'd loved her. Not until I saw him after the accident. His face was grey – it looked like gravity had stretched it down overnight, and there were deep, dry wrinkles that I hadn't noticed before. He seemed empty. The wave of guilt was so forceful, it almost sank me. He told me, then, about when he heard the sirens. He said, 'I had this... this fleeting worry that it was her, but I just continued with whatever it was that I was doing. I can't even remember what that was...' The words are etched on my memory. There was this awful choking sound, like grit in his voice. The despair I felt for him... well, it stopped my heart. To him, she was everything – and I had never realised."

"I see. Do you worry it was too soon for him to get with Evelyn?"

Jack knew the answer was yes.

"Well, who am I to say" she responded, trying to sound brighter, leaning back in her chair. "I certainly want to try harder, for his sake, this time. I know he was lonely without Helen, so it's just got to be a good thing, hasn't it?" Jack rubbed Amelia's shoulder affectionately.

"Yes, that's what we said about Granddaddy when he met her too! And she did seem to have some sort of hold over him. You know, he seemed enchanted with her, like he was under some sort of spell."

"She obviously has a way with men," Amelia said, "to make them such... so spellbound. But it's good that Dad has someone to share things with. I can't imagine him on his own – I can't even picture him before he met my mum, you know, before he was married, as a young boy or a teenager. I've seen old photographs, but it's almost as if I'm looking at a celebrity, or a character out of a book, and not him, the real him. I just can't imagine him alone, so I'm very happy he's not." She was smiling and Jack could almost read her mind. He knew this was true, but also that she wished it could be with someone easier, and altogether more amenable and fun. She'd never say it out loud though.

Laura held court for a while with how her great-grandfather first came to America from England as a child, by which time they'd opened another bottle of wine, to "celebrate the success of the lawyer's lunch". At 11p.m., Jack sent them to bed, before clearing up.

"You girls need your beauty sleep – big day for you tomorrow, Laura, travelling across London by yourself."

Jack had warmed to Laura and felt almost brotherly towards her. She seemed to have a brightness around her, which made him happy. He smiled at her while he put his arms around his wife. "Go on up – I'll finish the cleaning up."

"You sure, darling?" Amelia asked.

"Of course," he said and whacked her bum with a tea towel.

"Night Laura," Amelia said, and yawned as she began to climb the stairs. "Sleep well."

"You too, Amelia, thank you." Then she look directly at Jack and grinned. The gesture was rather suggestive, Jack thought, as he stood opposite her.

"It's been great," she said, as she gripped his upper arms and reached up to kiss his cheek. "Wow," she said, as she lowered herself. "Great biceps – you work out, don't you, Jack?"

He just gave her goofy smile and said, "Well... a bit," even though he didn't.

She turned and looked behind her at him, her blonde hair moving graciously over her shoulder as she moved up the stairs. "Nighty-night. Oh, and thanks to you both for making my last night with you so special."

CHAPTER 9 (JACK)

They finally arrived on Roger's Long Island doorstep at around 7p.m. The studio above the garage was finally painted and furnished. Roger had done this so that guests could come and go as they pleased – it had a fully-equipped kitchenette with a dining area, a lounge, a separate bedroom with a shower room, and its own entrance inside the garage. It was roomier than some one-bedroomed flats he'd lived in.

"It's sparsely furnished, but very comfortable and fully private," Roger had told them as he left them to unpack. Jack was grateful – the spare room in the house was small and not en-suite – last time they stayed, he had felt uncomfortable, especially when he bumped into Roger on the way back from cleaning his teeth – like he shouldn't really be there. And he definitely couldn't be physical with Amelia in any way. Shagging her was completely out of the question.

The Treehouse, as Evelyn had annoyingly called it, was indeed very comfortable. There was a big double bed with an old-fashioned quilt, a good-sized sofa, a pine coffee table, a stacked bookcase, and an Indian rug on the floor. It was all shades of brown, from light to dark. The kitchenette was modern and offered everything required for light cooking, and washing up. As Amelia looked around, she pointed out a tray-table, a small pewter model of an old MG, the throw on the sofa and finally, the painting of the cottage above it.

"I knew it," she said sadly. "I bought him that, that... and that. Oh my goodness, the painting. I can't believe that was his choice to put it here."

"Oh darling," Jack said, sympathetically, "It probably wasn't."

"Drinks?" Roger offered, back over at the house, in the conservatory. "Would you like a cup of tea, or a glass of wine, a beer, Jack?"

Before they could answer, Evelyn swanned in, wearing white trousers and a long, floaty top – her perfume trailed behind her.

"Hello all. Shall we go? I'm all ready. How are you both?"

Roger continued as if he hadn't been interrupted. "I thought we'd pop out to Girasole once you're sorted, as you must be hungry and tired. I called them earlier and they're keeping a table for us." Girasole was a local Italian restaurant where he and Helen used to go on Fridays, and they treated him like royalty there. Roger liked that a lot, and enjoyed being the centre of attention – especially when it was in front of his daughter. Benson, the tabby cat, padded in to greet them both like long-lost friends. Helen had acquired Benson from a local farm as a kitten, with his brother, Hedges. Sadly, Hedges was run over soon after. Helen had been devastated and Amelia had sent flowers. Benson had pined, but carried on stoically. The cat now curled around each of their ankles in turn, and purred loudly at the touch of their gentle, familiar hands. He ignored Evelyn.

***

The waiter greeted them like long lost friends. "Welcome, Mr Kavanagh, welcome, welcome." He over-smiled and kept bowing, as if Roger was the king.

They unfolded their napkins and their aperitifs arrived immediately.

"Oh, I wish I could cook, Jack – but alas, I've never found it necessary," said Evelyn, looking at him. "Now, I want to talk to you about Laura. It's so amazing how you've helped her, getting that meeting together. You know she will be very grateful indeed."

"Nothing to do with me," Jack said, loyally. "That's all down to Amelia. She's very well-connected in that industry. She has a great reputation and knows all the right people."

"I'll bet," said Evelyn. "Well, it's very charitable of you, Amelia," turning now to her. "I am sure Laura should thank you deeply."

Amelia smiled, grateful for the credit. "Well, I just happened to know the right person. That's what they say, isn't it – 'it's not what you know, it's who you know'. But she can thank me IF she gets the job – there's no guarantee."

"Yes, I'm sure you're right. But, you know, she could have thrown it all away when she was younger. She was a terrible student at college, tried to cheat in all her exams."

"Ahem. We probably shouldn't bring that up, Evelyn," Roger said. "It's in the past and all dealt with." He held her look for more than a couple of seconds and she eventually lowered her eyes.

"Yes, my love, you're right. I'm sorry, it certainly is in the past," she agreed, and giggled girlishly as she sipped her Martini. Jack and Amelia exchanged a knowing glance. It occurred to him that, for some reason, Evelyn didn't like the fact that he and Amelia had befriended Laura, let alone tried to help her.

Roger said, "Anyway, Laura can tell you how it went on Thursday. David and Elizabeth are coming too. Ali and Raymond couldn't make it – they have family upstate. I'm picking up the Thanksgiving turkey tomorrow."

"That's great," said Amelia, and then she blurted out, "I saw the painting of the cottage in the studio..." Jack squeezed her hand under the table, but knew she couldn't help herself.

"Oh darling," said Evelyn, "the style of it doesn't suit the house. It's perfect where it is because it's more contemporary."

Amelia looked at Roger, who looked calm, and directed back. "Yes. I'm sure you're right," she said, and looked down at her lap. Roger smiled and leaned over to squeeze her other hand, resting on the table, as if he knew what she was thinking. Evelyn had trumped him, the gesture said.

***

On Thanksgiving Day, they all slept late and shared brunch happily, just like a close family. Amelia thought it made a pleasant change, and wished it could be like that always. There seemed to be no underlying maliciousness, no furtive glances. They chatted light-heartedly about the previous day's trip to Jones Beach, and the refreshing stroll along the boardwalk, until the breeze became an uncomfortable wind. Miriam, Roger's Mexican housekeeper, arrived to help with dinner, and Amelia offered her assistance.

"No need, sweetie," interjected Evelyn, before Miriam could accept. "I want everything to be a wonderful surprise," she replied. "You go and keep your father company. Miriam and I shall prepare everything."

"As long as it's not like the last surprise," Jack whispered to her, as they made their way to the conservatory.

David, Elizabeth and Laura had arrived together at exactly 7.30p.m., and Miriam poured them all a glass of sparkling wine as they greeted each other in the lounge. Amelia was fond of the housekeeper because she bustled and clucked like a mother hen, and cared for Roger as if he was her own. She arrived on the scene not long after Helen was killed, when Roger realised he simply needed the help. Amelia had wholeheartedly agreed it was a good thing.

"Champagne for everyone," said Evelyn. "We're celebrating." She reached over to touch Roger's arm. "Aren't we, darling?"

"Oh, is this champagne," remarked Amelia, as she looked at the label. "'Gloria Ferrer, Carneros, California'," she read aloud. "I didn't think that an American wine was allowed to be named champagne."

"Well, as *I* understand it, it *can* be called that if it's made by 'méthode champenoise', which means it's been fermented twice in the bottle," Evelyn stated.

"Oh, I see," Amelia replied, matter-of-factly, knowing confidently what she was doing. "Well, I'm sure it doesn't matter whether it's champagne or not, it's still absolutely delicious."

"Yes, it is," agreed Elizabeth, "totally delicious," and everyone smiled, except Evelyn, who was staring pointedly at Amelia.

"Laura," said Roger, "how did it go yesterday, with your meeting?"

"Oh my Gawd." Laura was visibly excited "It was totally amazing... they all seem so nice in that office. And I've been invited back to meet the Vice President, so I think they liked me. The job is mine, as long as he approves."

"Of course he will approve," Evelyn said, confidently.

"Fantastic news," Amelia said. "Double celebration then, cheers," and she raised her glass to the room. Everyone joined in, with, Jack noticed, the exception of Evelyn.

When they entered the dining room, they were all amazed by the beautiful autumn leaves, spread artistically among the knives and forks. There were baby pumpkins, squashes and nuts, surrounding the deep-red votive candles. A large, harvest-themed floral arrangement took centre stage in the middle of the table. Everyone gasped in awe and a series of "wow" and "beautiful" were whispered.

Evelyn proudly welcomed her guests again and muttered, "All my own work," as they moved by her to their seats.

"Do you think she picked the wheat by hand from the farm down the road?" laughed Jack quietly to Amelia, referring to the centrepiece, tied neatly with a terracotta ribbon, as they unfolded chestnut-coloured napkins.

"Shh," she said, smiling and taking a quick sideways glance at Evelyn, who was looking at Roger, silently begging his approval.

"Very impressive, Evelyn, well done," Roger said, and Evelyn beamed.

Jack thought he noticed a lot of furtive glances over dinner, but as he relaxed into the flow of the conversation, he told himself it he was making it up, just because Evelyn slightly annoyed him. There was a lot of laughter, jokes, stories, recollections, and witticism. The meal was fit for a king – the turkey tasty and cooked to perfection. Laura had brought strawberries from California, which were sweet and firm.

"Ironically, I bought them here in New York," she told them as they tucked in.

Jack leant back and took in the scene. Amelia was smiling as she listened to Elizabeth expressing something amusingly shocking. The table was full of dinner party debris, each dessert plate scraped clean. Evelyn had clearly gone to a lot of trouble to make this a success. Maybe he should try harder, for Amelia's sake – try not to let her get under his skin. Yes, she deserved a chance after the last time. He decided to propose a toast. After all, if he played into her hand, she may become easier to deal with. He clanked a teaspoon gently on the rim of his glass and said, "Everyone, thank you for including us in your harvest celebration and allowing us to give thanks with you. And a special thank you to Evelyn, for being such a wonderful hostess and making us so welcome. To Evelyn!"

"To Evelyn," everyone repeated with a raised glass.

"Why, thank you," she said, with a fake coyness. "I had no help. Amelia, perhaps you would assist now with clearing the table."

Amelia, thoroughly embarrassed, bowed her head to hide her eyes and immediately began to help Miriam stack the plates, but only Jack noticed she was hurt, and he immediately regretted complimenting the woman. He followed the other two into the kitchen.

"Pretty flowers," Amelia said, as she set the plates down. He followed her glance to the jug of yellow and white stems on the sideboard. "I love gerberas, Miriam, and that lily of the valley – they're like little fairy bells, so pretty."

"Just like you, gorgeous," Jack said, as he came up behind her and curled his arms around her waist, kissing her neck. "So, so pretty."

CHAPTER 10 (AMELIA)

It bothered me that no one seemed to have noticed Evelyn's comment. Maybe I had taken it too personally, or was jumping to conclusions, but Miriam confused me further.

"Yeeess. Evelyn has gone out all afternoon, for the shopping and nail salons. It was me who make you decorations and dinner. But she wanted you to be happy, and make surprise for you. She didn't want you to come here in kitchen, because that would spoil it, you see? It worked, no?" We *had* all enjoyed the meal and had fun together, especially my father. It would be a shame to taint it with unnecessary hostility. What did it matter who did it all? Then Jack was there behind me and told me I was pretty like the flowers... I sighed. It was ok, we were all ok.

***

After breakfast, we packed, said our goodbyes and thank yous, and headed for Manhattan in a taxi. It was warm, despite being November. We saw *Chicago* on Broadway, dined late, and walked back to our cheap hotel, through the madness that was Times Square, with its bright lights flashing neon, the street teeming with crowds of tourists and party-goers. Sleep came easy to us both.

***

The following day's airport trip was quick for once and the queues were short. I watched the people in front and behind us, taking in their moods, their colour, their attire, what they were carrying. There was such a variety of cultures – I spotted a pair of erstwhile Hasidic Jews, business people, Chinese, African, smart, casual, lazy-looking, happy, fat, thin, hurried, laidback. I saw light hair, dark hair, greasy hair, bald heads, head scarves, black jacket, no jacket, ties, t-shirts. There were heels, flats, trainers, pumps, boots and flip-flops.

Through all this, I perceived similarities between many Americans – their gestures, their expressions. All of them reminded me of my father. He was English through and through, but his mannerisms were American – the way he waved his hands about, or pursed his lips when thinking of what to say, or how to explain something, the way he said "goodbye now", when a simple "bye" would suffice, the way he would say "and so on", instead of "etc.", "garbage" instead of "rubbish". His accent was mixed – transatlantic – he sounded American to me, but to the Americans, English.

Once through security, we meandered around the shops, pleasantly filling time. I was surprised when my mobile phone began to buzz in my bag.

"Hello?"

"Ameeelia," said Miriam, her accent shrill. "Your father, he is in the hospital."

"What? What's happened? Since when?" I grabbed at Jack.

"Yesterday. She did not tell you, so I phone you. He fell. Fell from a ladder."

"Oh my God! When? How badly is he hurt?"

"We think a couple of bones maybe. His, how you say, his collarbone? Maybe his ribs, I dunno. Since yesterday, he been there."

"Which hospital, Miriam?" Now, I was throwing things out of my bag, on the hard floor and wildly searching for a pen and paper with one hand, pulling out random items, scattering them around me, Jack picking them up. I found an old, folded envelope. Miriam slowly dictated the number and the name of the hospital and ward.

"Thank you, Miriam, thank you. Thank you for letting me know, bless your heart."

We found some nearby seats and then the airport disappeared around me while I dialled the number. Jack waited calmly by my side, still holding the handbag debris.

The nurse knew everything and had a calming effect on me. I listened patiently – she was very precise, like a newsreader.

"Mrs Jones, your father has broken his collar bone and fractured two ribs. The injured bones cannot be splinted. He is on strong pain medication and needs to take it very easy. He can't do anything for some time now and must rest. His pain is controlled so he can come home in a day or two. He is right here; you can speak to him if you wish?"

The next voice I heard was his.

"How are you feeling, Dad?"

"Very sore, my dear, but I think I'm improving."

"What happened, how did it happen?"

"Up in the attic, after you left yesterday, lost my footing on the ladder on the way down. Complete accident. Should have been more careful."

"Oh Daddy, we're moving our flights now – we'll be over to the hospital to see you later."

"No, no, there is no need. I thought you had already left. Don't change things around just for me – there's no surgery so it's not serious."

"Don't be silly. Of course it's serious. We haven't left yet so it's easy. And we have insurance." I think he was quite relieved because he said we could use his car once we were back at the house. I immediately called to let Evelyn know we were returning, but she didn't answer. We waited impatiently at the ticket desk whilst they checked availability on next week's schedule, and removed our luggage from the hold.

Jack was slightly embarrassed: "I wish I could apologise to all those other passengers who will be cursing us right now."

"They'll get over it." I said, unsympathetically.

It was mid-afternoon when the taxi dropped us back at the house. Our plan was to drop the bags and then drive ourselves to the hospital. Evelyn was there, but strangely, seemed put out that we had come back. She came out of the house as we heaved the bags from the trunk. Benson slid quickly around her legs to the freedom of the garden with its refuge and prey. I had already opened the garage door and found the key to the studio in its hiding place.

"I can see you have been told about your father's accident." It sounded terse, and it occurred to me that she hadn't wanted us to know.

"Yes. Miriam called us."

"Well, he seems to be doing better and hopefully will be home by early next week."

"I know. We've spoken to him."

"Oh, you have? Well, I'm glad. But we don't need you here, Amelia. You'll just be in the way. I'm sure you can get a flight home tomorrow."

"No, we've already arranged to fly next Friday. We'll try not to be a burden, Evelyn."

"Fine, but don't expect me to look after you."

I looked at Jack, because I was too stunned to think of a response. He thought of one for me.

"It's ok, Evelyn, we won't need you to help us with anything. We're happy in the studio or 'Treehouse'. We have the key and Roger said we could use his car. If you can get the car key, it would be helpful."

"It's out of my hands then. Get the car key yourself, you know where it is. I'll leave the door open." She turned to march back into the house. As Jack followed her, I knew that she had more than irritated him; I also felt an alarming stab of anger.

Dad was lying in the hospital bed with a nasal cannula on his face, to help him breathe. He seemed surprisingly relaxed. We stayed with him for just over an hour, by which time, he was sleeping soundly. The painkillers probably. I was fraught with worry. It blocked out everything else.

Later that evening, we were preparing a light supper when there was a knock on the door. It could only be Evelyn. I trailed Jack downstairs to answer it.

"I was hasty before and I apologise," she said, guiltily. "It's just that I'm worried about Roger. Climbing up into the attic at his age... it could have been much worse, you know, he could have hit his head."

Jack didn't invite her in. He stood at the door, with a small smile, and accepted her apology. It was drizzling outside, but we were in the shelter of the brightly-lit garage. Evelyn pulled her cashmere shawl around her.

"You know, I'm struggling because the doctors won't reveal everything to me, because I'm not his wife. They can only release information to the next of kin – which is you, Amelia." She looked over Jack's shoulder and caught my eye, appealing for understanding. "I wanted to ask..." she paused, "Amelia, ask them what medication he is on, so I can research it and remind him to take it when he comes home. Help me, please. They will speak to you if you are next of kin. They won't tell me anything."

I took a deep breath; a sudden surge of sympathy overcame me. Jack turned to watch my face. "Oh. Of course we will, Evelyn – I'll ask them then for you tomorrow; find out everything we can."

"Thank you, Amelia. I appreciate it. I won't have time to visit tomorrow myself, but please let your father know I'll be here Monday when he arrives home. I'm assuming you will collect him – now that you are staying on and can use the car?"

"Yes, we will, Evelyn. Is there anything else we can help with?"

"No, just that – thank you. Goodnighty now." She lowered her look and took a step back, before turning her strained smile away. As she strode purposefully toward the house, she flicked the light switch, plunging them into darkness.

***

The next couple of days flew by with visiting, meeting doctors, shopping and arranging the furniture so that Dad could move easily around the house with a stick. Once home, we helped him out of the car, through the door and into a big, comfortable, leather chair in the lounge, next to the fireplace. He could walk, but very slowly, and his instructions were not to take the stairs unaided, or go outside, or drive, or cook, or do any exercise whatsoever. The nurse was to visit on Wednesday. All his drugs were in his checkout pack, with instructions on the labels.

Benson was suddenly there at our feet. He meowed softly and rubbed his face across my shins. I bent down to stroke him.

"Hello, you gorgeous kitty," I said in a silly voice. "How are you holding up, have you missed your daddy too?" He meowed a response, and I had to restrain him from jumping onto Dad's lap.

"Here," said Jack, "I'll take him," and he picked him up, put him on the sofa, and sat down next to him. The cat stepped immediately onto Jack's lap and curled his furry, white paws under him. His loud purring seemed to emanate calmness.

I bent over the armchair and kissed my father's forehead. He smelled of soap. I noticed how much older he looked. He had never been an "old man" until this moment. Over the years, I'd seen the thinning silver hair, the liver spots on his hands, the yellowness in his eyes, but this all seemed more vivid now. He was fragile. His mouth was a thin line across his face, rather than the soft place his gentle, quiet, comforting voice would emerge when bedtime stories were whispered on those rare childhood occasions so long ago. I clung to the memory and hugged him gently.

"How are you feeling, Daddy?"

"You know what? I'm about as ok as you would expect. It hurts occasionally but not all the time, and I'm happy to take it easy and let you lot look after me for a change," and he did that little laugh that I loved so much.

"Tea then?" I suggested.

As I took the teapot and mugs from the cupboard in the kitchen, I noticed one that was emblazoned with a picture of a gold cup and the words "Happy Father's Day to a Champion Dad!" It perplexed me because I had never sent this. I didn't celebrate Mother's or Father's Day any more. It was my little private protest against them splitting up. They both knew about it and understood. My 10-year-old self had explained it to them and they had accepted it with grace. When Evelyn walked in, I asked her about the mug.

"I bought it for him last year – such a shame he doesn't get a gift when he's such a good father, don't you think?"

Evelyn smiled triumphantly, turned on her heel, picked up a fashion magazine from the table and walked through the door. "No sugar for me, thank you," she said over her shoulder, before disappearing.

CHAPTER 11 (JACK)

"Aw, look at you all comfy in the armchair, darling." Evelyn bent to kiss Roger on the lips. Jack looked away. As she placed herself next to him on the sofa, Jack held his breath as her expensive scent drifted under his nose.

"Oh, I see you've made a little friend there, Jack. How sweet."

"Mm," mumbled Jack, looking down at Benson, who was curled sleepily in his lap, while he continued to gently stroke his soft fur. They had been discussing the intricacies of engine parts, until Evelyn entered.

Amelia came in with a tray and started pouring.

"More tea, vicar?" she said, in a staged English accent, and laughed. Roger and Jack laughed too. Whilst they were sipping, Miriam arrived.

"Eeeeee!" she shrieked when she saw Amelia. "Wonderful, wonderful that you are back, eh, Mr Roger? Wonderful children you have! They will look after you now." Roger chuckled then winced. She cuddled each of them in turn like they were long-lost offspring, holding their cheeks and kissing them strongly. Then, still smiling, she waddled out to the dining room and they heard her laying the table, singing.

"Miriam is here to prepare our dinner," Evelyn explained, looking over the top of a fashion magazine. "It would be appreciated if you would stay out of the way until she is finished. Perhaps a shopping trip?" She caught Amelia's look of indignation. "You will have plenty of time to spend with your father over the next few days. I am going to the city on Wednesday, after the nurse's visit, and will be back on Friday night, probably after you have left for the airport."

Jack's relief was almost visible. He knew Amelia would feel the same. They exchanged a knowing smile, not visible to Evelyn. He wondered if Roger ever noticed that Evelyn was so bossy, the way she craftily worded things.

At 7p.m., they were back in the house and seated around the large dining table for dinner. Roger at the head, Evelyn to his left, and Amelia to his right. Jack was next to Evelyn, so that Amelia was alone on her side of the table. The silver cutlery was out, the fine china plates, wide bowls stacked on top, and Waterford stemware. A glass of water was placed delicately to the right of each setting.

"How lovely," Amelia commented. "The table looks gorgeous, Evelyn," as she noticed the lily of the valley in the centre.

"Thank you," said Evelyn, and then she put her hands together on the table in front her. "And now we should say grace."

Whilst she was praying aloud, Jack looked at Evelyn. She was holding Roger's hand on the table. She was wearing a stark white blouse with sheer, full-length arms, which bloused around her skinny wrists. The top button was probably a bit too low for anyone's liking, except her own. The light from the window shone on her face and he noticed her skin was glowing. Finally, he looked at Amelia, who had noticed him staring. She looked back quizzically. He rolled his eyes and winked at her.

Suddenly, there was a loud tinkle of a small bell. Evelyn returning it to next to her place setting as she said, "It's to save us shouting through to the kitchen for the housekeeper's attention."

"You mean Miriam?" Amelia said, with a smile.

"Yes, Amelia, I mean Miriam."

At that point, Miriam brought through a bottle of red wine and began to pour it into the crystal glasses.

"Oh, let me do that, Miriam – you can't cook everything AND serve us," Amelia said, as she reached for the bottle.

"AMELIA," said her father, as if she had said something shocking, making her jump. "Leave it."

"But it doesn't seem right..." Amelia pleaded, though her sentence trailed off. Roger shot her a look that willed her to stop. She looked apologetically at Miriam, and in return, Miriam squeezed Amelia's cheek with her free hand.

When the wine was poured, Roger raised his glass and said, "Welcome Amelia and Jack, and thank you for changing your plans – I am sure you will be a great help over the next few days."

"Oh. Thank you, Daddy. I do hope we can help," Amelia said.

"Thanks Roger. Yes, Amelia and I have worried about you, so it's important to us both to be as supportive as we can be."

Evelyn said nothing, but did raise her glass slightly, as she looked pointedly at the two of them, her head lowered. In fact, she said nothing for the rest of the evening, even though the others talked animatedly throughout the meal. Miriam only dared enter when the bell was rung, to fill glasses, clear plates and bring the next course.

After dessert, Amelia said, "I would like to make coffee. Let's enjoy it in the conservatory. And then Jack and I will leave you two in peace, Dad, you look worn out and probably need to get some sleep – maybe tea would be better."

"Good girl, Amelia" said Roger, as if Amelia were a little child. "We have decaffeinated." He flashed Evelyn a "be quiet and let her do it" look, and she recognised that Roger was giving her a rare opportunity to help, be involved. "Come on everyone, let's... retire." He said the last word in a mock upper-class English accent, as if he were a lord of a manor, and it made everyone smile.

The conservatory was located at the back of the house. Jack helped Roger up and escorted him there. As he was returning, he heard Miriam and Amelia stacking the dishwasher together, chatting happily and laughing.

"What's so funny, girls?" he said, as he placed some used glasses and napkins on the kitchen table.

Amelia looked up. "Miriam was just telling me about how Dad and she exchange a look sometimes when Evelyn gets a bit bossy, and he rolls his ey... oops."

Evelyn walked in and the atmosphere changed immediately. Amelia silently filled the cafetiere, smiling. She wasn't sure if she'd been caught or not.

"Miriam, you can go now. Thank you for your help," Evelyn said, tonelessly.

"Ok," replied Miriam, and quickly washed her hands, stretching over the sink. She hummed a happy tune.

"But your coffee..." Amelia said.

"That's ok, I can have some at home," replied the housekeeper, with a sideways glance at Evelyn. She took her coat from the back of a chair and stepped out through a glass door into the "mud room" – an enclosed porch, where her shoes were. She closed the door to, but not shut.

Jack went to the dining room to collect the place mats. As he returned, he saw Evelyn push past Amelia. His wife had just picked up a steaming mug in order to take to her father, and he saw the older woman, with her shoulder, almost barge directly into his wife, so that the scalding hot coffee jumped out of the mug and spilled onto the delicate material of her own thin, white blouse.

"*OH MY GOOOOD!*" Evelyn screamed. "You stupid, little bitch!"

He found himself immobile, as he continued to stare.

"Oh, I'm so sorry, Evelyn," said Amelia, embarrassed. "Let me get a wet cloth. Has it burned?" She quickly set the coffee down by the sink as she doused a clean cloth with cold water.

Evelyn was frantically wiping the blouse with one of the napkins. "You silly girl, you stupid, stupid woman. Oh my beautiful blouse."

"Here," offered Amelia, and handed her a cool, wet cloth. Evelyn snatched it and muttered something about how it was completely ruined.

"I'm so sorry, Evelyn. Perhaps Miriam could take it to the cleaners for you tomorrow morning, she hasn't left yet." She turned to see if Miriam was still in the porch. She was, watching the scene, aghast, and she nodded to signify her agreement.

Evelyn was not consoled. "Oh look at you, Missy Amelia, with your bright ideas. You probably did this deliberately. You're hateful and spiteful, I don't know why he puts up with you."

"Look – why not go and change? Let Miriam take the blouse. You guys can afford that small luxury, can't you? Let her take it tonight and have it laundered properly tomorrow for you. I can pick it up later in the week if you like, and have it back here all clean and fresh, before you return from the city."

Amelia's composure impressed Jack, but she didn't seem to realise that the older woman's move had been deliberate. He was still rooted to the spot, but taking in each word and action. Miriam stepped back through to the kitchen.

"You think you have all the answers, don't you?" Evelyn continued. "Well, I'm telling you right now, you know nothing, Amelia. NOTHING. You hear me?"

Amelia looked at her, losing patience now, and raised her arms slightly, recognising the hopelessness of the situation. "I don't know what you mean," she sighed, as she walked past the woman, back to the sink, to pick up the mug again. "But I don't like the sound of it."

"Don't you dare walk away from me when I'm talking to you," Evelyn hissed to her back, as she reached out to grab the younger woman's wrist.

"Leave her," Jack said, loudly. Evelyn swung around to look at him.

"Shut up," she said slowly, over her shoulder. He felt anger rise and walked defiantly towards her.

"I'm sorry? What did you say?" he said, leaning close to her. He saw red blotches on her neck, and the wet patch on the shoulder of her blouse. It had stained.

"You don't frighten me, Jack," and there was a loud smack as she swiped her hand swiftly across his face. Jack laughed. "Oh, you are the most selfish people I have ever met," she continued, tears in her eyes now.

"Evelyn," Jack said more quietly, taking hold of her shoulders, calmly, the action dissipating the anger in them both. "What's the problem here – why are you so upset? It's evidently more than the spilt coffee." Maybe, just maybe, they could get to the bottom of this – the hostility that was now getting out of hand.

"You think you can control Roger, don't you?" She shrugged free of Jack's grasp and turned again to Amelia. "Well you can't. He loves me, just me. You have no idea how to please him, Amelia. There can only be one winner in this game, you know, and that will be me. Only I can win this."

Amelia looked softly back at her, encouraged by Jack's sympathetic try. "Evelyn, I don't know what you're talking about. Try to calm down and let's take the coffee in to the conservatory?" Jack watched her walk determinedly to a cupboard, retrieve a tray, place two mugs on it and hand it carefully to Evelyn.

"Take it in," she said, more firmly. But Evelyn didn't move. She was pressing her fingertips to the corners of her eyes, as if pushing the tears back in.

Jack said, "Evelyn, Roger's alone in the conservatory, why don't you just go and join him with the tray and we'll bring the milk and sugar."

"You. YOU!" she yelled, as she stomped over to Jack and smacked his face. "Why don't you just shut uuuup?" and now she had both hands around his neck.

Jack was surprised, but it was easy to simply take her wrist and calmly say, "Evelyn... pull yourself together or Roger will hear."

"Please, Evelyn," said Amelia – she was next to them, the three of them in a close huddle – "Please, let's just leave things for tonight. Take the coffee in. Please?" she begged.

Evelyn dropped her hands. She seemed exhausted. She took a deep breath and wiped her hair to one side. 'Humph,' she murmured, before taking it and walking out. Jack closed the door behind her.

"What the hell was all that about?" he said, looking at Amelia.

"I have absolutely no idea."

Miriam was next to them now. "My, oh my," she said. "She ees losing control, I think."

"What did she mean by she'll 'win this'?"

"Too much wine, I reckon, or the Martinis... she's drunk, Amelia. It's all in her head," Jack said. "But we're going to have to ignore it for now – for your dad's sake. It will probably all be forgotten in the morning."

"I hope so – I feel a bit... a bit upset," Amelia said, taking a breath. She was trying not to cry and Jack put his arms around her and squeezed. She sniffed and ran her finger under her lower lashes.

"Not surprising."

"Not surprising at all," agreed Miriam. "That ees a very rude woman. You ok, Ameelia? You ok, Jack?"

"Yes, I'm fine, thank you," Amelia said, with a sniff, and then stroked Jack's cheek. "Are you ok?"

"She didn't hurt me, if that's what you mean."

They heard a car pull up in the driveway, the headlights illuminating the room quickly as it turned – Miriam's husband. As they waved goodbye, Benson returned through the cat flap, in from the cold, shaking himself as soon as he felt the warmth of the house. He trotted into the kitchen, looking for a warm lap.

He knows how to time things well, thought Jack.

CHAPTER 12 (AMELIA)

I kept my distance after that, and my mouth firmly shut. Jack and Dad bonded over cars. Dad and Evelyn laughed sweetly together. He even complimented her hair.

"Why, Rogey, I just had it done yesterday, thank you so kindly for noticing." I had to admit, the style made her look younger than she was, and it looked nice. I was on the verge of agreeing, but she shot me a smug look. I felt troubled and out of my depth somehow.

I quietly made a filling lunch for everyone, following which I managed a short walk in the garden. After that, I ensured my father was comfortable and he napped on the sofa. That night, Jack held me close and we made love. It was comforting and I fell asleep quickly. But I woke just before dawn and sleep wouldn't return. I began to worry that my relationship with my father was being tainted in some way. Perhaps I was somehow subconsciously sabotaging it. But that could only happen if I let it, surely, and I wasn't going to do that. If I could just forgive Evelyn... understand her... sweep what happened under the carpet, then everything could be fine. Or was I just over-analysing? Reading too much into everything.

While we were waiting in the conservatory for the nurse to arrive, I was preparing questions for her, so that I was clear on Dad's medication and care. Dad and Jack were discussing classic cars and Evelyn read a book. Three empty mugs sat on the glass coffee table in front of us, one of them leaving a sticky ring. At exactly 10.30a.m., the doorbell rang. Evelyn shot up, dropping her book on the chair.

Dad nodded at her. "Evelyn will get it," he said to the room, and went back to engine parts. She strode confidently out of the room towards the front door. It amazed me how much energy she had for her age. She was wearing grey leggings and a long, black and grey cashmere pullover, which would have looked better on someone younger, but fair play to her, the outfit worked. A few seconds later, she reappeared with a lady, dressed in fitness clothes, following behind. She looked more like a physiotherapist than a nurse. She introduced herself as Karen and shook hands with us all. I offered to make tea.

"Just water please, thank you honey."

I was back in an instant with her glass, not wanting to miss anything.

"The most important thing," nurse Karen was saying sincerely, "is that you need to take it easy – big time..." and she went on to explain about breathing exercises, ice packs and ways to support the chest if coughing. She took him on a detailed tour through his medication, how many, why and what for, and ensured that we all understood too. "Your rib injury should have healed within three to six weeks, and I'll be back regularly, starting from next Monday, although I'll ease off after the first three visits." She was so thorough that I felt wholly reassured that Dad would be in good hands. I felt myself relax for the first time since we left the UK.

"When do you guys leave for home?"

"Friday night," I said, smiling.

"Well, I wish you a very good trip – don't worry about your dad... we'll take good care of him," and she stood to leave. "Remember, Roger, if you're unsure about anything, if you get shortness of breath, or any other kind of chest pain, call us – that's what we're here for, ok?"

We all thanked her and Evelyn began to show her out. I slowly picked up the mugs and glass and quietly followed them. As I approached the kitchen door, I heard Karen talking. I hovered just behind it, out of sight, listening closely.

"I bet you're glad you have Jack and Amelia here, right? Even if it's just for a short time?"

"Well, to be honest with you," Evelyn replied "they're sort of... in the way. They both of them seem to have more respect for themselves than they have for her father. I am sure the daughter is after something. I can't tolerate people like that, can you? Well, bye-bye now, Karen, and thank you again."

"She seemed nice. And very capable," I said, loudly, pushing through the door and placing the mugs in the sink noisily.

"Yes," was the only word Evelyn responded with, before she flitted hurriedly out of the kitchen like a startled bird. I heard her run upstairs.

Jack said she was just jealous.

"But how can she be jealous? She has him all the time – I live in another country and see him a few times a year. She sees him a few times a DAY! It should be me that's jealous."

***

Evelyn kept her word and left for the city on Thursday – we waved her off politely after lunch. She drove my father's BMW and it crunched slowly out of the driveway. As she lifted her left hand to wave at my father, I noticed it dripped with jewellery.

Jack went over to the studio, leaving Dad and I alone. He turned to me and said, "So... what was this I heard about you insisting to the doctors that you were next of kin?"

"I'm sorry?" I was shocked at the acuteness of the question.

"Evelyn said you'd called the hospital and insisted that you were next of kin, almost as if you were afraid that they might think she was." I remembered her weak protestations that the doctors couldn't furnish her with facts.

"Oh. Yes, well, I did call them. She asked me to – she said that they wouldn't speak to her about your medication etc. because you weren't married, so she's not next of kin – that they'd only speak to the next of kin, which is me. I just thought I was helping her. I didn't *insist* on anything."

79

"I see," he said, without expression. "Evelyn said you'd been asking her about my will as well."

"Oh my God. I've been doing nothing of the sort." Now I was insisting. "That's a ridiculous thing to say, I can't quite believe I'm hearing it."

He smiled a suspicious half-smile. "Well, if it's any consolation, there is nothing to worry about."

"I'm not worried... I... I..." I couldn't work out if he was joking. Or angry. The last thing I wanted was to start an argument with my father now. Especially when I didn't really understand what I was arguing about. "Never mind." I said, feeling pathetic.

"Come on then, I need to take my pills and then you can help me upstairs for my afternoon nap." He patted me on the shoulder to reassure me, but it didn't.

Benson followed us upstairs and jumped on the bed as I helped my father into a comfortable position. He purred loudly as he settled on the corner. and didn't seem bothered by the gasps and groans that Dad made as he struggled to lie down. They were both sleeping soundly in minutes.

Later that day, I felt nervous as I finished a handwritten note to my father. We were sitting in Starbucks, after having grocery shopped for Dad. It was a plea, a last-minute appeal for our relationship. Jack thought I was worrying too much, but I felt I was losing him somehow. To her, to Evelyn. I hoped the note was short and sweet. To the point. How he liked letters to be.

Dad,
I've always loved you, you know that. I care about you with all my heart and you (along with Jack) are the most important man in my life.
I wanted you to know that I was a little hurt by what happened between Evelyn and I. I'm sorry, I have tried to get along with her and I will continue trying. I worry she is

*depressed, as her behaviour is somewhat alarming. She's very
rude to us when you're not about. Yet, I will try to be kinder,
Dad, as I know she cares about you. It's hard though, if I'm
honest, because she doesn't make it easy for me, or for Jack. I
just wanted you to know.*

*Now, concentrate on your exercises so you can get
stronger. Please get better soon and let me know how you
progress. Talk next week on the phone?*

With love and kisses
Your daughter, Amelia. xxx

***

The following day, my father's mood had lifted too. He
was getting around well with a walking stick, and he was
following all of Karen's breathing exercises. As we packed
for our return trip, we took it in turns to joke about how
we would actually make it home this time. I felt reassured
about leaving Dad. The nurse was clearly very good, and
Evelyn would take care of him too... I had begun to dislike
the woman, but that didn't infringe on her capacity as a
carer. But there was something missing. The special thing
that was always between me and Dad. The father-daughter
thing that always surrounded us when one of us departed.
Something untouchable, so special that only him and I could
experience. A look, a touch, a laugh. I hadn't found it this
time, and now we were leaving. I hoped the note would
break the ice. I left it on the kitchen table, big bold letters on
the envelope – *FOR DAD.*

My heart broke a little and a sad sense of loss swept
over me as we left New York one more time.

CHAPTER 13 (JACK)

Jack rarely drove his Porsche in London. It was made for long, uninterrupted journeys in the country, or blasting on the motorway – not the constant stop-start-stop-start of the city. It wasn't good for the engine. Plus, he worried it would get scratched or damaged when he parked it. But this had been a quick meeting locally and so he'd taken the chance to blow the cobwebs from his beloved automobile. He was on his way home now, and his spirits were high. The street was full of Christmas lights and decorations. They'd been back from New York for a week, and it was the first time he'd felt really festive. He'd passed through Tooting, where the lights went up in October for Diwali and Eid. They sufficed for Christmas too, so signifying three religious celebrations, side by side. A shame we can't all get along like that as people, he thought. The heavy traffic didn't bother him today. He wound the window down and took in a curried aroma. As a kid, it would have been roasting chestnuts. He sang along to a festive tune on the radio and thought about those long-lost Christmases in Peckham with his mum and dad. He found it strangely lucky that his parents had died years ago, because it meant he and Amelia could be genuinely together without feeling guilty. Amelia's mother had passed away too, way before he had met her, from a sudden heart attack, apparently. And now her father was incapacitated, he, of course, wasn't visiting either. So – he had his wife all to himself. He felt smug and happy.

"Hello gorgeous," he called, as he let himself in the wooden front door, with the stained-glass window. A waft of garlic and onions embraced him. "Smells great."

His coat hung, he smiled as his wife breezed into view.

"Only onions," Amelia said, as she kissed him. He enveloped her in his arms and squeezed her bum.

"What time are they coming?"

CHAPTER 13 (JACK)

"I told Tricia seven-thirty, but they'll probably be late as usual, so I'm planning on eight. How was the meeting?"

"Really good, yeah. Very good, in fact – got about six months' work, so will keep us going for a bit. Anything I can do?"

"Can you lay the table? Everything else is prepared, wine's in the fridge, meat's on, veg ready to go, starters done..." She had that look about her - the sparkly one, when she'd been so involved in something that her hair was mussed and her complexion pink. He kissed her softly and thought, this is right where I want to be. But he didn't say it.

"Right sir," he said instead, with a smile, and walked into the dining room to do as he was bid.

John was Jack's good friend and best man. They went way back to drug squad days, when John trained and supplied detector dogs to the force. He'd been married to Tricia since they were teenagers. Their only son lived in Dubai and Tricia missed him madly. They arrived at seven-forty-five and all hugged and kissed noisily, the men slapping each other's backs. The spent a little while in the kitchen with a bottle of Cava before settling at the table for their meal. Jack and John reminisced about various people and projects, while Tricia and Amelia caught up on various travels, including the recent trip to New York.

"And how is your father's lady?" asked Tricia, inquisitively, knowing that Jack thought Evelyn slightly odd, to say the least.

"Oh fine, they seem happy, you know. She *is* a bit strange, but that seems to work for Dad!"

"Did they get married, darling, in the end?" Tricia referred to most people as "darling".

"No. I don't think they've ever planned to get married. I don't think Dad wants to."

"Yes, I thought they were engaged? That's what Evelyn told us at your wedding. She said she would be next and they were already planning dates and venues. I thought it would have happened by now."

"Well, that's the first I've heard of it. That would be four years ago now – and no one has told us anything. Unless they've done it in secret. Are you sure that's what she said?"

"Couldn't have been clearer. I remember thinking, what an odd thing to say on your wedding day... I just said 'Oh how lovely' and changed the subject. Never thought to mention it to you, as we were all having such a great time. What a super day that was. Four years, really? Gosh, darling, it seems like only yesterday."

"Yes, it was a good day," said Jack "A really good day... remember the speech... maaaaaan... you naughty bastard... you embarrassed me!" he said to John.

They fell about in raucous laughter as they reminisced.

"Your money wouldn't go so far now," said John, sighing.

"I know," said Jack, as he nodded. "You know, they're calling it the Great Recession in the States?"

"Really, darling?" said Tricia. "That's a bit much, isn't it?"

"Well," added Amelia, "isn't it always the greatest if it's American?" They all laughed.

John agreed. "Yes, and now they've got the world's greatest bankruptcy with Lehman Brothers... what a shocking state of affairs."

"Evelyn is the world's greatest bitch," said Jack, with a chuckle.

"Now, now," Amelia said, quietly.

"She can't possibly be that bad, surely," said John, with genuine disbelief.

"I can't stand her." Jack was honest. "She's sort of... disingenuous... fake. She has this really annoying habit of touching people's arms and saying 'daaarliing'. But Amelia tolerates her for the sake of her father."

"I just want him to be happy. And it's only Dad's arm she touches – she does rather fawn over him. But he likes it and I want him to happy, like I said."

"Of course you do, darling," said Tricia, reaching for her hands.

It was 2a.m. before they left, leaving behind a Christmas gift "for under the tree, darlings"; and taking with them two wrapped bottles to help with their own celebrations.

"Wonderful – we will share one of these with my darling Robert. So wonderful to have our son home for Christmas."

"Lovely," agreed Amelia.

As they closed the door, Amelia immediately turned to go upstairs. "I'm going to bed. I'll finish clearing up in the morning."

Jack knew she had shut down. He knew the story of an unlikely engagement of her father would have upset her. He saw that flicker in her eyes.

"I'll do it, baby," he said, as he watched her go. He wasn't quite sure what she was most upset about – the conversation about what Evelyn said, or the fact that when she'd called her father yesterday, Miriam had answered, and told her she had found her letter in the garbage bin, ripped to pieces.

CHAPTER 14 (JACK)

"Are you sure she's looking after you properly... Sorry, it's just that... I know... I know... Ok... Well it sounds like that's going to be a great trip. Call me when you're back. You could always send us a postcard. Yes... ok. Bye Dad, bye-bye. Please take care."

Jack heard Amelia replace the receiver before joining him in their tiny garden. The summer evening light was fading. The birds were tweeting gently in the warm dusk. Floating in the air was the faint smell of grass cuttings.

"I worry about him," she said solemnly. A brief anger flew over her. "But he won't open up... somehow, he seems to be distant with me – a bit short. And I just don't seem to be able to do anything right. I wonder if it's because of the note... It must because of that note – he's never mentioned it – maybe he thinks I want it to be like it was with Helen. What shall I do, Jack?"

"Amelia, don't over-analyse – you spend your life worrying and trying to please that man and his stupid woman-friend. I don't know why you just don't leave them alone."

"Because he's my father, Jack. Don't bite my head off."

Jack took a deep breath. "I wasn't." He knew it wasn't easy for Amelia. But he struggled sometimes not to just walk out of the room, turn his back. She never seemed to understand that this was hard for him too.

"They're going on holiday. Taking a trip to Grenada to stay with David and Elizabeth. He said that they can't afford the Bahamas this year, what with the recession, so they're cutting back and the Caribbean will just have to do."

They both laughed lightly at the contrasting prosperity of each couple. Jack knocked back the last of his beer and put the bottle down on the table. "Well, when I drag my business out of the gutter, I'll be able to afford to take you to Bahamas too, my darling," he said, with a rue smile.

"I will look forward to that day," and she flashed him an affectionate grin in return.

Jack wondered if it was the right time to tell her about the new TV. It was still in its box in the downstairs toilet. It was reduced to half price, as it was a line-end and the last one in the shop. He couldn't resist it. He wanted to surprise her with something they could both enjoy.

"I wish he would come here instead of Grenada. I know he's just got over his ribs and everything, but what with us not affording to go, and I worry that Evelyn's not good for him, not that I said that to him."

"I see." He didn't.

"I'm just worried, that's all. I asked him about the email I sent, suggesting I go over for a weekend, but he said he hadn't seen it. Then he said I shouldn't put myself out, that he was fine, and he would try to visit later in the year. I just wish he'd share more with me, so I knew more about what was going on with his health. He never seems to want to stay on the phone when Evelyn is around either."

"He'll tell you what he wants you to know, no more, no less – whether or not Evelyn or Helen or whoever is around. He's his own man, Amelia. He wouldn't let anyone run his life, including you – just accept it darling, otherwise it will eat you up."

"Yes, I know, I know you're right. I just... I just feel a bit like she's taking him away from me... like a childhood thing."

"Baby, up to now, you've been so good at dealing with it... keep strong – your dad admires you for that, you know."

"He's been poorly again too. Said his stomach had been playing up. He did say he'd been to the doctor though, but they can't seem to find an exact cause. I wish he was closer."

"What difference would it make if he was? He'd still be the same – there's nothing more you can do."

In truth, something about what she was saying made Jack uneasy. Even more than he hated that woman, Evelyn, he hated what was happening to Amelia.

"What I mean is, you've done everything you can. Hey, I've got a surprise for you," he said.

When Amelia opened her eyes, her mixed feelings showed all over her face. "I can't believe it."

"In a good way, or a bad way?"

"I think I'm livid. So it's bad."

"Why? I thought we could snuggle in front of it, as we're not going out much?"

"We already have a perfectly good television."

"But it doesn't do this," and Jack showed her a list of things it could do, including connecting to the internet and downloading films.

"All I want to do is go to America to see my sick father, and you... you spend our hard-earned cash on this contraption. What were you thinking of, Jack?"

"You, Amelia, I was thinking of you. And US. I was trying to think of ways to make our time together nice and enjoyable, give it a lift, give it a bit of a kick, you know? You've been obsessive about your father and now you're shutting me out. I can't bloody win, can I?"

"But we can't afford a new TV. If we can afford a new TV, we can afford to go to America – at least I can."

"Oh, just leave me at home to look after our degenerating companies then?" It sounded childish. "Look, I just want to make you happy in all of this – help you, protect you, somehow." He realised that was the wrong thing to say, as she raised her voice.

"I DON'T NEED PROTECTING! Especially with a stupid TV. What do you think I'm going to do? Immerse myself in soap operas every day and forget everything that's happening in the real world. Get real, Jack. I'm worried. You're worried. We're all fucking worried, and won't stop until we find out why."

He watched her back as she stomped outside to collect his beer bottle. He heard a muffled smash of glass as she threw it in the wheelie-bin. He went to the kitchen to fetch another. Amelia passed him indignantly in the corridor, her anger clouding around her, like a swarm of bees.

"I'm going to bed," she said defiantly.

He didn't reply. He was hurt that she'd chided him, felt patronised. He thought she'd love it. He'd take it back tomorrow. Then he got down on the floor and put it all together. Once up and running, he connected it to the internet. Then he settled on the sofa and began to play. He downloaded a film and began to watch it. The next thing he knew, Amelia was there in front of him, gently stroking his shoulder. He had fallen asleep, of course, and it was the middle of the night. The new TV had switched itself off. The yellow glow from the lamp, that was still on, glimmered through her cotton dressing gown. She looked sexy.

"I'm sorry," she said softly, as she got on the sofa next to him and snuggled in.

"I'm sorry too – I'll take it back to the shop today." He put his arm around her, pulling her in.

"Let's see what it can do first," she said, as she picked up the remote control from the floor.

CHAPTER 15 (AMELIA)

"Guess what?"

"What?"

"Dad's coming in two weeks – I've agreed to pick him up at the airport and take him to the cottage. He gets in around nine in the morning... I'll take him straight to the cottage and get him something to eat, help him get things done, spend some time, and I'll be back by late afternoon. Also, he invited us to dinner at the pub the following night – that's the 20th – are you free? Is all that ok with you? Oh, I'm so happy, Jack... and there's more... he's not bringing Evelyn, so I can have him to myself all of the first day and, of course, I don't mind sharing him with you in the pub, ha-ha. Ah, it will be lovely, I can't wait."

"Amelia... can we talk later, I'm with someone right now."

"Oh, darling, ok... sorry, I didn't realise – should have asked... sorry."

"Its fine... I know you're excited and its great news... I'll call when the meeting is over, ok?"

"Ok, darling. Bye."

I probably wasn't giving Jack enough time. He was there for me every time I moaned about my father. I'd been so up and down this year. I felt guilty. But I was so happy my father was coming to visit. I went back into the office, humming a tune, and settled back into my day. I'd called regularly over the past nine months, since December, our last trip, and emailed too, but often, he couldn't recall receiving anything, and at first, I deduced that he had deleted some messages by accident. He was often tired or sleeping when I called. Again, I brushed this off, and put it down to old age. If Evelyn picked up the phone, it had come to mean that he was snoozing, or busy. But there was an annoying niggle that wouldn't go away; I wondered if much of the time Evelyn "forgot" to pass messages on. Something just didn't seem right.

***

CHAPTER 15 (AMELIA)

Those two weeks passed so slowly. It was early autumn and the nights were still light, but the leaves were just beginning to change. My father had always loved this time of year, the golden mornings and misty evenings. He insisted on continuing to call it autumn and not fall. I remembered kicking leaves in tiny red welly boots, with him holding my little hand, and considered it special that he was coming now.

***

I was breathless in the arrivals hall. When I saw him come through the door, I was quite overcome with emotion and actually jumped up and down. To see his face, and have his eyes meet mine, was overwhelming. I tried to hold back the tears, but they were too strong. The child in me wanted to jump up and throw my arms and legs around him. But when I saw how thin he looked, I suddenly needed to be gentle, in case I knocked him over, like an over-exuberant dog, galloping to greet his master. I waited for him to carefully bring his trolley to a halt, before he opened his arms wide and welcomed me into his gentle and warm embrace.

"Well, well, Amelia. You have missed your old dad, haven't you?" he chuckled. I loved that chuckle.

"You don't know how much, Dad. It's great to see you. How are you? How was the flight?"

"The flight was good, the food was nice and it was comfortable." We started walking towards the car park. "I've had Gwen, the neighbour, switch everything on at the cottage for me yesterday, so it will be nice and warm when we arrive." He always added "the neighbour" after Gwen's name, just in case I ever forgot who she was. I found it endearing. He admired and respected the little, old lady, and trusted her completely. He'd bring her gifts from the States and she always kept them fondly, knowing she would never visit such a vast country, so far away.

"I've picked up some food for you, so you don't have to shop straightaway. And for lunch, I've got us some soup and salad, and a bit of cheese and some fresh, crusty bread. And some fruit too, if you like."

"That's great, Amelia, thank you. Actually, I wasn't too well on the plane. I think I'll just have a small amount and then go straight to bed and rest. I don't want to mess up tomorrow night's plans. There's a lot to catch up on... I want to know how you two are faring with this so-called doom and gloom economy... oh." He put his hand to his head.

"Are you ok, Dad?"

"Yes, yes, fine... I just need some more sleep... didn't get much on the flight, you see."

"Let's get you home... we can catch up tomorrow, as you say. Is your tummy ok now?"

"You know, I'm not sure... I can't really seem to shift it – most of the time, its fine, but sometimes... I'm just terribly sick."

They were reaching the car by now and I helped him get into the passenger seat. His elbow felt bony.

"I suppose you will think I've lost some weight."

"I did notice. Has the doctor come up with anything?"

"Nothing very conclusive... but they did a test before I came away so I'll have the result of that next week when I'm back." I made a mental note to call and check the outcome.

"And I've got pills for the nausea so they seem to be helping." He said this as he took a little packet out of his jacket pocket. I handed him a bottle of water and he swigged it back.

Luckily, the traffic was clear and the journey was quick. I helped him unpack a few things, made him the soup, which he didn't finish, and then took him upstairs for his nap. Once he was comfortable, I left him to sleep, with a promise I would call later. I arrived home to an empty house, subdued. Jack came in later – he was tired.

"I dunno... I think I may have to pack all this in and become a kept man," he joked. "Is your dad ok?"

"No, he's not well. He went straight to bed when he got in. He's only here for three nights, so I hope it goes, whatever he's got. Otherwise, the whole trip will exhaust him."

"That's not even enough time to experience the jet lag," said Jack, as he went up to his office and shut the door.

Dad sounded much brighter that evening – the sleep must have helped him. So, plans were to remain the same. I looked at my watch. Two hours to get some ironing done... then dinner. I was going to make Jack's favourite.

***

We were in the Four Horseshoes, a traditional, old pub nearby with short doorways, creaky floorboards and two big, old fireplaces. Two men stood at the bar, pints in hand, with green wellies and caps, their checked shirts rolled up at the sleeves – each had a well-behaved collie at his feet.

We were sitting at a farmhouse table, in a barn-style room next to the bar, where there were just a handful of other diners. There was an old cuckoo clock on the wall near the table, next to an old hunting print. It tick-tocked loudly, but the bird had been quiet for years. A delicious aroma of roast lamb hung in the air. I thought Dad looked tired and it did occur to me that after his eight-hour flight with an upset tummy, perhaps we shouldn't have come out, but he had insisted, and he seemed so happy, smiling and laughing. The warmth of us three together, in this cosy country pub, chatting and sharing food and wine, comforted me. It felt good.

We all talked non-stop about our lives. My father was attentive, he smiled and nodded, and took a real interest. More so than usual, I thought. I think I even caught him looking at me fondly, once or twice, but then it could have been him noticing my new haircut. He spoke about his house, his friends, his new classic car... he didn't mention Evelyn, except to say that she had gone to her house "upstate" while he was in the UK. He seemed happy and bright – no longer the sick man I saw the day before.

"It's a good job she's got so many houses, Dad!" I joked. "With all of those, I don't suppose she'll be after yours!" It was just a flippant remark to fill the gap, but I did wonder if it came out wrong.

He talked "business" with Jack, and he even flattered me on how well I was dealing with my company too. In passing, I mentioned the missing emails (I was sure there was more than one). He glossed over it.

"Well, you know I'm no computer whizz kid. I struggle each time the technology changes, and that seems to happen so often. A 'technophobe', isn't it, Jack?" he said, laughing.

But as I watched him closely that night, as he laughed with my husband, I saw them, separately from me, as two friends, having a catch-up. It was then I noticed something missing from Dad – something so small, naked to the eye. I felt the urge to ask him "What's wrong, are you really ok, is there something troubling you?', but it seemed the opportunity never came, and even if it had, the words wouldn't come – it was impossible to form even the syllables. I couldn't open my mouth and let out the question. It seemed wrong.

And then it was gone, the thing I thought I saw. And I just saw the two men I loved the most, smiling and laughing, chatting and talking. The thing I thought I saw was a shadow and now it was gone. It probably wasn't even there in the first place.

CHAPTER 16 (JACK)

Jack was shocked at the sight of Roger. He looked as though the life had been sucked out of him. He wasn't sure that Amelia had noticed. She was so enthralled at seeing him after so long that maybe she blocked it out, lest it mar the reunion's enjoyment. But he was a ghost of his former self – thin, tired, shaken. It was the colour of the man's face that he couldn't shift from his mind. The greyness. It reminded him of someone, something. He racked his brains but the memory wouldn't come. Despite it, the evening at the pub was great, and the way he looked didn't seem to affect Roger's good mood. Amelia was relishing her father's company and Roger hers. It warmed him to see them together like that.

"Well, Jack, how's business?" Roger had asked him, as soon as they were settled and had chosen their meals.

"Roger, I have to say, it's pretty challenging right now. Everyone's thinking they can bring the expertise in-house to save a few bob. Trouble is, it's just not that easy. It seems they can pass the effect of drugs off as another illness and deal with it more cheaply that way, than actually accounting for addiction."

"Yes, I understand. It's tough for everyone at the moment. Lots of cutbacks everywhere. My stocks and bonds have had a battering and the property is losing value too. Everyone's worried the markets will crash big time and it makes sense to wind in the spending a little." He sighed. "It will all blow over in a few years though. People don't realise its cyclical. Remember 1990? And the 1973 oil crisis... and it will happen again. We do it to ourselves – each generation thinks they can do better than the last and they just create the same old problems, again and again."

Jack imagined how it would feel to own a property worth three million dollars and see it reduced to two. He could not muster much empathy. But he nodded anyway.

Amelia interjected before things got too depressing. "Hopefully, it won't be that bad this time, though. I remember 1973 – the strikes, the power cuts... I was only a child... I think it was the same year you went to America. I remember food rationing, even... milk, bread... Mum did a brilliant job."

"Yes, she did – it was just after our divorce so times were pretty rough for her then – rest her soul."

"I still sometimes miss her, Dad."

"That's understandable. You did a fine job of holding everything together at that time. You're a very level-headed, young lady – that's why you've done so well with your business too. I am sure you'll make the right decisions when you need to."

Jack felt a swell of love for his wife when he saw her become bashful. It wasn't often she blushed, but then, it wasn't often her father complimented her. He found himself vowing to help create moments like these in the future. To get Amelia and Roger together so they could cherish each other and realise what they meant to one another. Before it was too late. Amelia hadn't seemed to notice how awful Roger looked.

After they dropped Roger at the airport for his flight home, Jack voiced his worry.

"I think your father looked quite ill," he said to her, in the car on the way home.

"Really? I thought he looked thin... but he smiled and laughed so much, he didn't seem ILL ill. He looked better than when he arrived. But he had been unwell on the journey, I suppose. I'm sure that's what did it."

"Mm. I was a bit shocked, if I'm honest. I know he's been up and down, but to me, it looked like he's had a bad illness." He stopped; he didn't want to worry Amelia any more than she already was. But he couldn't help his nagging conscience. "I wonder if he's telling you everything."

***

He woke very early the next morning, and as soon as he opened his eyes, it hit him. The greyness in Roger's face had reminded him of Tony Vincent. Marie and Tony Vincent and their greedy son, Paul. He was just a young PC at the time. His first big case. It all came flooding back. Marie was very often ill and finally collapsed in their home – her death was recorded as infectious hepatitis. Around that time, Tony began to suffer the same symptoms – sickness, vomiting, and nausea. It was their daughter, Carole, who alerted the authorities – she'd noticed the strange behaviour of her brother, Paul, who had already cashed in a life insurance policy on his mother. Jack had been at the hospital the day before Tony had died, investigating Carole's claims – he had been struck by the greyness of Tony's skin. They found arsenic in his body. Marie's body was exhumed and they found it in hers too. Paul eventually admitted in court that he was putting rat poison in their drinks. His plan was to cash in on a life insurance policy he had on them both. He was taken to an asylum – as they called it in those days – before serving three life sentences for the murder of his parents.

Evelyn is poisoning Roger! His investigative cells suddenly woke up and the blood began to pound in his veins, making him nervous, and a little sick. Then, another thought; did he really fall from the loft, or was he pushed? What was it she said? 'We don't need you here; you'll just be in the way.' She wanted them out of the way, so they wouldn't notice what was going on.

It all began to make sense. If Roger wasn't to going to marry Evelyn, or if he didn't change his will to include her, could she have a life insurance policy? Where to start, where to start? Could she have done this before? What about Thomas – how did he die? Wait! He took a deep breath. Was he letting his imagination run away with him? He'd seen stranger things before. Yes. This was totally possible.

Amelia lay quietly beside him, still asleep. It was still dark. He got up and went to his office, and the internet.

***

"Hi Laura, how are you?" It was early evening now. Windy and dark already. Lunchtime in the States. There was a stack of books from the local library, piled up high in front of him – some were overdue. Over the past few days, he had gathered a large amount of information, and his theory was gaining magnitude. He'd said nothing to Amelia.

"Jack, hi, I'm fine, thank you. I'm LOVING my internship."

"Oh, that's great... yes, that's good. Amelia told me you moved to New York." It was important that he didn't sound over-interested.

"Yes, I have and I love it, but I have to live way out in Queens, in a horrible place, because it's all I can afford, sadly."

"But you could stay at Evelyn's, couldn't you?"

"Oh my God, no. She wouldn't have me there. Says she enjoys her privacy too much."

"But I thought your grandpa left it to you."

"Yes, he did, and I should be able to share. But she can live there forever, it's in the will, remember I told you back when I came to stay. So, yeah, even though I'm working here now, and can't afford anywhere central at all, it still doesn't seem right to ask her."

"How long has it been since Thomas died?"

"Six years now. How I miss him – he was wonderful, Jack – you would have loved him."

"I'm sure I would. How did he die?"

"Heart attack. One day in his office... he just collapsed... they tried to help him, but he died in the ambulance. Tragic. We were all devastated."

"Of course. How awful."

"Yeah – Evelyn was, like, way out of control. She didn't know how to handle it, it was weird. She was so cold. We all thought she must have been in shock, but she was so heartless to all of us. It was as though she was... I dunno... *relieved* he'd gone. Anyway, around that time, she seemed to take exception to me somehow. Stopped inviting me to New

York. She seems to hate me being in the same city even. It was so sad, especially after the college accusations."

"What do you mean 'college accusations'?"

"Well, Jack, it's a long story. Oh please don't say anything to Roger because I don't want to upset the applecart, but basically... oh, how can I put this? Well, Evelyn accused me of *cheating* in my exams at college. She told EVERYONE. And they all seemed to believe her – even my parents did for a while, and Granddaddy – that's why he changed the will, to let her stay. Of course, I didn't do it, but it left such a bad impression of me on people I know here in New York. That's why I was so grateful to Amelia for getting me in at Brown & Burton, because they looked at my real results without knowing the rumours. Evelyn did it to keep me out of the city, and out of the apartment, I know it; she told me as much one day. But it's over now. We've all moved on. And I'm here, no matter what. But you can see why I couldn't live there, and why she wouldn't have me."

"Yes, yes I can see that. But you both appear to get on so well with each other."

"She's not right in the head, Jack. Plus, my parents intervened, got us all together one time, just after she met Roger – told us to put down our weapons and make up – life is short, make the best of it. She recovered totally, but she's fragile, and I felt... still feel, a little guilty. I don't think she meant it. Life is so short, and she's an old lady now... how much damage can she do, you know?"

His mind shot back to the surprise birthday party, when Raymond Schilling had warned them about Laura... *"From what I hear, she's not to be trusted."* So that was all down to Evelyn.

"I'm sorry, Laura... that's got to be really tough. But you're right, you're in the right. Anyway, listen, Amelia and I wanted to wish you a happy Thanksgiving for next week, and to know if there was anything from England you wanted for Christmas so we can mail it to you on time."

"Oh you are sooo sweet, Jack. Yes there is – Marmite! Please could I have a big jar of Marmite! I love that stuff."

"I'll rake up all those leaves this weekend," Jack said to Amelia over dinner. "It won't take long." He leant back in his chair. "I'd still love a really big garden, you know. So we can properly enjoy the outdoors in the summer. Like your dad's garden in America. Would be nice to grow herbs and stuff."

"Mm," agreed Amelia, chewing on a potato.

"Did your dad help design his garden, or was it Helen?"

She swallowed. "I think Evelyn changed a few things after she arrived on the scene – remember how she said it was neglected and she was replanting? Helen wanted more evergreen shrubbery-type things, you know, so it was low-maintenance. But I remember Evelyn saying she likes petals and flowering plants. She had some things dug up and re-planted; pretty stuff, you know, like that lily of the valley she had in the kitchen at Thanksgiving last year. I can't believe it's been a year..."

Bingo! There it was. Amelia was still talking, but he didn't hear the rest of the sentence. The words "lily of the valley" resounded around his head.

CHAPTER 17 (JACK)

- *A popular garden plant, native to the Northern Hemisphere in cooler climates, popular for the flower's pleasant scent and its ground-covering trait.*
- *Covers large areas by spreading underground colonies and shoots attractive upright stems called pips.*
- *Its defence against animal consumption is its strong toxicity. ALL parts of the plant are extremely poisonous.*
- *Symptoms of ingestion – blurry vision, diarrhoea, nausea, vomiting, abdominal pain, flushing, drowsiness, disorientation, headache, hot flashes, dilated pupils, red skin rash, excessive salivation, coma, death.*
- *The plant contains glycosides, which can cause deadly altercations in cardiac rhythm, leading to sudden collapse and death.*

His notes on lily of the valley spanned a good few pages in his A4 notebook. Evelyn's motive was clear to him – inheritance or an insurance policy claim. If he could only prove that she'd caused the heart attack of her last husband, with the same motive, and was trying to do the same to Roger, they could officially accuse her and she could be out of their lives. In *Sherlock Holmes* (one of his favourite reads), Sir Arthur Conan Doyle wrote, *"It is a capital mistake to theorise before one has data."* And he had no data. No evidence. Just presumptions. And theories. Even a medical analyst could do nothing without evidence, and even then, the direction of a criminal investigator would be needed. And an investigator would only become involved to prove a crime was committed – a deliberate poisoning as an act of evil intent.

GILDING THE LILY

This is mad. It can't be right. I'm not thinking straight. I'm going around in circles, he thought. Doubt flooded Jack's mind, and he momentarily felt guilty and ashamed. But the suspicions nagged him like a thorn in his side. "Doubt is the beginning, not the end of wisdom." Who said that quote, he thought. Or was it just something he'd heard a police officer or judge say once. He couldn't recall. He thought to the future – what if he was right; Roger dies from poisoning, and he'd said nothing. What if Amelia's beloved father died and an autopsy proved he was right? How would he feel then? It would destroy her – he couldn't let that happen.

"Don't think I'm mad or anything, baby, but I've got a weird feeling about Evelyn." He'd cooked for her, placed candles on the table.

There was a loud snort that came from Amelia's nose. "I know you don't like her... but what do you mean by that?"

He took a deep breath to slow his thoughts down.

"Look... we think she's a bit odd, don't we... but I think it could be more... you know, her erratic behaviour, the outburst at Thanksgiving, the fact she told people at our wedding that she was getting married to your father. I think she could be concocting something... something evil."

"I agree... but those things are just eccentric... not evil, Jack."

"Ok. But why do you think your father hasn't allowed us to visit this year? Do you remember what she said to the nurse when he broke his ribs? And why have your telephone messages not been passed on, why does she tell you he's busy, when he's not? Remember that time she told you he was out to dinner with a friend, but when you asked him about it, he wasn't. I think she wants your dad to think that you are not contacting him – that you don't care."

"It could also be that she just doesn't like me – like you said when we were there, there's jealousy."

"No. It's more than that. I think... well, I think... she's poisoning him."

CHAPTER 17 (JACK)

"WHAT?"

"Look... listen to me. I spoke to Laura. It's not beyond the realms of possibility that Evelyn's a gold-digger – marries for money." Amelia tried to object, but he raised his hand. "It was Evelyn who spread the rumour about Laura cheating in her exams, to damage her reputation, so it was difficult for her to come to New York."

"That was Evelyn?"

"Also, your father doesn't have to marry Evelyn to include her in his will. I think she could have married Thomas for money. He died of a heart attack."

"Yes, a heart attack Jack, not a poisoning."

"Heart attacks can be brought on by poisoning. Think about it... Evelyn came into a lot of money then, and got to live in that apartment, which is rightfully Laura's. The only reason Laura's not there is because Evelyn lied about her, and Thomas changed his will. I think she could be doing the same again... but this time, it's you she's lying about. Even if your dad doesn't change his will, there could be a life insurance policy. And... what if... maybe he didn't fall from the loft last year..."

"What? You think she pushed him?" Amelia was dismayed.

"*Maybe*, I said. It didn't kill him, so now she's trying to poison him instead – or bring on a heart attack."

"Oh my God, Jack... this is mad. But I can see. I can see what you mean. But what would she be poisoning him with?"

"I don't know yet, but a good guess is the lily of the valley. That stuff is highly toxic. Even the leaves are harmful. She could be doing anything with it... putting it in his food, making tea with it."

"She grows that in the garden. Oh no, this is crazy... Shit... Dad mentioned his will when we were there last year... I couldn't understand why he, or she, had brought it up. Let me remember... he said, 'Evelyn said you'd mentioned the will'... and then he told me that there was nothing to worry about. I was a bit put out actually, and said I hadn't done anything of the sort, but I don't think he believed me, and we didn't mention it again. Oh God... that manipulative bi... she's told him I only care about his will. And he hasn't answered that last email I sent him... has he even seen it? But how can we be sure? This is madness. We need to find out for sure, before... before... we... you... say anything else. To anyone."

Jack reached for her hand across the table. He could tell she was going to cry.

"We need to tread very carefully. We know she can't be trusted."

"Let's call him – its mid-afternoon there, he should have napped already."

Amelia stood up and went to the telephone in the hall. Jack followed her and sat on the bottom stair. She pressed a button to put the receiver on speaker and then anxiously dialled her father's number. They listened to the ringing tone. One... two... three.

"Yes, Roger Kavanagh's residence," said Evelyn with her pompous American accent.

"It's Amelia."

"Yes, Amelia?"

"Can I speak to my father?" She looked at Jack and rolled her eyes – as if she would ring for anything else.

"I'm sorry Amelia, but he's resting – can you call back another time?" Jack nodded in an "I told you so" kind of way.

"No, I'm afraid I can't. Can you let him know I'm on the phone?"

"He's unwell, Amelia, but as you insist on disturbing him, I will ask if he would like to speak with you."

Amelia grabbed Jack's hand and squeezed it. They exchanged a look. A minute later, Evelyn came back to the phone.

"Roger is sleeping. Please do not call again. I will ask him to call you."

Amelia's grip tightened on the phone again before she almost dropped it.

"Evelyn, I'm not sure it's really your place to tell me that." Evelyn tried to interrupt, but Amelia raised her voice. "PLEASE pass the message to my dad that I have called. I will know if you don't. And I WILL call again, in an hour. Goodbye Evelyn." She cut off the call and looked directly at Jack. "Oh my God, Jack, what if you're right? Surely it's impossible?"

"It's just a theory at the moment, baby, and it will be very difficult to prove, but you're right – we need to find out, fast."

"But how?"

The phone rang suddenly and they both jumped. The speaker was still on. Jack pressed the button and pointed to Amelia, who instinctively knew to answer.

"Hello?"

"Amelia, it's your father."

"Dad, how are you? Are you ok? I'm worried about you. Evelyn said you were sleeping – sorry if I disturbed you." It all came out in a rushed garble.

"She told me you sounded panicky about something and that you were rude." Jack looked at the ceiling and breathed in loudly through his nose.

"Dad, are you ok?"

"I'm a bit under the weather, to tell the truth, Amelia – but it's nothing to worry about."

"Yes, yes it is, Dad. I am worried – I was worried you didn't reply to my last email, and that you hadn't got the message I'd called last week."

"Amelia, pipe down!" It was an order. "I need to get some rest – I'll be in touch soon, ok? I just wanted to let you know I got *this* message, even if I didn't get the last one."

She knew when to stop. For all her life, she'd always known when to stop. "Ok. Please phone when you can, Dad, I love you."

"Don't worry. Bye now, Amelia."

She threw her hands up in the air.

"I'm going to run a bath," she said, as she sullenly climbed the stairs.

Jack cleared the kitchen then made them both a hot chocolate and took the steaming mugs to the bedroom. He heard the bath draining and then Amelia padded in from the study (which was really a small bedroom). She handed him a piece of A4 paper. It was an email from Evelyn and it made his blood run cold.

Amelia,

Please stop interfering in our lives. Your father does not want to hear from you all the time, especially when you are as excitable and weepy as you were tonight. You are disturbing him with your persistency and your calls are annoying. Please stop telephoning us – your father will call you when he is good and ready to talk to you.

Evelyn

CHAPTER 18 (AMELIA)

I couldn't believe what I was hearing. But a strange dread ran through my veins, as I lay there in the dark. Jack was finally sleeping soundly – the odd snore and mumble emanated from his side of the bed. We'd talked for hours. And now, each thought linked to another in a never-ending chain. "She has enough money of her own so I know she's not after mine" was what my father told me when they first met. Ironically, it comforted us both. Staring into the blackness, I began to get carried away with Jack's theory. If it were true then we had to stop it. It would be murder. No, that couldn't happen, surely, not to us. I tried to mentally rein in my thoughts, as they began to hurry away with me, like a runaway train. Who were we to interfere so belligerently when we could be so wrong? And then again, if we did nothing, and then something terrible happened... that was simply unthinkable.

I turned over to put my arms around my husband. He was warm and his breathing was soft and slow. I tried to relax into his body, and allowed his raising ribs to rock me.

I woke at 6a.m. with a feverish energy. A strange vitality or stamina had suddenly appeared in me – a drive to endure, a surge of power, like a battery charger. I wouldn't let anyone hurt my dad. Something had to be done. Today.

Jack was already up and bent over his keyboard in the study – his eyes fixed to screen, his reading glasses perched right on the end of his nose.

"How long have you been up?"

"Since five. I've been doing a little internet research. At first, I couldn't find anything about Evelyn and I was beginning to wonder if she's even lied about her name, but then I found her addresses, age, names of relatives and so on, on a public records site. The most interesting thing to come out of this," he said, dissatisfied, "is that she has two so-called criminal convictions, but they're only parking tickets, which were paid up."

"Oh," I said, as I sat down next to him – he wasn't yet dressed either, and we both looked at the screen in our slippers and dressing gowns. "I was thinking... maybe we should go... I think we need to go. Do you want a cup of coffee?"

"I know there's more to come, but yes, you're right. We could find out more from Laura too, maybe meet up with her. But let's not tell your dad and Evelyn. Possibly until we are there. If I can find the tickets cheaply enough, I'll pay on my credit card. I've got a bit of space on it now – paid a chunk off last month. And yes please."

"Eh?"

"To the coffee."

I left Jack to his internet bashing and went to the kitchen. After a bowl of cornflakes and two cups of coffee, I finally found it easier to focus. I put all dubious thoughts aside, showered, dressed and went to the office.

When I got back that evening, I was astounded at what Jack had found out. Evelyn was born in 1936 and her family originally came from Germany in the late 1800s. Aged seventeen, she had married an estranged member of the Austrian nobility, but it only lasted two years, and that had ended in divorce by 1950. Her second husband passed away after a serious food-poisoning incident in a hotel in Florida in the mid-seventies. There had been several other casualties, but no other deaths. The hotel's insurance had paid out, as well as her own. Her third marriage to Thomas had actually lasted twenty-three years. We already knew how that one ended. She'd lived in Europe, Florida (where she owned a condo), New York, Connecticut, Harrisburg, Chicago and Washington, DC. She holidayed regularly in Hawaii, where she also owned a house, the Bahamas and Mexico. She shopped regularly at Brooks Bros, Saks, Gucci, Prada, Luis Vuitton, and Macy's. Her car was leased. She was a member of a book club and a restaurant club in New York, and sat on the committee for a local cancer charity. She was a regular private buyer at Christie's. She usually flew first class but hadn't travelled for some time. She owned one other property in Connecticut.

"Wow," I said. "How on earth..."

"Like you say, it's not what you know, it's who," Jack smirked.

"It's great information, but it doesn't help us work out if she's capable of killing someone though, does it? Did you speak to Laura?"

"Yes, I did. I said we're planning a surprise visit in January – the fares are cheaper – she was delighted and said we could stay with her on the first night."

"Great."

"So we leave on 4th – it's only a couple of weeks."

"Oh my God!" I said, sounding like Laura. "I'd better get time off work then."

***

The streets of London were alive with the party season. Our office joined up with a few other companies at a pre-organised party at a hotel in Regent Street. It started off with a drinks reception, in a grand hall with stacks of cornicing, huge chandeliers and a painted ceiling. There were probably 200 smartly-dressed individuals, mostly young, sipping from champagne flutes, the girls cooing over their neatly-done hair dos, lipstick and heels, the boys comparing bowties and shirts. We were called through to dinner and sat at a large, round table, which seated all 10 of us. Jack was at my right, and Sarah, my trusted accountant and fellow director, to my left. Her current partner was to her other side. Partway through the turkey course, I leaned over and brought Sarah up to date with what was happening.

"I'll only be away a week. And I can't imagine what will happen, but Jack is convinced there is something going on."

Sarah hadn't responded all the way through my story. She had often behaved as though I made mountains out of molehills, as though nothing could ever happen to anyone we knew, least of all ourselves. Sarah had never married, but had a son, who was on the brink of a divorce. Although he was "the best thing that ever happened" to her, he was also her "only irresponsible choice". She'd recently passed the massive half-century birthday – she'd had a sedate dinner party for six in her flat in Balham to celebrate. She'd worn a long, woollen, brown skirt, which suited her thick, straightened, ginger hair, and thanked everyone for coming at least six times each. I was very fond of Sarah – she'd helped me set up the business all those years ago, and joined me when it was making enough money to pay us both. We always joked that we were good at running a business together because I had the creativity and she had the sound sense, and wouldn't let me get carried away or spend too much money. When I stopped talking and put my knife and fork down on the plate in front me, I turned to her to see if she was still listening.

"I think you've finally gone mad," she said, looking me straight in the eye.

"Oh."

"I think you should leave your poor father alone – he's obviously found a partner that makes him happy and now you're going to try to sabotage it. That's rotten."

"Oh no. I don't mean it to be rotten, I know it could seem like that, but what if Jack's theory is true?"

"Unlikely, but if you've got it in your head, I suppose you've got to try and follow through a plan to get it out of your head. It's destructive though – to you all. The woman's probably just jealous. Just be careful, Amelia, please."

"You're right, I know," I said, shrugging. "But even if we put the whole poison thing aside, I still need to find out what's wrong with my dad."

"Yes, you do. I know you do, honey," and she put her arm around me, "but don't go upsetting yourselves for no reason. Be sensible, ok?"

She turned to Rob, her partner, and squeezed his knee – in case he was feeling left out. The rest of the team were itching to get on the dance floor, and it wasn't long before we were all up. Sarah and Rob got a cab at around midnight. Jack and I stayed with the others and danced slowly to a poor cover of *I Don't Want to Miss A Thing* by Aerosmith, before joining the merry throng for high-kicking to *New York, New York*.

"How apt," I giggled to Jack, as we applauded the end of the night.

As we wobbled down Regent Street in our big coats, we gawped at the brightness of the city in the crisp, winter night. Masses of bright white bulbs in festive shapes were stretched high across the road, shop windows were ablaze, and the traffic surged, even though it was past one. It was beautiful. Jack flagged down a taxi. As soon as we were on our way, he continued with the party song.

"Start spreading the news..." he sung tunefully to me, *"we're leaving in two weeks... We're gon-na... be a part of it, New York New York..."* He squeezed my shoulder as he drunkenly continued. *"That vagabond woman... is a very bad person... she's in the heart of it... New York, New York... but she won't get her way, she'll take a long holiday, and then it's up to you New York, New York..."* His left hand was conducting an invisible choir, as his wide eyes looked into mine to check I was getting it. Once finished, he fell about laughing, and I joined him.

"Very clever, Jack" I said, convincingly. "Very clever."

When we got home, there was a medium-sized box on the doorstep.

"Lucky that's still here and not nicked," said Jack, as he stumbled over it and pulled it through the door.

I picked it up and took it through to the kitchen. It was the hamper full of English goodies that I'd sent to Dad for Christmas. There was no hand-written note inside, just a printed docket with the words "NOT REQUIRED, RETURN TO SENDER". Underneath, in an unmistakable, black scrawl, was Evelyn's signature.

CHAPTER 19 (JACK)

The following week leading up to Christmas seemed busy in every way. Jack completed an important report for a new client whose premises he'd visited with the dogs and testing kits. The work quality of some members of their team was diminishing, and the HR director had called in Jack to investigate. The dogs found traces of drug use in the toilets and the kits had identified two members of staff who had still been under the influence of drugs or alcohol during working hours. His report offered various solutions. He'd asked an old police friend, who now ran a rehab centre, Peter Brown, to work with him on various recovery options. Peter had inserted a few extra pointers, which had added clarity to the report, and Jack welcomed that. After they had finalised everything, they went for lunch at a busy pub near Elephant and Castle. At some point, Evelyn came up in conversation.

"She sounds offensive," Peter had said.

"Yes, I'd like to wipe her off the planet, to be honest, out of our lives anyway," Jack had returned.

"Ha-ha. Old Skilling would be the one then," Peter laughed, as he took another swig of his pint.

"Yeah, you're right. He'd make a brilliant assassin." Jack said, as he remembered Bill Skilling, the ex-user turned informant who had helped him climb the ladder of drug-squad success in the '90s.

***

Jack submitted his report confidently the day before the deadline (Christmas Eve). Then he'd sat down with Amelia to plan seasonal visits to Kevin, his younger brother, at the care home, and various friends. He'd managed to get some DIY done in the house, whilst he put up the lights and the decorations, including choosing, buying and transporting home a tree. He was grateful that Amelia had done all the present shopping, including stocking fillers. Though, he had shopped himself for her – a gold necklace was hidden in the drawer in his bedside table. It had a little heart pendant and he couldn't wait to see her face light up when she saw it. He'd also planned the trip to New York with brilliant efficiency. He knew what time they were leaving, which route to take to the airport, what to do when they arrived, how to get to Laura's apartment, and which bell to ring once they got there. He'd arranged tickets, money, passports and visa-waivers. He'd packed his research on Evelyn, and poisonous garden plants, in a neat folder and created various places for it on his laptop, so it was all easily referenced, found and backed up.

As usual, Evelyn had succeeded in continually blocking Amelia's calls to her father. After Christmas passed, his wife was becoming more and more angry that she'd not managed to speak to Roger at all. She didn't give up. Jack admired her persistence. Saturday came, Boxing Day. Finally, Miriam answered.

He could only hear one side of the conversation, but he knew it was deadly serious. Amelia was crying as she finished the call.

"He's been in the hospital since last Sunday! He had blood clots in both his legs and couldn't walk. They fixed him, and he should come out tomorrow. But he's not going home! They are staying in the city at Evelyn's place. Miriam said she assumed we knew. What's more, she said there was a lawyer at the house the day before he went to the hospital. They were signing documents, but she didn't see what. She's going in each day to feed the cat. Oh my God, Jack – he's been in hospital for a week and no one told me!"

She was beside herself for a full 30 minutes. Jack tried to console her, but could only watch as she sank further into a kind of depression. How or why were there blood clots in his legs? Was that a symptom of poisoning?

Once Amelia could speak again, she called the number Miriam had given her.

"Dad...? I tried and tried to call you – I didn't know what was happening to you. Did you get any messages? I'm so sorry that I didn't know that you were in hospital... We can come over, shall we come...? But I do worry... How are you, what's happened...? But how, why? Dad, wait..."

"What did he say?" Jack asked, squeezing her hand.

"He said he didn't want me to worry, that we shouldn't come, and he was too tired to talk."

***

The next day, she tried again, and the conversation seemed much brighter.

"He's getting out today. They are going to Evelyn's. He said it's closer to the doctor and the hospital for check-ups. And he'll be having occupational therapy for a while; it's closer and easier for them to travel, especially with all the snow."

Not for the first time, Jack speculated that Roger wasn't telling her everything. But it wasn't his place to say.

"We have to get over there. I can't bear this. What if you're right, Jack? She'll lock him away and never let us speak to him. She'll sprinkle arsenic on everything. Even when we get there, she won't let us in. I don't know what I'm going to do. I can't believe he is letting her do it."

"She's too clever for the arsenic. That would show up in a post-mortem. If she's doing it, it's subtle. And slow."

"And painful! Oh God, he must be in so much pain, Jack."

And that's how it went on. Their suspicion growing daily, the worry driving them mad. They continued to call every day, sometimes twice, and more if no one answered. But they didn't manage to speak to him.

***

On New Year's Eve, an email arrived in Amelia's inbox.

> *December 31st, 2008*
> *Amelia and Jack,*
> *I am afraid to say that we are finding your persistent phone calls intrusive and counterproductive to Roger's wellbeing. Henceforth, we will accept calls from you at 12 noon on Sundays only. Roger already told you this yesterday evening, when you called three times and woke us both up. Please be positive when you call – if you have nothing helpful to say, don't phone. By the way, we had a cosy, meaningful Christmas. A coffee table book and CDs arrived from Laura, and my family has showered us with more goodies. It was sad that we received nothing from you. Roger was very disappointed.*

They stuffed themselves, in their winter coats, into the back of a yellow cab. Their breath steamed up the windows. The rain did not show any signs of letting up. Instead, it turned to sleet, and later snow. It was a dark night – the weather had been appalling – much worse than in London. Soon, they would be at Laura's apartment.

"It seems weird – that we're here and they know nothing about it," said Amelia, pensively, as the skyline panned out over the river; the blackened clouds behind giving it an ominous glow. She fingered her gold heart pendant gently.

"Ignorance is bliss, so they say," Jack replied.

For half an hour, they criss-crossed streets through Brooklyn until they reached Queens. In between a nail bar and a dry-cleaner's was a narrow glass door with a double-locking handle. They heaved their cases out of the trunk and wheeled them into the tiny, square vestibule. Jack paid the driver and Amelia pressed the button marked with a "D". Seconds later, the intercom crackled and Laura's voice answered.

"Oh my Gawd, are you guys here?" There was a loud click, followed by feet hurrying down the stairs at the far end of the corridor. Hugs and kisses took place there, under the dim, bare bulb.

"Second floor – no elevator, I'm afraid," said Laura. "Here, I'll help," and she took the smaller case, as they climbed the stairs clumsily and noisily. "My roommate, Jackie, is still at her folks, so I will have the sofa bed and I've cleaned up my room for you guys. You'll see why it's probably only convenient for a night... but we can go out for dinner once you've freshened up."

The apartment was tiny. Jack didn't think it should be called an apartment. More like a cupboard. He remembered how Amelia had worried about their spare room being small. No need for that now.

"How on earth do two of you fit in here?" Amelia asked, as she looked around the small space. There was an odd smell in the main area – something like stale food. There was a sink, cooker and a fridge along one wall by the door, then a big TV. Opposite, a sofa behind a coffee table, and a small dining table with two chairs either side. Beyond was a small double bedroom. On the other side, a shower-room, with old, mouldy tiles and a craggy, brown crack in the ceiling, where an old leak had been fixed more than a few times. Amelia noticed that the taps were coming loose, and the hot water didn't work in the basin. The only window was in the bedroom, and it looked as though it was about to fall out – the wood was completely rotten at the bottom.

"I can't open it – but the landlord says it's too expensive to fix."

Amelia drew aside the net curtain and looked out, past the fire escape stairs, into the junky, snow-covered backyards opposite. A couple of weathered American flags hung, dripping over concreted areas, fenced with chain link.

"I pay more because I have the bedroom and a part-time waitress job in the diner around the corner. Jackie lives in here," she explained, as they stood huddled back in the main area. "It's not bad for 1,800 a month. We're hardly ever here so it works out well."

"Ha! Nearly two grand a month when you could be on First Avenue for nothing – that doesn't sound right to me," Jack said, bitterly.

"Well, that's just how it is, I guess. I'll get the apartment one day."

They both admired Laura's acceptance of the situation and told her so over dinner. They'd gone to a low-key Italian place. Laura was in the mood for talking.

"She made my Granddaddy happy, and I'm thankful for that. Yeah, she can be a real bitch, but I don't think she can help it – especially now. She seems to have become forgetful the past couple of years – you know – names, places, holidays – she doesn't seem to remember as well as she used to. Sometimes, I see her just sitting there... breathing deeply – as if she is trying to remember something. Then she just snaps out of it. Sometimes I hate her, I really do. But it doesn't last long." She smiled and looked first at Jack, then at Amelia. There was something unconvincing about that grin. They watched her, as she animatedly told them how she felt about Evelyn. How a small part of her resented her lies in the past, but that she had been able to put it aside. There was something in the way that she expressed herself that Jack thought was disingenuous. But then again, maybe it was just because she was American and much of her storytelling was lost in translation. They decided not to mention their theory to her. It would be pointless, right now. She had tried very hard to be the good person here. Why spoil it?

***

The next morning, they woke late. Laura had already left for work. There was a note on the tiny table.

I hope your trip goes well, guys. Say hi to Roger and Evelyn – I hope they like the surprise, ha-ha! It was great to see you. Don't do anything I wouldn't, ok? Laura x

CHAPTER 20 (AMELIA)

"Mr Kavanagh, you have visitors... Your daughter and her husband, sir." The doorman spoke politely and clearly into the receiver. I heard a faint voice on the other end reply with surprise, whilst he nodded, and then said, "I'll send them right up, sir."

The elevator seemed slow. We turned right and walked down the thickly-carpeted corridor. Expensive artwork adorned the walls. I had not noticed this before. Dad was already waiting at the apartment door. I breathed in audibly. He was a hunched, ghost-like, pale form, clothed in a checked dressing gown and warm pyjamas. He looked so much smaller than normal, I found it hard to believe it was him. And this person was most definitely sick. The face was gaunt, the eyebrows grey, white stubble on the chin. He stepped back to invite us in. And he smiled.

"Amelia. Jack. What are you doing... h... h... here?" His weak voice cracked and he coughed, as though he had a bad case of bronchitis. "Come in. But I thought I told you not to come." We all shuffled into the living room and Dad sat down in his normal chair, the leather one with the high back.

"I'm sorry to surprise you like this, Dad, but we HAD to come. I had to see you, I've been worried sick. We brought you this." As I hauled the hamper onto the coffee table, I fought off every urge to tell him that Evelyn had cruelly sent it back to us. But I kept quiet – he had enough on his plate right now.

"Nice," he croaked, as he looked at the list of ingredients. "Very thoughtful of you – some of my favourite things," and he smiled again. "Evelyn will be back momentarily. She's only popped out to the drugstore. She won't be happy to see you – we've been trying to keep everyone at bay, not just you. Where are you staying?"

"We've got a hotel in Queens – we're not too far away if you need us to do anything for you. Is this all about your stomach problems, Dad, or something different?"

"I'll explain later. I am too poorly today – let's just sit for a while. At least until Evelyn is back. And then, I do have to go back to bed. It's a variety of things, Amelia – all you need to know is that I am sick. I didn't want you to know how sick – I know what you're like. I didn't want you to see me like this, and panic, be upset. It won't be long until I'm better, and then we can talk properly."

"But I need to know what's wrong so that we can help."

At that moment, they heard the entrance door slam shut and Evelyn swung in. She wore a fur coat and threw a brown paper grocery bag down on the table – a few bits of fruit fell out. A bottle of pills too.

"What in hell's earth are you two doing here?"

"We were worried, Evelyn. It's my father, he's clearly sick." I was determined to remain calm.

"He doesn't need you here – especially after what you did. You are both most unwelcome and you need to leave."

"I don't know what you mean, but to me, it looks like he needs medical attention."

"He HAD medical attention – do you think I'd just leave him if he were sick?"

"Calm down everyone," yelled Jack – it was the first time he'd spoken.

"Well said, Jack – I'm going back to bed, please try to keep the noise down," said Roger.

"I'll help you, Dad..." and I joined him, as he allowed me to take his elbow. At the door to the bedroom, he said, "Thank you, Amelia – I can manage from here."

"You're sure?" I thought about asking him what Evelyn meant when she said "especially after what you did", but he was stressed enough, so I let him go. I half expected to hear shouting as I re-entered the living room, but it was quiet. Evelyn had gone into the kitchen.

"She told us to leave, so come on, let's go," said Jack.

When we arrived back at the hotel, we started on our list of people to call. Although shocked by our arrival and worried by our news, Ali promised to help us as much as she could without crossing the line, and invited us to dinner the following evening. She told us she shared the same medical practice as my father. So she wouldn't feel that she was doing anything unjust or immoral by sharing contact information, I asked their name and looked up the details on the internet.

"I'm his daughter," I said to the nurse. "I just need to find out if he's being treated. He's so ill – he looks terrible. I'm so worried and I just don't know what to do."

"We suggest your ask you father to inform us that it's ok for us to speak you. It's all we can do."

"Ok – thank you." Fat chance of that happening, I thought, as the call ended. He clearly thought I was interfering as it was. "Jack, we'll just have to go back again tomorrow and keep trying to make sense of the whole thing. We need to get to him when she's not there. That means watching the apartment and waiting for her to leave."

"You clever little detective, baby! You can be my undercover partner any time! We start tomorrow."

***

Evelyn didn't leave the building until the afternoon the next day. We phoned as soon as she was 200 yards away.

"You two aren't going to give up are you?" Dad said. "You'd better come up."

"We just need to make sense of what's going on, Dad," I said, as soon as we were seated. "You seem so ill but also closed off, and as though you are angry with me for some reason that I don't know about."

"Well, I am ill, but you know about that. I haven't tried to hide anything – you know what's been going on. With regard to my being angry, it would be a lie to say I'm not.

Evelyn told me about what happened last time you were here. About the argument you had."

"You mean when you broke your ribs after Thanksgiving? That's over a year ago now."

"The time lapse doesn't make it any less true."

"Doesn't make what less true? What did she tell you happened that night?"

"She told me that... that you seemed to be under the impression I was very rich. That you made a rude comment about us having a maid to send to the cleaners with our clothes. Or something like that. That you deliberately spilled something on her dress."

"WHAT?"

"That she overheard you telling Jack how much you were looking forward to inheriting the house in Long Island."

I was stunned. "And you believed her?"

"You know how hard I've worked over the years, Amelia, and how sensitive I am about these things. It's not an out of the ordinary thing to happen. It's possible. That you would want that. She just thought I should know your motives, that's all."

"I can't believe it, Dad. I... I'm shocked... Do you mean that's the reason you've been distant all this time? Why didn't you ask me about this when you came over at the end of last summer? I thought it was about the note I left you."

"What note? I didn't see any note. I wanted to test you. I told you about Evelyn staying at her house in Connecticut, and you said something about her not needing my house. That's when I knew she might be right. Why would you say something like that if the subject matter is so irrelevant to you?"

I went cold. He said he hadn't seen that note. Miriam had found it in the bin ripped to pieces... I thought it was him and never mentioned it again, because I thought it had angered him. But now, I realised it was her – she must have ripped it up before he'd seen it. And now this... about the house... I could only vaguely recall the conversation in the pub that night. But I remembered what I had said, then, because I had worried that it had come out wrong.

"Dad. That's ridiculous. I'm sure that was a joke. The argument Evelyn and I had that time was all one-sided. She just seemed to explode for no reason. It was very strange behaviour. I didn't want to say anything in order not to upset you. But I left you a note – to explain."

"So it's not true then – you don't care about my will?"

"Of course it's not true, of course you can leave what you want to whomever you please, I told you that before," I implored. But as I thought of it, I realised, I did care – I did care that he could change his mind and leave things to her, because she had cruelly manipulated him. It's not that I *wanted* him to leave things to me – it's that I *didn't* want him to leave things to her. "I can't believe you've been thinking that about me all this time."

"Look Amelia. Evelyn is not a terrible person. She's brought me great happiness since Helen died. Before I met her, I was very lonely. Evelyn makes me laugh. She is kind and she cares about me..."

"I know, but..."

He cut me off. "I haven't finished... It does appear that you have been fairly spoilt in your behaviour towards her. Could it be because you are jealous?"

Me? ME? I opened my mouth to say more but the words wouldn't come. I looked at Jack, pleading for his help, as tears blurred my vision.

"Roger," he said, "Amelia isn't jealous. Evelyn has not been nice to either of us over the past year or so. It's true that she's been two-faced – we've seen two sides to her. In actual fact, we think that Evelyn is plotting something dodgy and has been for some time. The thing is..."

"The thing? What's the thing, Jack?"

"We think that you're ill because she's... she's..."

"She's what? Spit it out Jack – what's on your mind?"

"Well, to tell you the truth, we think she's manipulating you, not Amelia. We think she is after your money and... and is trying... trying to..." Both Amelia and Roger's eyes were burning into his face. "We think she may be trying to poison you."

My heart did a funny jump in my chest and I searched my father's shocked face, waiting for a response. It had sounded ridiculous, laughable even.

"After you change your will, of course" Jack added, making use of the pause. It made it worse. The absurdity of it was horrifying.

Dad starting coughing again. When he stopped, he wiped his mouth with the back of his hand and said, "That's the most preposterous thing I've ever heard and I think you'd better go."

"But..."

"Now, before I completely lose it."

I knew we had no choice but to leave. The look in his eyes reminded me of his anger when I was a child, when I'd screamed about how I hated Helen when she'd locked my puppy in the shed at the cottage.

"Bye Dad," I said quietly, as I got up from the chair. Jack did the same. "I'm so sorry."

CHAPTER 21 (JACK)

"Oh my Gawd," said Ali. The four of them were seated around her dining table in their pretty house in Manhasset. It was a typical American family home, with a large garage, complete with basketball hoop and an American flag. Her children were the same age as Amelia, and had families of their own.

Amelia began to clear the debris from the table. She stacked the bowls in front of her but didn't get up.

"Help us, Ali. Ray, what do you think?" Jack said.

"Well... "Ray replied. He breathed in deeply and slowly while he looked at Ali, who was looking anxiously at Amelia. "I'm not sure we should get involved."

"I agree," said Ali, still looking directly at Roger's daughter. "You look so like your dad tonight, honey. It breaks my heart to not help, but you must understand, we just can't."

"Oh... I'm so sorry," said Amelia, apologetically. "Of course, it's a silly thing to have asked. It's just that we... I... well, we're just running out of ideas. I am sure Dad is ill and hiding something serious from me, from us. We're supposed to go home tomorrow night, but I can't leave things like this."

"I see your point... I think," continued Ali, "but really, honey, that is a huge accusation. I'm not really sure it's your place to delve so deep. I know you are worried, but I think you need to respect your father's wishes. He's a good man. And he's fond of Evelyn, and she's doing what she thinks is right. If they don't want you involved then they don't want you involved. We did try to visit ourselves, but he said he needs a bit of time to himself right now. He's not at death's door – you need to worry less."

"You think we should keep our noses out?" asked Jack, bluntly.

Ray nodded. "To be frank, yes. I'm sorry, but we can't support you in this. On our part, it would be... well – it's disrespectful. You're going to have to find another way."

"Ok," said Jack. He looked down at his hands.

Amelia stood up with the bowls. "We understand. Sorry to have burdened you with it all, but thank you for listening anyway." She walked toward the kitchen.

"I'm sure the woman is not as devious as you are making out," Ray said, his eyes following her. He patted Jack on the shoulder after he put on his coat. "I agree she's not everyone's cup of tea, but a killer? I don't think so."

Amelia returned and Jack helped her on with her jacket and scarf. They felt embarrassed.

"Take care, you guys. We hope you find what you're looking for."

Jack swallowed his anger, not just for Amelia's sake, but for his own. Their drive back to the hotel was quiet and uncomfortable.

***

The next morning, they extended their stay. Among telephoning the airline and the car hire people, Jack contacted the DEA to catch up with James Eagle. He'd last seen James at a conference in Washington three years ago, just before Jack had retired from the force. James had moved on to another department, but he was easy to track down. Amelia emailed Sarah at the office, saying she would be away for a little longer than planned. Then she purchased a pay-as-you-go mobile phone and texted the number to Miriam, Laura and Ali. The first call was from Laura. They were in their room at the hotel, drinking coffee and looking on the internet for short-term apartments. Amelia put it on loudspeaker so that they could both hear.

"Are you guys ok? Ali called me and told me about your lily of the valley theory and what happened last night. She's concerned for you guys. Look, I want you to know I don't think it's a stupid idea – I can totally see why you could think that. It's even something I've thought is possible before, but I never dared voice it."

"Thank you, Laura, it's great that someone believes us," said Amelia.

"I feel for you guys. But I think I can help you make more sense of it all."

"Oh?" She looked at Jack urgently.

"I've received an email from Evelyn about your dad. You weren't copied."

"What does it say?"

"It's not good news, I'm afraid. But Evelyn isn't poisoning your father, Amelia. He has cancer."

Amelia was immediately still. She was standing by the bed, speechless. Jack stood up from the desk and went to her side. He saw her eyes mist over, her mouth open. She became ashen, and as she audibly drew in a gulp of breath, her knees seemed to slowly give way beneath her. Gravity dragged her to the floor, her shoulders slumped forward.

"Hello?" came Laura's voice from the mobile.

Jack took over the conversation. "Laura, its Jack. Amelia's a little shocked. Can you please email me a copy of Evelyn's note? Once we've made sense of it all, we'll get back to you. Thank you. Thanks for letting us know. We really appreciate it."

"Sure," replied Laura. "I'm so sorry to be the bearer of this awful news. So, so sorry. It's hit us all hard."

Jack put his arms around Amelia's racking torso, as she tried to catch her breath.

"How long has he known? My God, Jack, I can't believe it."

The email came through within minutes. Jack had picked up Amelia from the floor and she was now sitting at the table with a warm cup of coffee, and a blanket around her shoulders. He passed her the laptop so that she could read it for herself.

It is with sadness that I must inform you that Roger has been taken very ill over the past few weeks. I have been attending medical appointments with him of late, but we have now received the terrible news that we did not want to hear. Roger has stage 4 pancreatic cancer. Due to his direct family not being around, he will now be cared for by myself when he is not in hospital. He is to start chemotherapy immediately. For now, please email instead of calling, but I will be in touch again soon and let you all know his progress. Fond regards, Evelyn.

***

The doorman at Evelyn's apartment block had been instructed not to let anyone visit. Jack was very insistent, but the doorman was more so.

Amelia finally spoke. She'd said nothing since the email. It was getting dark now. They had resolved to go to Evelyn's apartment to apologise, and then go and find something to eat. "Can we leave a message, at least?" she asked.

"Sure. Just leave it here with me. I'll take care of it, ma'am." He handed her a notebook and a pen. Efficient, thought Jack.

She scribbled a few words and handed the note back. "Thank you," she said, as she looked into the doorman's eyes. It read, "Dad, I'm sorry. I'm sorry for what we thought and said. Please call us on this number. We will be in NYC for at least another week. Laura has told us the news. I'm desperate to see you. Your daughter, Amelia."

Later, the aroma of stale coffee surrounded them in a diner. It made her feel nauseous. The bright lights made her headache worse.

"How could you let me believe that awful story about the flowers? How STUPID. How utterly ridiculous, Jack. He'll never forgive us."

"Oh, so it's my fault, is it? Well, I explained my theory. Yes, I got wound up in it, but I needed to tell you. It could have been true, you know it could. You believed it too."

"No. Not at first. You MADE me believe it."

"I HAD to Amelia..."

"No. You didn't. Shut up. You didn't have to. You're always so ready to play the 'good cop, bad cop', aren't you? You're not a cop anymore, Jack. Stop trying to relive your 'good ole days'."

Jack felt a surge of anger and his voice rose, making people look at them. "I'm not trying to relive ANYTHING. I'm trying to help you, Amelia. I'm trying to help you get through this situation, can't you see that, can't you understand? I'm trying to be a supportive husband, for fuck's sake. Not that you'd notice anything, you're so wrapped up in your own world."

"ME?" she screeched. "Well, thinking up a ridiculous Agatha Christie plot like that is NOT helpful, Jack. For God's sake. It's... desperate. What were you thinking? It's you that's wrapped up in your own world."

"What if it was true, Amelia, what then? You'd have been bloody thanking me then, wouldn't you? And what if I'd said nothing and it were true. And I'd known all along. And I didn't say anything because of how pitiful it sounded. How would you have felt then?" He could hear his voice rising again. "Just think about that for a minute, will you?"

"STOP SHOUTING!" she shouted back. They each took a deep breath. "God, it's miserable, no wonder everyone had been so upset. How are we ever going to get through this? It's pathetic. It was pathetic, Jack."

Jack leant back into the leatherette seat, threw his hands in the air, and let them slam back down on the table. But he said nothing. They were silent for a while. He picked at a burger. Amelia couldn't face food.

"What I don't understand is how he didn't know sooner," she said eventually, a look of total abandonment on her face.

"He did," said Jack. "He simply didn't want you to know."

***

The next day passed in a blur. All the research they did was negative.

"Pancreatic cancer is the fifth most common cause of cancer death in the UK."

"Pancreatic cancer has the poorest survival rate, with just 15% surviving one year."

"Research into pancreatic cancer lags well behind almost every other cancer."

"... probably weeks, as opposed to months..."

It didn't help soothe Amelia's fears.

"But what if it's spreading?" Her questions came. "And how much pain is he in? How are they controlling it?" And then: "Is he going to have chemo? And anyway, would he even feel ok to go through that?"

They called the hospital where they treated the blood clots but were rejected.

"I'm sorry, ma'am. We are not authorised to give any information except for the proxy holder."

"What's a proxy holder?" replied Amelia.

"Ma'am, it's the only person we're allowed to talk to."

***

They found a cheap, short-term let – a grotty studio apartment on the Upper East Side, not far from Evelyn's. Forty-eight hours passed with no contact. Countless times, they telephoned and only reached a voicemail message. Twice more they visited, to the shake of the doorman's head.

When Evelyn finally answered, it was late.

"It's Amelia," Amelia said, as she spoke into the receiver, with a certain desperation.

"Yes Amelia, what do you want?"

"Please can I speak to Dad... please Evelyn?"

"He doesn't want to speak to you or see you – no visitors whatsoever, I'm afraid."

"Please, I need to see him. We just want to apologise. We're still here in New York. We'll be here a while. I need to see him. Please Evelyn. Be reasonable. Laura told us about the cancer. I need to see my dad. Have you given him the CD we sent with our Christmas card?"

Jack remembered the CD. It was a compilation of rousing, light classics, and included *I Dreamed A Dream* and *Both Sides Now*, both of which he knew touched Amelia's heart. She had wanted to send a message of love to her father. It didn't come back like the hamper.

"Your father is not here. We are 'living on the wind', Amelia, as the sailors say. He has the CD – I gave it to him myself. He was most impressed I had done the research and thought of something so tender. But you two have no sense of what 'care' means. Please don't call again."

CHAPTER 22 (AMELIA)

On the morning of the seventh day in New York, another email came.

Biop results avail Tues. Roger will call you Tues p.m. Voicemail or emails will not be responded to. Evelyn.

Tuesday was tomorrow. We met up with James Eagle for lunch near Central Park. He was younger than Jack, by about 10 years, but looked older. He had an understated, experienced aura – like he'd been there, done everything and collected all the t-shirts, but he wouldn't show you any of them. As well as working for several law enforcement agencies, he also held a JD degree.

He and Jack shook hands warmly and patted each other's shoulders then Jack introduced me. I liked James at once. His tall frame, his big smile and tall shoulders offered certainty somehow. He seemed trustworthy. And not only did he believe us, but he took us seriously. A lot had happened for them both since they last met. Their happy demeanour promised to catch up later. Right now, there was important work to be done.

Jack had explained the situation to James on the phone, but now wanted him to know just how desperate they were.

"So, as far as Roger's medical condition is concerned," Jack explained, "we both think it is very serious. Evelyn is heavily guarding him and preventing us both from seeing him, or finding out information. He may, or may not be agreeable to this, we don't know. All we know is that he has not contacted us himself – but she may have not passed on our contact details."

"Ok." James said the word slowly, as if he had just finished the exhausting process of taking it all in. "There's one thing that's loud and clear. If he doesn't wanna see you, then he doesn't wanna see you, right? How can you prove otherwise? Could he still be rattled by the poisoning theory, do you think?"

"It's her influence," I said. "Of course he won't reject us, I'm his only family. No matter what's happened or been said, he's not that bitter. Not in this situation, you know, with it being... well... stage 4 cancer. Someone was at the house – a lawyer. The day before he left for hospital with the blood clots. Miriam, his housekeeper, told us. They were signing documents. It would have been... around the 20th, 19th maybe? I'm frightened he's changed his will. She has still poisoned him... poisoned his mind, if not his body – against me."

"But if he changed his will before Christmas, well, that was before the poison fiasco, right?"

"Yes, but I'm sure now that Evelyn has been manipulating him for years. Turning him against me. Us. At first, I just thought, like Jack did, that she was weird, possessive - but there's so many lies against us. She's got her claws so embedded in him and he doesn't see she's taking him for a ride. She's been telling him we don't care and setting things up to look like I'm the evil one. The poison accusation was just the nail in the coffin for him, you see. Now, he probably believes everything she told him and her plan has worked." I stopped abruptly when I realised how utterly feeble it all sounded, how petty and lamentable. I was embarrassed. I sounded like a jealous teen.

"I see," said James, stoically. He pursed his lips and audibly breathed in. "Now, if he's stage 4, shouldn't he be in hospital? Have you had a doctor confirm it's cancer?"

"I tried calling the hospital," said Jack, "in case he'd been admitted since we saw him last week. But they won't give us anything. They won't recognise Amelia as next of kin and they told us we don't have a... what was it... a proxy? Whatever that is."

"I see. Well – coupla things you should know. Here in the States, doctors are limited in what information they can give about their patients. Normally, the closest relative will have access to all information, but that is complicated by the fact that she, Evelyn, is his main carer. Plus, could she have told the hospital she is his wife? There would be no reason not to believe her if Roger is too ill to speak for himself. Perhaps she is that unsound. Plus, you guys reside in England – they won't like that – but the fact you are physically here is good. The nurse was talking about a healthcare proxy. We need to find out who holds it. It's a legal document that gives power to a nominated person to make all his medical decisions if he can't do it himself. I am sure it's probably Evelyn that holds your father's healthcare proxy. Either way, we need to find out. We need to get you guys in to see him and we need to find out the truth."

It was after 4p.m. when we got back to the apartment.

"He's an ally, isn't he, Jack? I like him. He'll help us, won't he?" I asked, after we took off our wet coats. It had begun to snow again.

"Yes, he's our man, baby."

"Oh, I don't know what I'd do without you, darling," I said to him, truthfully, as he brushed my cheek with his lips. I threw my arms around his neck. "I'm sorry I was angry about the poison theory. I'm sorry I said it was pathetic."

He looked at me and smiled. "It's okay, darling. It's okay."

***

My dad didn't call the next day, as promised. We called on Wednesday morning, but, as we predicted, there was no reply. We visited. Again, the doorman would not allow us through. We called Ali and Miriam, and begged them to let us know if they heard anything.

The little apartment we had found was becoming our refuge – it was warm, cosy and had everything we needed, except a bath. I longed for a deep, hot bubble bath. The snow flickered down, slowly and silently. We bought snow boots and some warmer clothes to help us get around the city without freezing to death. But we had to watch our spending – we'd already missed two mortgage payments, in order to pay for the flights and our accommodation. We needed to do more walking and less cabbing to save money. Luckily, the apartment was fairly central.

That afternoon, while we were still madly trying to research Dad's healthcare proxy, which was proving very difficult, the mobile rang shrilly and Miriam's name popped onto its screen. She begun talking quickly and hardly stopped for breath.

"'Melia – your father ees in the hospital, the biopsy not good – you need to go to heem, pleeze. But please, you know you may have problems getting to see heem. She will not want you there. She is saying naasty things about you to the nurse – that you hate him and will pull out his wires... and that she is hees wife. He wen' there yesterday. She ask me to clean her house while they wen' there. I heard her say the name of the hospital, just once. She say 'The Cornell Medical Center'. Ees not far from her house – or where you stay I theenk? I wen' there and she went maaad, soo mad – oh, you should have heard her – she ees telling the nurses that you should not be allowed in. I cannot believe my ears when I hear thees. So I leave in a hurry. But your dad, he is very tired. Please go to him. I think he wanna see you. I got the number from the nice nurse."

I scribbled down the number and repeated it back carefully.

"Miriam, thank you, thank you, you're an angel. Thank you." I didn't wait for her to say "you're welcome", and was already dialling the hospital. Jack was by my side. A nurse answered and I told her who I was.

"Ah, Mrs Jones, yes, your father is stable. He'll be with us for a few days, but he's not critical yet. The chemotherapy is not working as we would have liked. I can't tell you much more because, as I understand it, it's his wife that holds his healthcare proxy, and she should be the one to pass on the information."

"That woman, the one who brought him in, Evelyn DeGrawe – that's not his wife. You mustn't believe her if she tells you that," I pleaded.

"I see. Well, you are more than welcome to come visit your father, of course. When you come in, please bring your passport and any other identity with you. We will ask Mrs Kavanagh to bring the same. In the meantime, don't worry too much; we're here to help your father be as comfortable as possible."

"Can I speak to him?"

"Certainly, I'll put you through to his room."

I heard several clicking noises and then the ringing tone. One. Two.

"Hello?" It was Evelyn.

"Evelyn, it's Amelia. Is Dad awake, can you put him on?"

"He's very tired, Amelia," she whispered, "and it's very inconsiderate of you to disturb him. You know, as far as I'm concerned, you don't exist anymore, and as you haven't communicated, you obviously have no interest in your father's health." I heard my dad call her name in the background. It sounded as though she covered the phone with her hand while she spoke to him, but the next voice I heard was his. The relief was magnificent.

"Dad, how are you? Are you ok? I'm worried about you. Evelyn said you were sleeping – sorry if I disturbed you. I know... I know about the cancer. And I'm here. We're both still here in New York." It all came out in a rushed garble.

"Amelia, it's not good, I'm afraid." His voice was weak – croaky and slow. "I'm very tired. I do want to see you. But things have been so active in making arrangements with the doctors and this place, travel back and forth. The chemo is very hard and is not working. Amelia, come when you can. I'm sorry about our disagreement. There's not time for angry words."

I heard him gulp. Was he crying? I was bursting with overwhelming compassion. He continued. "Please prepare yourself. I'm afraid you will be surprised when you see me. I have lost a lot of weight. It's why I didn't want you to come before."

A sense of dread travelled up my spine and a familiar ball of lead bounced once in the pit of my stomach. Even just these few words had expended his energy. He couldn't say any more.

"Oh Dad, it's me who should be apologising. We've been trying to speak to you ever since, did you get any messages?"

"No messages, Come when you can," was all he could manage.

"We'll be there as soon as we can. You sleep now, Daddy."

I put down the phone and realised I was crying too. Jack's arms around me helped me control the flood. To think that he was so ill, and I had hurt him so much, unnecessarily, crushed me – that he didn't know I had tried to say "I'm sorry". The wretchedness of the situation gripped me like a vice. I felt ragged, but then, every atom, every instinct in me was suddenly alive with urgency. I washed my face and freshened up. Within minutes, we were in a cab towards the hospital. It was still snowing, but the roads were clear.

The Cornell Medical Center at the New York Presbyterian Hospital was an imposing building, with several towers, its white facade rising majestically out of the ground like an old, gothic fortress. Laced with tall windows, allowing in floods of natural daylight, it faced the east end of 68th Street. The building was so big, it dwarfed its own entrance block, which displayed three separate Asian-style arches. We recognised the area – it was indeed close to Evelyn's apartment, just a few blocks. The taxi dropped us by the huge doors, and splashed away through the slush, back into the city. Jack and I walked across the cold, tiled entrance hall, holding hands. The receptionist was smartly dressed and very polite. She spoke quietly in the dim light, almost as if not to disturb the patients.

"You need to take the elevator to the fourteenth floor."

"Thank you."

This lift seemed to take forever – it was even slower that the one in Evelyn's building.

The elevator opened onto a set of double doors, which automatically opened as we approached. Another brightly-lit reception desk was behind us, to the left. Another pretty receptionist welcomed us.

"Mr Kavanagh is in room 1436. Back down the hallway and on the left," she pointed. "I think his wife is already with him."

CHAPTER 23 (AMELIA)

The door to room 1436 was ajar. I pushed it open and immediately, my eyes found my father. His head was turned towards the door, toward me, and away from the window opposite. He was covered neatly in a thin, white blanket over a clean sheet, but had clearly not moved much, for it was still tucked neatly. The late-afternoon light flooded in. As my eyes travelled up from the foot of the bed, I thought that at first it was the wrong one. The bony angle of his knee was sickening. It looked as though the blanket was covering a skeleton. Then I saw his face. The shock was like a punch. His skin was grey and thin. His eyes hollowed in his head, and he seemed to have lost his already thin, grey hair. His eyes were glazed and staring straight ahead, focused on nothing.

"Daddy," I breathed. I walked quietly to his side and touched his arm. There was no response and he didn't seem to see me.

Evelyn was sat on the other side of the bed. The window, behind her, silhouetting her frame. I shaded my eyes to see that she looked straight at me. She sat still as a millpond, and her watery, grey eyes never moved from my face.

I heard Jack say, "Evelyn, would you mind leaving Amelia alone with her father for a few moments?"

Her eyes shot from me to him swiftly, like a trapped animal. "I will not," she hissed.

I bent down so that I was in front of Dad. "Hello Daddy," I said more loudly than before. He focused then but he still looked sad and lost.

"I'm here, Dad, it's Amelia. I'm right here." I pulled up a chair and sat, moving my face into his vision. He smiled and touched my face. His skinny fingers opened to caress my cheek. In that moment, everything and everyone was forgiven. There was only love, even for just a few seconds.

He opened his mouth, I think to say "Amelia", but only a wheeze came out. Maybe the breathing tube in his nose was uncomfortable or made his throat sore. He closed his eyes. I touched his face.

"Perhaps it would be better if you just didn't speak!" Evelyn said, abruptly. The cherished moment fled. But the importance of the connection with my father gave me a surge of strength and I found I could ignore her. In an attempt to comfort him, to transfer some energy, some strength, I stroked his shoulder. But the gesture seemed weak. So I took his hand in both of my own and put it on my chest so he could feel my beating heart. Then I moved his hand, still in mine, to his own chest, completing the bond.

Evelyn flicked my hands away like they were dirty flies.

"Get off him – don't touch him! Just don't touch him. You shouldn't even be here, you're not welcome."

I knew for a fact that wasn't true. "Evelyn, please be quiet, it's not the time or place."

Dad didn't look at her. He continued to look at me, as if he was pushing me on, I think, but I couldn't be sure. He moaned quietly and indicated that he wanted to sit up. Evelyn and I both helped him, by lifting him under each arm and pulling him, ever so gently, up the raised bed. I was surprised how easily we did it, such was the lightness of his body. His arm had felt excruciatingly thin. It was the first thing Evelyn and I had ever done together, but I didn't give her the satisfaction of acknowledging it. I felt that she was poisoning the air in the room, and that I shouldn't be breathing it, let alone my poorly father. I just wanted positivity for him, not a negative aura. So, for his benefit, I looked at her and tried to smile. She didn't return it. Instead, spitefully, she suddenly put her upper body over my father, simultaneously pushing me away. Then she put both her hands either side of his face, wrenched it toward her and attempted to passionately kiss him. I watched with horror, as he lay there helpless, motionless, while she put her tongue inside his open mouth. Bile rose in my throat and I was speechless – couldn't move. Then she suddenly dropped his head back on the pillow and walked out of the room.

"Are you ok, Dad?"

There was only a croak in response. His eyes were still closed. I offered him some water and he nodded. I put a straw to his expectant lips and he drew in the liquid slowly – I noticed it travelling up – and then he gulped, once, twice. I talked to him on and off for a while – the more I did, the more alert he became. After an hour, he was awake and talking back. Jack came to stand behind me, so it was easier for my father to focus on us both. Finally, he asked affectionately about Benson, before he drifted away.

A nurse was there. I hadn't noticed her come in. "I just have to ask him a question, if you wouldn't mind?"

I moved out of her way as she took his hand out of mine.

"Roger? ROGER!" His eyes snapped open. I couldn't work out if his look was startled, or angry that she had disturbed his sleep so abruptly. Probably a bit of both. "Do you want your daughter here? Is it ok?"

"What?" I questioned, quietly.

Roger managed a definite nod and looked directly into the nurse's eyes.

"Ok, Roger, I just needed to check." His hand was returned to mine and he faded back to sleep.

"Can we see you privately to speak about his treatment and progress?" I said to the nurse.

"Yes, we can talk to you outside whenever it's convenient for you, honey," she replied with a kind smile, which I warmed to. "I'll go get the doctor."

"Thank you," I whispered. I was truly grateful.

Outside Room 1436, the lounge area was bustling. Even though the light had faded, dinnertime had passed, there were doctors and nurses to and fro, a surgeon walking quickly down the corridor, and groups of smartly-dressed people discussing something serious as they moved towards the doors. Suddenly, the nurse, whose name badge said Cindy, and my father's physician, were in front of me. Jack, as always, was at my side. Cindy checked my passport against a document in a folder and said, reassuringly, "Ah yes, you are on his file as next of kin. So, Doctor Brown will bring you up to date."

Doctor Brown shook our hands. He was tall, slim and of an Asian ethnicity that I couldn't place. He moved the spectacles on his nose so that he could read his notes in the file and focus on us at the same time.

"Well, Mr and Mrs Jones. The prognosis, I am afraid, is not good. The cancer has spread to your father's liver and his stomach. It has gone too far for us to operate. The chemotherapy is not working as we had hoped, and Mr Kavanagh has decided not to accept any further treatment, except for painkilling drugs. He is recovering from a short anaesthetic from when we looked into his stomach, but he should have recovered from this by tomorrow. He can go home, but he will need to come back after about a week, or two, at the most. Now, I understand you have not been kept as informed as you would have liked, however, we suggest you grab as much quality time with your father now as you can. Try not to be irritable around him. We can provide a mediator if you need help getting along with Mrs DeGrawe."

I looked at him, feeling a little nervous, and then at Cindy, who said, "Yes, we're here to help you and your father get through this together. He is the important one now."

Then I uttered the worst question: "How long?"

"Probably months," said the doctor, "but it's difficult to ascertain just now exactly how many – it could be weeks."

"Oh." It was all I could say. And then, to Cindy. "Why did you check with him earlier that it was ok that I was here?"

"Well, honey," she put a hand on my arm before gently continuing, "Mrs Kavanagh told us that he didn't want you there – that you had had some sort of disagreement."

My mouth opened to protest. "But..." but Jack pulled down my raised arms and soothed me.

"Don't worry about it, baby, it's sorted."

"She's NOT Mrs Kavanagh!"

"Yes, Mrs Jones, everything is all sorted now. You can stay with your father as long as you like. He's a dying man and needs you."

I don't remember what happened then, it's a blank. I can just recall endless cups of coffee... and the security guard. I was returning from a trip to the ladies, and as I walked backed down the corridor, I was surprised to see him outside the room, talking to Jack.

"Mrs Kavanagh has reported that your husband has a history of violence, ma'am, and I am not to allow him into Mr Kavanagh's room. But you, Mrs Jones, please go ahead and enter."

I looked at Jack, quizzically.

"It's ok, Amelia. I'll sort this – you go in and spend time with your dad. I'm explaining to the officer what's been happening," and they walked off down the corridor together. He was back within 10 minutes.

"It was just another cock and bull story of hers. As soon as he knew I was a cop too, we became friends," he whispered, winking at me. "I've explained everything. He understands and is on our side too."

I was too exhausted to discuss it. I couldn't help but feel sad when I heard the word "side". There shouldn't have to be sides when someone you love is dying. During the evening, my father woke once or twice, and seemed grateful we were there. His lucidity was good and he even chatted a while. We helped him to the bathroom twice. We stayed until 1a.m. and left him gently snoring.

We chose to walk home through the cold night air. On the way, we stopped at a 24-hour restaurant. Jack ate a whole pizza, while I chose spaghetti and meatballs. As I picked, still without an appetite, I was reminded of the film, *Lady and the Tramp*. Both my parents had taken me to the local cinema to see it when they were still together. The memory of it came to me so strongly, I could vividly see the colours of the animated dogs in the soft candlelight, as if the screen were there in the diner. The long eyelashes of Lady and her coy, upward look, as the spaghetti strand led her nose to Tramp's, and his scruffy grey whiskers. I remember giggling so hard and my father chuckling, his shoulders moving up and down next to me, making me laugh harder – he was more amused at me giggling than the film. We had looked at each other with such acute happiness, and the magic of that moment washed over me. I choked on a meatball as I welled up and sobbed uncontrollably into a napkin.

CHAPTER 24 (JACK)

The next day, Roger's brightness was manifold. He was alive, coherent and looking forward to going home that afternoon. Jack and Amelia had checked out of the apartment and arranged with Miriam to stay in the studio. She had told them the bed was already made up, as well as the dinner prepared and the log burner ready to go.

Jack was driving, Roger was in the front seat. Evelyn spoke from the back. "Amelia, Jack – I must apologise for the way I have treated you – it's not been fair. It's just that I've been under so much pressure. Please understand this is a very difficult time for me – I'm trying to be civil, not to break under the pressure – but I'm finding it very hard." Jack was sure she was acting up for Roger's sake but strangely, something made him want to believe her.

Amelia looked at the woman next to her and said, "Evelyn, it's hard for everyone, but most of all for Dad." She leant forward and touched Roger's shoulder. "Let's just try to make the best of the situation."

"I know honey," Evelyn said. Jack caught his wife's look in the rear-view mirror – he knew she was inwardly balking at the fake use of the endearment. "Yes, you're right. Let's all try to get on over the next few days, huh?"

It would be great if they could all get along, he thought. Evelyn had used a tone that he had not heard before. It was neither malevolent nor kind. The sentence hovered in his head while he tried to work out if there was any sarcasm behind it. But he could only detect hope. Perhaps there was a very small chance that things could be reconciled after all.

When they arrived home, Roger was so happy, he began to hum. Benson was purring a welcome noisily, interspersed with a few "mews". Roger was delighted that the cat was so happy to see him and talked to him fondly. They settled together in the conservatory and Roger began to catch up with the mail and last weekend's papers.

After dinner that night, Amelia helped her father climb the stairs and then immediately retired with Jack. They both hoped this would avoid any conflict.

"I'm happy he's home. But I do wish we didn't have to pussy-foot around her," Amelia said, as she climbed into the bed beside Jack.

"I know and I agree – but your dad's doing great. He's walking about, chatting, reading. You know, we can be here with him for as long as you want. Now we're here, there's less financial outlay. I've called my clients, you've spoken to the office. Everyone understands. Your dad's going to be around for a few weeks longer, definitely. Maybe we should take a break – just for a night. Go up to Montauk for a couple of days. Just to get a breath of fresh air. This is taking its toll on both of us and there is, I hate to say, probably worse to come. You need your strength for that."

"It's a nice idea... but I'm not sure I could leave him. Not now," Amelia said, pensively. "But I'll think about it."

"Don't forget, he may not want us around so much too... he may want some alone time, and he will deserve that."

***

The first day went well. The sun shone and melted some of the snow. The spring-like air breathed hope across the beautiful wintery garden. Roger managed a shuffle to the conservatory door, to look out, but decided to wait a bit longer before venturing into the garden. Amelia cooked a light supper for everyone that evening. Jack helped with the clearing up in the kitchen. As he was putting away the last of the plates, Amelia put down the dishcloth and was about to leave the room to wish her father goodnight, when Evelyn rushed in with a face like thunder.

"What's happened?" Amelia asked, immediately concerned.

Evelyn paused and took a breath, before she looked directly at Amelia's face to say, "Amelia, you know, there is one thing that that I can do for your father that you can never do." She curled her top lip in a malicious grin and her chin lowered. She continued quietly. "It's sex, Amelia. You can never please him like I can. I can give him all the sex he wants. Oh yes, that's what brought us together. Our voracious appetite for it. And believe me, girl, that keeps him going." There was a shocked silence, and then she was gone. Amelia stared at the space where the woman had stood, open-mouthed, a tear slowly brimming.

"My knees," Amelia said. "My knees have gone weak," and she held onto the sink to steady herself. Jack pulled out a chair for her. "I don't know how much more I can take," she said, as she sat, putting her head in her hands, her elbows on the table.

"Maybe that's it," Jack said.

"What?"

"Well, I know you don't want to hear it, but I can see that could be what he sees in her. I mean, if the sex is great between them, well, maybe it's keeping them young. Maybe that's why your father is sticking by her. I mean, it doesn't account for some things... but it's a type of explanation for some others. Amelia?"

"La-la-la, la-la-la." Amelia had her fingers in her ears and was trying to block out Jack's voice. He laughed. "It's not a laughing matter," she said.

"Oh, ok – I was hoping it may help us all get along together... but I can see that it won't."

"Try again, Jack." She smiled for the first time in days.

***

"I'm going to the city for a couple of days today; I have some errands to run. I have given Miriam a few days off because she was so tired. You two can look after Rogey, right? He doesn't mind that I need to be away, do you, sweetheart? It's only for a couple of days. Thanks goodness the two of you are here." They both looked at her over the toast and eggs, but didn't respond. Roger seemed agreeable, though, and it was a relief to wave her off after breakfast.

It gave Amelia the chance she had been waiting for. This was the time she could be with her father, and she literally threw herself madly into the nursing role. It was as if she was obsessed – needed to take on the responsibility, not so much to help her father, but to help herself – help relieve the years of guilt, her own desperate compulsion to please her father. She was unleashed and nothing was stopping her. Ali came over and so did Laura, and other visitors who they had never met, but she rejected the help from everyone, even Jack.

"Please let us know if there is anything we can do," they all said.

"Of course," Amelia replied, "it's all under control though."

She spring-cleaned the kitchen, emptying, scrubbing and restacking the cupboards, in the name of hygiene. Then she moved on to the other rooms. She prepared all the meals, she sat with her father and read to him; she shopped, did the laundry, made the beds, vacuumed, polished and washed. She monitored Roger's medication with an eagle eye, helped him get up and down stairs, shave and dress. Jack could only watch her exhaust herself.

"This is the last chance I have," she explained, each time he tried to calm her. "Please let me have this time."

Roger also seemed moved by how she had exerted herself. When they were alone, she told Jack, "When I took Dad to bed earlier, he said, 'I'm sorry, Amelia, that we fell out about your theory. I'm willing to let it drop if you are. If there's one thing I've learned this past week, it's that life is short. Let's not argue, eh?'"

"Wow. That's great."

"Yes, AND he also said he'd transferred some money for us to stay a little longer... he said he knows that we must be struggling. I had to say yes, and I admit, it's a relief to know we can bring the mortgage payments up to date."

Jack was also comforted by this news, as his bank card had been rejected at a cash machine that afternoon. Roger's support was so welcome, he felt happy.

***

By the time Evelyn returned, Amelia was run ragged. Her hair was lank, she wasn't bothering with make-up, and she was quiet. Roger suggested they take a break.

"Evelyn and I thought you may like to take a couple of days away." Jack knew it was Evelyn's idea, not Roger's, but it did sound plausible. "I'm well looked after, the nurses are coming in each day, and I'm not going anywhere. Lord knows you need some sleep, Amelia, look at those dark circles under your eyes."

"They can go to my house upstate," suggested Evelyn, happily. "It's only an hour's drive, maybe two." Jack jumped at the chance, as this could give him the opportunity to gather more information for his file on Evelyn, and before Amelia had the chance to protest, it was all arranged.

"But..." said Amelia.

"It's ok, baby – you need the sleep. It's kind of Evelyn to offer," and he looked at the woman. "Thank you, Evelyn, it's very kind of you."

"I'll still be here when you get back, my dear," agreed Roger.

"Sweethearts, you both look positively awful – you need a deep breath of the country air," said Evelyn.

"Ok," Amelia said, finally. She conceded – she had no choice. "But only for one night."

CHAPTER 25 (AMELIA)

The journey took three hours. The long, straight roads were clear of snow, but the landscape looked like an iced cake – the blue sky reflected so brightly that we both wore sunglasses. We stopped at a deli to pick up some provisions for our stay so we didn't have to go out whilst there. Our bag included four lagers and a bottle of Californian wine.

I think we were so tired, we hardly spoke the whole journey. Cornwall was a quaint, old town with its own mountain skiing area and old, covered bridge, right out of *The Bridges of Madison County*. Evelyn's house was on a hillside at the end of long driveway. It was a 1960's redwood, brick and glass structure, with cathedral-type angles and large, covered balconies. Inside, there was soaring space, sheepskin rugs, open fireplaces and retro furniture. The dated kitchen housed a cavernous 1950's-style fridge, and a table big enough to seat eight. At the back was a relatively small conservatory, which looked out onto a tiny garden, beyond which was a dense wood. There was garden furniture stacked high in here – we guessed for the winter. There was a faint smell of damp throughout the whole place. It seemed worse in the hallway, where the carpet was thin and the windows huge and rattly.

The first thing we did was switch the heating on to high, remembering to turn the dial to LF (lower floor). Then we found the bedroom that Evelyn had asked us to use, which offered a four-poster bed and an avocado en-suite. It was downstairs – that way, we'd only need heat the ground floor. Jack had commented that this was an odd comment from someone who didn't need to worry about money.

"Put it in your research notes," I had suggested, with a wry smile.

We took sheets and blankets from the wardrobe and added an old-fashioned patchwork quilt to the bed for extra warmth. After a quick cuddle on it to settle in, we unpacked our shopping and made lunch.

We took a walk back to the bridge in the afternoon. Back outside, the cold air made our cheeks red and our eyes water. Our breath was visible in puffs of cloudy air. We were following a cleared track about half a mile from the house on our way home. As we turned the corner, we were struck by the beautiful sight of an avenue of pines. Frozen dewdrops hung from the branches, which were topped with frost, and holding dazzling rainbows of colour. When the gentle breeze blew, they tinkled magically, and each one sparkled with wonder. Then I noticed that someone had decorated one of the pines. It had red, green and gold glass balls, bows and tinsel, which went about halfway up the majestic tree – it must have been too tall to complete the job.

"I wonder why this tree, of all of them," I said to Jack.

"Probably a family tradition – there's bound to be a story attached to it."

"I'd love to know what it is." I thought about the imaginary family that could have decorated it and how we would never know them. I imagined they were all kind and good-looking people – mum, dad, four kids, spanning fourteen to twenty, a boy's girlfriend, an aunt and an uncle, two grandpas and a grandma. They were sitting around a feast, all lovingly cooked and prepared, laid out on a red gingham tablecloth, everyone laughing, chatting, drinking wine and juice. This tree was special to them – could it be where grandpa and grandma came to picnic, or was someone – or a pet – buried here, and then I thought how they would never know we'd seen it and been touched by its beauty. Somehow, this image made me want to hold on to the short, happy moments, to embrace what might not be with us forever. But it also reminded me of what I might have lost in not being able to have children of my own. I'd always thought you couldn't miss what you didn't have, but that day, it didn't apply.

Please hang in there, Dad, so that I can appreciate you for a little longer, let you know how proud I am to be your daughter, no matter how bad I've been.

It was late afternoon when we returned – the house was lovely and warm. We telephoned Dad's place, but it went straight to voicemail.

"It's me. I'm just checking in. We arrived safely. I'm sure you're sleeping or busy. Hope everything is ok. Phone if you need us, otherwise, we'll be back after lunch tomorrow."

We actually relaxed then, and laughed together as we prepared an early supper. We settled down in front of the TV to watch a film, in front of a blazing log fire. It was bliss. The beautiful sleep that followed lasted 11 hours.

***

Late the following morning, having washed and dried the sheets and returning things to how we found them, we began our return journey, which we managed to cut to two-and-a-half hours. We only stopped once for fuel.

"Cheap as chips here," said Jack, when a full tank cost less than a third than it would at home.

"Good thing too. Thank goodness for Dad's gesture – I don't know how long we could have stayed if we didn't have that."

When we reached the house, all looked quiet. Evelyn's car was gone, but Dad's was still in the garage. We parked up, approached the door, and rang the bell. Nothing. We tried again. Still nothing. We walked around the back to find no signs of life. I looked through the patio window and saw Benson fast asleep on the sofa. In the garage, the key to the studio was in its usual place. I took it out, but as I approached the door, I saw an envelope taped to it. I ripped it off and gave it to Jack. He opened it hurriedly.

Amelia and Jack,

You have had your chance. You abandoned your father. His health deteriorated while you were away and I have taken him away where I can better care for him myself. Your lack of care will now be obvious to everyone, including him. Who would leave their sick father alone like that? If you try to contact us, you will be ignored. I suggest you go back home. It's very sad that you have chosen to behave like this. Your father will be most disappointed.

Evelyn

CHAPTER 26 (JACK)

"She's bloody tricked us, the bitch." Jack was livid. The anger coursed through his veins, and he stomped about the garage, looking for something to throw, to smash. *That bloody cow, I'll fucking kill her,* were the only words inside his head. "I'll fucking have her," he said aloud. Then he thought of Amelia. He turned to see her standing there, shivering, a wreck of a girl with fat tears moving silently down her reddening cheeks, and his anger was gone. "Oh God," he breathed, as he walked over to her, took her in his arms. "I'm sorry darling. I'm so sorry this is happening to you. It's just a trick. It won't work. She's not that clever."

"I can't believe I actually thought she was trying to be nice. I thought she had seen the light. I felt relief. For moments, I thought we had a way of sorting it all out. Bloody hell, I can't imagine how it's all come to this." Another sniff. A wipe of her eye. "Where is he, where is he, Jack? What on earth are we going to do?"

"We'll find him, baby. Let me call James. He'll know what to do."

"I'll call the hospital first; see if she's taken him there – in case he took a turn for the worse."

But that wasn't the case. While Jack was talking to James, Amelia sent Miriam a text: "How was your vacation, Miriam? We are back from our trip but Dad and Evelyn are not here???" Miriam called her back immediately.

"I was no on vacation 'Melia... I offered to come, but SHE say no one here, so I just didna come. I will come now though. I can be there later. This evening? 6p.m. ok wid you?"

How many lies, Jack thought. How, in God's name, could he have started to trust her?

"It's basically a kidnap," James said, two hours later, over a sticky, coffee-stained table in a diner on 68th, "or abduction." The waitress had filled chunky water glasses and taken their order. "Keep the cawfee coming please, miss," James said, as she wiped the surface clean, and they all held up their arms for the swiping cloth.

"Will do, sir," the waitress replied obligingly, as she walked busily away.

"The crime of unlawfully seizing and carrying away a person by force or fraud, or seizing and detaining a person against his or her will. Now, it may be that he has agreed to the move, in which case, we can't call that card. But in the meantime, he or Evelyn have not communicated to you where they have gone, leaving you to think the worst. All you have is that note. Correct?"

They both nodded. "What about the police?" suggested Amelia.

"They can't do a thing."

"What, nothing?"

"Nothing... yet. He's a responsible adult. We have no evidence that he was taken against his will. He may well have said that he didn't want any more treatment and wants to be taken away to somewhere quiet to ease out the rest of his days."

"No. He wouldn't do that... he wouldn't. He knows we're here – he'd tell us, warn us, something – not just go."

"Well ok, that may be true, but we have to somehow prove that."

"How?" Jack said. "What if she has told him that we know where he is – that we're just not bothering to visit. Manipulation is her second name."

"He wouldn't believe it, surely."

"Ok. So in order to find him, we're going to have to ask around, you know, at the hospital, his friends, at the apartment. But the police won't do it officially because of the lack of evidence. They will report it, but it will just stay on file. So, I can help you. We can try and gather a little more information that could lead to something like evidence. If you're up for that, that is."

"Amazing!" breathed Amelia. "Of course we are – anything to find him. But how much?"

"Aw, look, I've known this guy a long time, and we're fellow protectors of the law, hey," he said, as he put his arm around Jack and patted his shoulder in a macho way.

Jack nodded appreciatively. "What do you need from us?"

"We'll start with a photograph, if you can source that. I'll need his full name, date of birth, height, weight, etc., and any specific things that identify him, such as birthmarks, spectacles, that sort of thing. Addresses. The names of his friends, doctors, any nurses at the hospital. If you can call anyone that could know something – it would be great if we could go see them – do you know any of his or her friends?"

Jack and Amelia both nodded. Amelia was scribbling notes.

"Now," James continued, "what worries me is that she has his healthcare proxy – that's a challenge. If he can't speak for himself then all the decisions are hers, but in that case, she should have informed you of her plans, as his next of kin."

Jack leant across the table; he took Amelia's hand and squeezed it. He could tell by the look in her eyes that she was unsure, frightened almost.

"Ok," she said.

"Ok?" said James. "You sure?"

"Sure," Jack said "Amelia has a photo on her phone; we can give you a whole load of information now."

"Good," replied James. "Let's get started. Now, where's that goddam pizza?"

The first person on the list of Roger's friends was Laura. She answered after four rings – Jack thought she wasn't going to pick up.

"Guys, I'm so sorry this is happening to you. I'm in California with my parents. I'm due back at the end of the week though, I can come see you, and this guy."

Ali and Raymond didn't want to get involved.

"It's not that we don't trust you, honeys," Ali had explained. "It's just that, well, you know, it's six of one and half a dozen of the other. You could be overreacting... like the poisoning story. We would feel disloyal to your father, Amelia, we've known him so long; we just couldn't go against him like that."

"But you wouldn't be going against him."

"Maybe he doesn't want to be found."

"He wouldn't do that."

"If you prove it, Amelia, we'll support you. But until then, we'd rather stay out of it."

David and Elizabeth were the same. David told Jack, "There's just not enough information to show she's kidnapped him – I think there will be a perfectly reasonable explanation for this – we just can't agree to help, I'm sorry."

"Laura's father," said Amelia, suddenly. "His sister, her aunt, lives in a huge house in Coney Island. I remember Dad talking about it on the night of the party. She could have taken him there – the aunt is a recluse and has tough security, and I have no idea where it is, but is that worth a shot?"

James took the information away, leaving Amelia and Jack with the remains of the pizza, promising to see them at the house later.

Benson purred on Amelia's lap, as they sat around the big, wooden table in the kitchen, steaming mugs in front of them, and a homemade walnut cake in the middle. Miriam was almost enjoying this.

"Shee has always been a leedle... strange... you know... unrelaxed. Yes, there was a lawyer here... he spend several hours with Mr Roger, looking at documents. She wants me gone soon. She say cat will go to vets to live in cage, and the house no need for clean if there is no one here. But I will come still, maybe even kidnap the kitty so she can't take him away," she laughed.

"This is great information, Miriam, thank you." James turned to Jack and Amelia. "I've collected a few more details too – the nurses at the hospital said that he should have visited for a check yesterday, but he failed to show up. They left voicemails here at the house, but didn't hear anything at all. The most leading piece of information came from the concierge at her building. He said they were there the day before – when you went upstate – and that Roger was in a wheelchair. He thought she said they were going to Coney Island. As yet, I haven't been able to locate the address of the mansion, but we could find it, or the sister, without too much searching. What d'ya think?"

Jack, Amelia and James met in a parking lot in Coney Island. On the way, they had passed Babushka's, the club where Evelyn held Roger's party, three years ago. The red curtain was still behind the front window – it was faded and cracked, and there was a hole in the glass in the bottom corner, like a tiny spy-hole, with thin, radial cracks. The morning sky was bright blue and cloudless, melting the last of the snow. Luna Park stood opposite them, beckoning.

"We need to search everywhere they could be, or could have been – stores, hotels, restaurants, the beach, the rides..."

"The rides? They're in their 70s." Amelia was aghast.

"Take these photos. Someone may have seen them arrive. Ask people; tell them he could be in a wheelchair. I will search for the house as well."

They looked at each other and then over towards the park. Surprisingly, it was open already, and a few groups of people mingled excitedly, but the vastness of the space engulfed them, making them feel small. Amelia wrapped her jacket around her, keeping out the cold breeze. She shivered. A loud burger joint that looked like a child's play store stood on the corner, with garish orange and yellow signs, also advertising soda and hot dogs. A type of water ride was in front of them, and the famous rollercoaster was to their left, its name in a 1920's font, up high on the summit of the highest peak: "Cyclone". Neither seemed to be in operation. 'Too early perhaps... or too damn cold. And how the hell did we end up in Coney bloody Island anyway, thought Jack.

"I'll start around here." James pointed to an area on map. "We are at this point right now." He indicated again. "You guys search all this area. Take this map and meet me at Frankie's on the boardwalk at noon. If we find nothing, we'll head back."

Jack found himself standing in the middle of the amusement park. Dark clouds were moving overhead, but it hadn't yet started to rain. It was dusk and the light was fading fast. Amelia was nowhere in sight. The wind was loud in his ears and the crowds were laughing and shouting. Pedlars on stilts and garishly-painted arcades seemed to swim in and out of his vision; multi-coloured machines, bejewelled fortune-tellers, characters from all the books he had read as a child, were in costumes, and shouting out that they could offer him "the best thrill ever, darlin'", "get your gimmicks 'ere", "'ere, love, ride on this...", as they moved past him, but he was rooted to the ground. It perturbed him that they were all speaking in English accents. Suddenly, the iconic Coney Island so-called funny face was next to him – or a man wearing a mask, cackling loudly, but the mouth not moving – the slicked-down hair shining like wet plastic. Thunder rolled in the sky now, and he looked up, only to feel a raindrop slashing his face, his blood hot, as it ran down to his neck. Now the face was Evelyn's. It was unmoved, but tears rolled down her cheeks as she stared at him. Eccentric, thought Jack, she could hide all sorts of illnesses behind that face. A ride with loud bells ringing was nearby – the tone was ear-splitting, trying to drown out the noise of the park

– it was distracting him from what he was doing, except he didn't know what that was. As he stared at Evelyn again, who was now in front of him, her eyes began to sink into her head, as if they were being sucked backwards, and he felt fear grip his ribs painfully. He tried to look down at her hands because he suddenly thought she could be thinking of killing him with something, or maybe she was actually stabbing him, but then he heard Amelia calling him.

"Jack," she shouted, "Jack." He whirled his head around and saw her up in the Cyclone rollercoaster – the only passenger on the ride, and it was going way too fast, up and down, out of control. Now it was raining wildly, and the daylight had disappeared – only a searchlight, like the one in a prison, was positioned on Amelia. Her lovely, blonde hair was now wet and bedraggled, and stuck to her white face, as she called him. He tried to shout to a controller, anyone, to slow it down, but no sound would emerge from his mouth, and he was still stuck to the floor with a thick, black glue. Amelia's head was being ripped back now with the force of the speed, her eyes were wild with fright, and she was fighting with the safety bar, which seemed to be getting tighter and tighter around her body, pushing the air out of her lungs. How could he save her, what could he do? He was utterly helpless and he began to panic.

"Jack? Jack?" she yelled. "Jack, are you ok?"

"Uh... What?" he replied, suddenly, his eyes wide, trying to focus, his forehead wet with sweat. She had switched on the bedside light; the covers were thrown back. He blinked – they were in the studio.

She held up her phone. "It's the hospital. He's there."

CHAPTER 27 (AMELIA)

The incessant wind that had been blowing all afternoon entered with us through the main doors to the lobby. It was 5.20a.m. but the roads had already been busy. Maybe they were never quiet.

"He's not in good shape," explained the nurse, as she walked us down the hall. "He's exhausted. He came in late this afternoon – we've no idea where Mrs Kavanagh went – she was here one minute, gone the next. We had to wash him – she hadn't cared from him properly – he was... you know... dirty, down there." I was shocked, but too despondent to react – it would all have to be dealt with later. It didn't seem important right now. The nurse opened the door to his room. A small lamp lit up his bed with a warm, low glow. A plastic jug of water and cup with a straw were on the bedside table.

Dad was a motionless skeleton. His cheekbones stuck prominently out of his face, hollowing horribly underneath, and his eyes, with dark shadows beneath them, were staring openly into the middle of the room, sightless. His dry mouth was wide open, as if in a perpetual yawn. I thought of the painting *The Scream* by Edvard Munch, and wanted to cover my ears in the same way. A vile sense of dread seeped into me, and I felt a vague sense of nausea. For a moment, I thought I could smell death. I sat down on the bed beside him, speechless.

"Dad?" I took his hand. "Dad, can you hear me?" I felt the gentlest squeeze on my finger. His open mouth formed a weak smile and suddenly, his eyes regained life as they met mine, I felt a surge of happiness, mixed with despair. Every atom of anger, worry and fatigue was suddenly gone. For seconds, I even forgot where we were, or who was there. I picked up his hand – it was a dead weight. I brought it to my face and kissed it, longing for him to touch my cheek as he had done before. But he didn't seem to have the strength. A painful sob grew in my throat and I forced it back down. I had finally made it to his side, and here I would stay.

"I won't leave you alone, Daddy, don't worry," and I watched his eyes close, his attention slip away again, his breath frail, as his waxen face fell to one side in a deep sleep.

The nurse spoke. "He had a nasal cannula for a few hours, but we took it away. We all thought that to be without it would help him pass quicker. Keeping it in would only prolong things. Mrs Kavanagh authorised it. It's his time now."

"Time?" I said too loudly. "What do you mean?" I signalled we should move away from the bed. "I don't understand," whispering now. "How could this have happened to him so fast? It was only four days ago that we left him at home – he said he was ok – he didn't look bad."

"He is on medication for the pain," the nurse continued. "He's comfortable now. But he doesn't have long."

"No. No – the doctor said months. He said months."

"He said *possibly*. His time has come; I'm so sorry it's sooner than expected."

I felt despair. It coursed through my blood and felt hot and bad. At the same time, I was relieved because he was comfortable now, after the unthinkable things he could have gone through in the last couple of days. I supposed we would never know what.

I felt Jack take my hand and I became still. As long as he's not in pain, I can bear it, for him, I thought – and my emotion ceased, dried up, like a raindrop in a desert. I took a breath, which I heard in a place somewhere between my ears, but also, far away. I was strong for my father, who was weak. I looked at Jack. He was crying.

I was aware that several people came and went. Evelyn didn't return. The air seemed cleaner for her absence.

At first, I found it difficult to think of anything to say to my father, as he lay there, unresponsive, dying. He didn't seem able to hear or see. But soon, the words came, and I

163

babbled on about anything and everything. Then, I'd find myself quiet again. Was it a waste of words? Should I only be saying deep and meaningful things to him? Or easy, everyday stuff? Did he care about the weather, or what was on the front page of the newspaper that Jack had bought? Occasionally, I felt tears well up, but on the whole, I held it together. I took his hand. It was bony and angular. The same hands that used to curl so gently around my tiny ones as a child. I noticed the skin almost hanging off them. They didn't look like my father's hands – surely, these hands belonged to another man – older and smaller. I couldn't work out if his face looked restful or pained. But I didn't want to look away, because that would be a wasted chance to see him, just to look at him and be there with him – if I looked away, he might leave, or open his eyes – I didn't want to miss a thing.

How long had we been here? I didn't hear myself ask, nor the answer. It didn't matter. What I really wanted to say was "Get better now, Daddy, don't go anywhere, don't give in, I need you." And the words banged around inside my head like a broken record. But I couldn't say them because I didn't want to put any pressure on him. I knew he was leaving and so did he. I wanted it to be easy for him.

"Maybe you'll see Helen soon," I broached. "I know how much you miss her, even though you never said. And Mum – you'll see her too. I know how you loved her once. I always forgave you, Dad, you know that, don't you? I'm very proud of you. I love being your daughter." I felt a faint squeeze of his hand, though his eyes remained closed. Brighten it up, Amelia, I thought – not so depressing, stop it – I told myself. "Anyway, it's been a lovely day outside – blue skies, really sunny. We may go over to Central Park soon. Won't leave you just now though. Want to be here, by your side." Another squeeze. "Rest now, Daddy, have a nice sleep – you're not missing much."

Jack entered now. Where had he been? How long had he been gone? "Hi Roger, how are you doing?" There was no response. Jack smiled at me and pulled up a chair.

At some point, it occurred to me that there were no gifts or cards in the room. I cried because I realised that get-well wishes would be pointless – but then forced myself to stop before the real tears came. So here he was, my father, in a small, white room, stark with cleanliness, with none of his own belongings, and his pathetic daughter, who couldn't even think of what to say. What a bizarre change this was. To the huge personality that he had been. I thought of him in his house with Helen, their friends visiting often, everyone laughing, loving pets constantly around. How brutal the change is. How awfully cruel.

Time passed but I hardly noticed. Jack took me to the canteen, asking a nurse to watch over Dad while I fed myself, quickly, so I could get back.

Laura came.

"Hey," she said quietly, "how's it going?"

"Ok," I muttered. "How was your trip?"

"Ok, but I'm glad to be back. Now, sweetie, you're going to need some rest. What about if I do the night shift? Its 10p.m. – I'll sit with him until you come back? You know I'll call you if anything happens."

Jack nodded. "Come on, baby, you need some sleep. We both do." I didn't move.

"Go for it," she said, almost bossily. "I will call you if we need you. I promise. You know he's being cared for and so does he, don't you, Roger." She squeezed his hand but Dad slept on.

For some reason, I suddenly noticed the view. It was a perfectly clear night; the stars shined liked tiny diamonds. The 59th Street Bridge, stretched over the yawning river, shimmered in the frosty air. The skyscrapers, still topped with snow, illuminated everything majestically, and proudly presented their height, as if they were alive and saying "look at us, just look, feast your eyes on our wonderfulness". Everything was reflected perfectly in the water below, making it all seem twice as big. I felt swallowed up, unnoticed and meaningless, dwarfed by the enormity of everything. It seemed to be crushing me, like an ant trodden underfoot. And suddenly, I was overwhelmingly tired – my eyes felt dry, the lids sticky, and my skin taut.

I don't remember walking out of Dad's room to the elevator, through the hospital lobby, across the road. Neither can I recall the cab that we took to the Holiday Inn that Jack had checked us into, in order to be closer. Nor him opening the door, undressing me or getting into bed. To me, the remainder of that night simply disappeared. I woke to the shrill tone of the mobile. I was awake like a shot, sitting upright. Thinking the worst, I snatched the phone up, saw it was Laura and felt my heart pound painfully.

"Is he ok?"

"He's still here, Amelia, don't worry, but you need to come if you can. Your dad's the same – it's just that I have received something you need to see."

It was 6a.m. We were back at the hospital in what seemed like seconds – in actuality, it took half an hour. I hadn't even showered. I kissed my father on the forehead. The fragility of his dry skin lingered on my lips.

"Has he had a drink?" I asked Laura.

She nodded. "About half an hour ago. But I need you to see this – can we go outside?"

She handed me a piece of paper with a printed email, from Evelyn. It was addressed to a few people I had heard of, but many others whom I hadn't. It began with yesterday's date and, shockingly, it announced my father's death

January 21st, 2009
To our family and friends,
At 2130 hours, in a little, quiet room, overlooking the beautiful East River, our beloved Roger passed away. He

fought the end, and death, like a brave soldier. His last words to me were, "Goodbye, my darling, and thank you." I am so sad to bring this news, but as there is one alive who remembers Roger then Roger lives on in our hearts.

CHAPTER 28 (JACK)

"Who the fuck does she think she is?"

Amelia had walked to the lounge area and slumped down on a faux leather sofa. Jack knew this was agonising for her. The dawn was just turning to day, but the sky was cloudy and a grey, subdued light rolled in through the large windows.

"You stay with your dad – I'll bring you some coffee then I'll call James."

Laura left, but not before she offered to do the night shift again later, if they needed her.

"God, Roger. What a mess," Jack said to the old man who lay asleep, nearly lifeless. "What do you see in that woman?"

"Shh," said Amelia, protectively.

He left the room to make the call and work on a calm and sensible response to Evelyn's email, copying in everyone (including her). Now people would learn how awful she could be.

22nd January, 2009
Dear all,
We know that some of you will have been very upset by the email that was circulated by Evelyn last night. We would like to provide you all with the facts and the latest condition of Amelia's father, Roger. When we returned to the hospital at 0600 this morning, after spending 17 hours by his side yesterday, we learned about the email that Evelyn had taken upon herself to circulate, announcing Roger's parting. In fact, Roger is alive and alert, and even still able to communicate with us. We will spend the day at his side to watch over him – he is still fighting back, although becoming weaker. We are sorry for the unnecessary distress that Evelyn has caused some of you and please be assured that we will advise you all when Roger finally gives up his valiant battle.
Jack and Amelia Jones (nee Kavanagh)

CHAPTER 28 (JACK)

By 8.30a.m., Jack was back at the hospital. His mobile began to ring. He fielded all the calls and put everyone straight. He went in and out of Roger's room. Amelia wasn't moving. He took her water and coffee, and made sure she drank. She made sure her father took sips, and occasionally padded his face and arms with a warm, damp cloth. He sat with them for various parts of the day but, on the whole, he left Amelia alone with Roger.

Jack strode up and down the corridor, watched the view, sat in the canteen, then in the lounge area, where Amelia had sat, so shocked, this morning. Was it only this morning? It seemed like they had been waiting days for Roger to die. He wondered where the old woman was, where she had hidden him, what she'd planned. He dwelled on how her twisted plans had so painfully estranged Amelia and her father. How she obviously couldn't wait for him to be dead before she lied about his last words. Bitch. He wished he could throw her out of that window. If she died too, it would solve a whole load of problems. He sat and shook open a newspaper, which was on the table in front of him. He turned the pages noisily, not really taking in the words or the pictures.

He couldn't seem to shake the anger, the hatred. His heart pounded inside his chest and he felt rage like a furious, caged animal. He wished it was her that was lying on her deathbed. Not Roger. He wouldn't care if she died, and nor would Amelia. No, he would laugh and spit on her grave. He wondered if he could kill her, but he knew he would automatically become a suspect. Then Amelia would be alone, and he couldn't do that to her, just leave her to cope with all that. He got up, threw the newspaper down, and paced the room. He thought about the conversation he'd had with Peter before Christmas, about Bill Skilling. Peter told him he'd reformed. Had done a two-year stint in rehab and was clean. But he was still a killer. Bill Skilling was a killer. Jack felt a calm gradually wash over him, as he remembered the man owed him one.

"You ok?" said Amelia, suddenly bringing him back to the present. "I'm going to use the ladies. Please go in – sit with him while I'm gone?"

There were some things that Jack hadn't shared with Amelia... there were parts of that job that weren't pretty, especially in the '90s, at the height of his drug squad career, and he never wanted to give her a reason not to trust him, or dislike what he did. A good example was the Vicky Crawford case, which he had investigated thoroughly. Vicky had been beaten up and raped by her drug dealer, David Luk, because she had not paid him. Jack knew David well. And his clients, and his supplier, Bill Skilling. David was addicted to heroin, but so far, had managed to hide everything and avoid arrest. In one sense, this time, it was actually lucky that Vicky couldn't pay, because that meant that David couldn't keep his deadline with Bill. At least Vicky stayed alive. Bill didn't mess with dealers that couldn't pay. It was bad for business. So, he went with his "team" to see David, in his flat, on a weather-beaten, run-down council estate, not far from Waterloo. They tied him up at gunpoint, but they didn't hurt him, on the outside. They injected a toxic and fatal amount of heroin inside him, cleverly using one of David's own syringes. They left it lying by his side, mixed up with other drug paraphernalia. He was found three days later, by a neighbour, and the cause of death was recorded as a "lethal overdose". Jack knew that Bill had been inside the flat, because one of his long, black hairs had been found on David's body. But Jack kept this to himself, at that point. A couple of months after David's death, Jack caught up with Bill, and arrested him for supply to someone else. Jack told him what he knew, and it was then that they struck a deal. If Jack dropped the charges, Bill would become Jack's informant.

Over the next couple of years, the relationship between Jack and Bill developed into a type of friendship.

They worked well together, identifying many dealers and suppliers over the coming months, and Jack's reputation as a DI was renowned throughout the city. Eventually, a rumour spread between dealers and other suppliers that Bill was informing, and his life became threatened. He ran to Australia. But within six months, his addiction had developed so much that he helped organise an armed robbery in order to get one small fix. He managed to flee back home before he was identified. Jack helped. Ensured that Special Branch let him through at the airport. They didn't communicate much after that – people knew him as a grass so Jack had to drop him. It was too dangerous for both of them.

Roger opened his eyes.
Amelia walked back in the room.
"He's just opened his eyes."
"Dad? Are you comfortable, Dad?"
But there was no response. Although his eyes were open, they didn't see anything. It was only later that they knew that that moment was the beginning of the end for Roger. As the afternoon turned to evening, they noticed a stiffening in Roger's body. He was no longer communicating. The hand squeezes had stopped. The stare was constant, and there was no longer any eye contact. Nurses came and went, checking his heart regularly.

Laura returned. Around six in the evening, she started to pray out loud. It surprised Jack – he didn't think she was into God. But then, he supposed you don't have to be religious to pray. He noticed her look directly at Amelia. Amelia continued to look at her father. She kept trying gently to brush his eyes closed with her palm, but they would not – they were stuck. His face was fixed palely in a mortiferous stare. She kissed his forehead.
"Why won't his eyes close?" she said, visibly upset. Jack couldn't answer. She looked back at him. "Safe travels,

Daddy. We love you. I'm so proud to be your daughter." She swallowed. She blinked. But she did not cry.

Laura prayed. "Oh Righteous Father, our Lord God, we know our days are numbered until we are with you, and that precious in your sight are the death of your followers. We are thankful that we know that when we die, we are with you in your holy presence and in your home. All of those who have gone before us, beloved friends and family, are there waiting for us, to welcome us. Blessed Lord, please comfort Roger at this time and have mercy on his family. We know that you will never leave Roger, nor forsake him. Oh Righteous Father..."

A quiet moment and then more prayer. And on she went. Amelia squeezed Roger's hand. Jack squeezed Amelia's other hand. Two sorry hours passed. Suddenly, Roger's breathing was shallow and sounded laboured. He stared into space. The breaths became ragged and slow. The prayer came quicker, as Jack and Amelia joined in.

Jack watched as Roger faded. He stopped breathing slowly and finally, they were able to close his eyes. Amelia had gone white but she was very calm. He heard her inhale so that she could let out a howl so sorrowful, it seemed to bring everything – the prayers, the building, the city, the universe – to a sudden stop. It echoed around his head. She didn't want to let go of Roger's hand. Laura left the room quietly to inform the nurses. Amelia stared at her dead father. Just stared, as if she may miss a speck of life that would bring him back.

"You ok?" said Jack.

""I suppose it's all over now."

"Come on. They will want to take him soon." But Amelia wouldn't move.

"Five minutes," she said. "Just give me five minutes more."

In the end, Jack had to physically pull her hand away and haul her up out of the chair.

"He's at peace now, baby. Probably with Helen."

CHAPTER 28 (JACK)

"Yes."

Amelia clung to Jack as they walked out of the room, into the corridor to the leather sofas in the lounge, where her knees buckled.

CHAPTER 29 (AMELIA)

As my father passed away, I seemed to separate into two parts – the real me and the dream me. The dream me, like a ghost, lifted up and glided into the corner of the ceiling in his hospital room, so that I looked downwards at the scene. I saw myself, saw my hand holding his. I saw his still, thin body, and his emaciated face, eyes closed, sleeping. Dead. I saw Jack behind me. People were talking, but their voices were muffled. The lights were on, but they were somehow dimmed and yellow. I watched as Jack took my hand out of my father's and helped me stand up. As we walked out of the room, I came down and joined my real self again. It didn't occur to me to cry. I didn't need to sleep – I was sleeping already. This was all a dream. A hideous nightmare.

Now, we were in the reception area of the morgue. We had come here on the instruction of the doctor, to begin the process of funeral arrangements. Some time had passed. I had drunk tea, but not sure when, or where. It was very late.

But as the mortician's assistant talked, I abruptly regained clarity.

"It was his wife, Mrs Kavanagh, who has made all the arrangements. Isn't she maybe your stepmom, dear?" he said, effeminately. I breathed in and bit the inside of my cheek to stop myself being rude – patronising git. He continued. "She was here yesterday to tell us she had arranged everything – he is to be buried in their family plot in... ah, let's see... Connecticut. We didn't know about you, until now. She said she was his next of kin, and his children were overseas."

"But she can't do that. He's not part of their family. They're not even married. I am his next of kin. I am his daughter. I am not overseas, I'm here, look." I realised how ridiculous this sounded, but exhaustion and stress had made me think perhaps I was invisible. I went on in sheer desperation. "She's NOT his wife. How many of you guys do I have to tell before that goes on his record, for God's sake" My voice was getting louder. "He doesn't want to be buried anyway, he wants a cremation, I'm sure of it." I wasn't sure how I was sure... I just was. My outburst must have surprised the assistant because he put his hands up, as if I were pointing a gun at him.

"Ok, ok. It seems there has been a little mix up. Are we talking about the same people here, I just want to be clear?"

I took a deep breath as Jack nudged me. Calm, I thought, I must be calm. "She has lied about being his wife all along. They were not married. Her name is Evelyn DeGrawe. She has no right to arrange anything. I am Mr Kavanagh's next of kin. Here's my passport." I'd been carrying it around for days. I turned to Jack. "Never in a million years did I think I would have to prove my own identity in order to arrange my father's funeral." Then back to the assistant. "Please... please believe me."

The official looked through the passport. "Well, I can see you are related. We will need to take this up with Mrs Kavanagh... um... Mrs DeGrawe. If I can take a copy of this? But there is nothing we can do tonight. It's too late to call people. It will have to be first thing in the morning."

I wanted to scream and strangle that young man as he handed my passport back. Jack put his arm around me.

"We have a legal representative here – his name is James Eagle," he said to the young man. "Please make a note of his name... he will call you first thing. What time will you be here?"

"Not me, sir, my colleague will take the call at 7a.m. That's when we sign off all the arrangements and papers for the day. He's due to be first out, so it needs to be as soon as possible."

I looked at my watch. 1.06a.m. An air of calm seemed to envelop me. As Jack pulled me in for a hug, I sighed deeply.

There was nothing more to be done until the next morning.

"Let's go back... maybe get a couple of hours' sleep."

"I don't know how I will sleep, Jack. Do you know, it's only been a two-and-a-half weeks since we knew he had cancer? If only..." I couldn't finish the sentence and swallowed hard, rubbing my eyes. I was breathing normally again, but I had a washed-out feeling, cleansed but quivery. "God, the back of my eyelids feel like sandpaper. Do you think things would have been different if we had found out about it earlier? Would it have made any difference? Was there anything we didn't do, Jack? Anything we missed? This whole thing seems so mad; it shouldn't be like this, should it?"

"Don't torture yourself, honey. There is nothing you, I or anyone else could have done."

The night air seemed quite warm, walking back to the hotel. It was only a couple of blocks, but in that time, I ran through everything that had happened over the past months. The slow changes – in my father's health, in Evelyn's behaviour, in my own – the reactions from other people – how we were disbelieved about the poison. The pointless discussions about Dad's will, Evelyn's stories, how he believed them, avoided me. Did he avoid me because of that, or because he knew he was ill and didn't want me to know? And finally, the desperate, ridiculous search for him in Coney Island.

***

Somehow, I did sleep, but I woke with a start at 6a.m. on the dot. Jack was in the shower. Something punched my stomach, as I realised where we were and what had happened. I had to face this day. It was still dark. I hated the dark morning. I hated the day. Forty-five minutes later, we were back in the morgue; it felt like we hadn't left.

"We're here about Mr Kavanagh," Jack said to the bespectacled lady that had replaced last night's studious, young man.

"Mr Kavanagh?" she blinked, not expecting a reply because she was searching the paper in front her, not looking at us. "Oh, yes – he's all ready... In fact, I think he just left..."

CHAPTER 30 (AMELIA)

"Let me check, because it says here to hold off on any movement, but I'm sure it was him that was just loaded..."

"Check, PLEASE CHECK," I said, as she adjusted her glasses and walked calmly through the door at the back of the reception. I paced the floor for a full five minutes.

"No, you're ok... he is still here," she said, loudly, as she re-entered.

I jumped as the phone rang loudly on the desk. "One moment please... Morgue.... yes... yes... yes, they are right here... Ok, Mr Eagle, thank you." The receiver was replaced and she looked directly at me. "Ok, your man's been on the phone. We'll back off from all instructions from Mrs... ah, Mrs DeGrawe, until everything is sorted." She looked at the computer screen. "I see you have already identified yourself. But she hasn't yet so that will be the next thing we ask for. Don't worry," and at me again, "your father's not going anywhere just yet."

We left the hospital feeling frazzled. Nothing could be done now, until Evelyn showed up with ID. At that point, I wanted sleep. Back in the room, I think I slept the whole day.

***

The next morning, James met us for breakfast in a diner near the hospital. He had spoken to my father's executor, Henry Attfield, another lawyer, whom he actually knew a little, and collected copies of relevant documentation, including a Letter of Wishes. I was right – this letter not only told us, in Dad's own words, that he wanted to be cremated, but that he wanted his ashes scattered in England, near his cottage, with the remains of Helen's ashes, which were in the basement of his house. It was a close call – I almost lost him to a deep, dark and wormy grave.

CHAPTER 30 (AMELIA)

"Attfield will need to meet you as soon as you are ready, Amelia," James instructed her. "He has a copy of the will, which he needs to discuss with you. You can wait until after the funeral if you like. But we need this..." he waved the Letter of Wishes "... to sort out the morgue issue. Attached to it was this – we thought you may wish to see this now." He handed her another piece of paper. "Attfield said he visited your father's house in December to collect it. He watched your father sign it. So the meetings at the house were for this – he didn't change the will. Evelyn was wrong to tell you that."

December 2008
To my daughter, Amelia,
If you are reading this letter then I have recently passed. I know you will be upset. But I want you to know that it won't help much, all that crying. I am at peace and resting well now. If I could squeeze your hand to let you know it's all ok, I would.

I have decided to write this letter to you, so that you can know that many, many times, I wanted to tell you how proud of you I am. I have always been proud of you, Amelia, since you were a tiny baby. But I have always found it hard to say the words aloud, for fear of showing weakness, I suppose. Stupid, you may say, but after your mother and I divorced, I shut myself up. It became easier to work like that, to socialise too. It was only Helen that found a way in. And only she that I could really be truly honest with. You were so young back then, and went on to have your own life. I never wanted to waste a moment of my limited time with you explaining something like that. Too much of a burden on your young shoulders. I knew it was your mother that helped you form your opinion of Helen in those early days. I couldn't bear to mix your young head up any more than we had already done.

I missed Helen very much after she died. I chose Evelyn because I was lonely – I am sure you are probably aware of this – you were never just a pretty face! I was never going to marry her. But I want you to be aware that, despite your differences, she has been a true friend to me. Whatever you think of her, she had made my last few years better than they would have been, had I been alone. I know you understand that – it comforts me that you tried so hard, and I thank you for doing that. Being with her never took me away from you.

I have known about the cancer for a few months, and I know there isn't long, and soon, perhaps, I will be unable to write. Amelia, it's changed the way I see everything. Even the weather each day is important and beautiful; bright, sunny mornings, crisp, white frost, and the big, blue sky – grey days are wonderful too, with their raindrops like crystals. And I find myself stressing less over small issues, something I think we all try to achieve every day, but never do – why does it have to be a terminal illness that enables you to appreciate most what you have? I am lucky to have a daughter like you. I will always be proud of you and I will always love you very much, even when I'm not there.

Don't forget – too many tears won't help – wear your beautiful smile daily – for me.

Your Dad xxx

It was problematic reading the last two paragraphs because my tears were coming thick and fast. Jack handed me a tissue. James signalled for more coffee.

***

Over the next few days, we visited the reverend that was to lead the service, invited speakers, organised obituaries, and went to the funeral home in Oyster Bay. I remembered it from Helen's wake several years before. We moved back into the studio and began to sort some things in the house. Dad had left very clear instructions. Attfield helped us understand the small differences between US and UK funerals. It was a moving and tiring time, but we felt that we were near a sort of completion. Once this was over, we could go home and begin our lives again. As we sorted various personal things in the house to take home, we chose some photographs to display at the wake. We put them to one side in the studio, along with the copies of the Order of Service and the special guest book we had bought.

We spent some time over at Ali and Raymond's. Everything was forgiven. It must have been whilst we were out that Evelyn visited the house.

"I got a call from Matthew Lapinsky, who is her lawyer," James told us on the mobile. We were driving back in the late afternoon. "She has accused you of stealing the photographs, and the silver frames, which she says were hers. Also, several other items that were apparently in the house that belonged to her. Of course, I have defended your actions entirely as appropriate, and Matthew had tried to be fair, so Evelyn has agreed to let you use the photographs, and the silver frames, at the wake tomorrow, providing you return them immediately. She sent a list of things you've taken and asked Matthew to ensure that none of these things are taken away to the UK. And one more thing – she has said she will not be coming to the wake."

I tossed and turned that night. Evelyn didn't seem to be going away. Miriam needed paying and so did the gardener and handyman, the utility companies needed informing, the bank, the insurance companies. The cat (oh, the *cat*, I thought, poor Benson) would need re-homing. Maybe Miriam would take him. He loved Miriam. The house would need to be put on the market, some items needed shipping back to the UK... on and on the list went.

Then there was the cottage at home. The last time we were there was that November evening, the fireplace alight, the chicken casserole on the Aga... my father sitting there, in his favourite chair, smiling, looking at me fondly. Did he know? Did he know then?

***

Eventually, I found a fractious sleep, only to awake a few hours later in a panic that I had overslept. I hadn't. Jack was already up and dressed, and I hauled myself out and into the shower. All my limbs ached.

We arrived at the funeral home about half an hour before the allocated time, so that we could be in the room to welcome guests as they arrived. The service was to be in a spacious, wood-panelled room, with a luscious red and brown carpet that was so thick and soft that footsteps were silent. One-hundred-and-fifty chairs were arranged, theatre-style, in the middle of the room, with an aisle either side and in the middle. There were mahogany sideboards and tables on every wall, and on these, Jack and I fondly and tearfully placed the photographs. They showed happy times: Dad with friends and family, with pets, indoors, outdoors, in summer and winter, autumn and spring. Many featured Helen, a few, Evelyn. At the top of the room was my father's coffin, securely closed, protecting him, in my mind, from the stares and tears of mourners. I didn't want him on show, all made up for the benefit of those of us who still lived. I knew he would feel the same way. More so, I wouldn't cope with seeing his dead body. The pale lilies and roses were arranged like a blanket over the top, and they draped beautifully down the sides to keep him warm and snug. They were a stunning work of art.

It was an effort to look smart in my black, knee-length dress and court shoes, which I'd bought in a hurry at Macy's the morning before. When I came to the States, I didn't realise I'd be attending a funeral, so hadn't packed a suitable outfit. I added a bright-pink scarf around my neck, to add a bit of colour. But I worried it only served to make my face look paler than it already was, and the dark circles under my eyes look deeper. It would have to do – I had nothing else.

People started to file in. A short queue formed to sign the book of condolences and there were suddenly people looking at the photos. I greeted everyone – some I knew by name, most, I didn't recognise at all.

"Thank you", "I see, how do you do?", "Welcome", "Thank you for coming", "Thank you", "Thank you", "Thank you". It was Jack I wanted to thank the most. He stood right there by my side the whole time. When the people I knew approached (Ali, Raymond, Elizabeth, David, Laura, Miriam), I reflected their tears. Attfield arrived. His short frame waddled toward me and I felt warmth from his hands when he shook mine. His black suit was too big for him, and he smelled musty. The room continued to fill. Sombre chatter floated in the air and grew thick like mist.

A lady in a long, fur coat and matching hat arrived. Her back was towards us as she signed the book. For some reason, I couldn't take my eyes off her. The body straightened and she slowly began to turn. It was Evelyn.

I nudged Jack hard in the ribs. He followed my gaze. I turned back to look protectively at the coffin, as if to check it was still there. We stood stock-still, side by side. Jack suddenly came alive and almost relished the moment – he was totally in control. He walked boldly and strongly towards the woman. This was his event now, he was in charge.

"Evelyn," he said. "We were led to understand you would not be coming today."

"How could I miss this day?" she replied, loudly, so everyone looked up. "The wake of my one true love? I was led to believe you would welcome me."

Jack turned to look at me. I was right behind him.

"It's fine if she sits quietly," I said to him, "at the back."

Again, she had lied and manipulated this situation. I was aware that only a handful of people knew what she had done. In everyone else's eyes, I would now be a dreadful person – relegating her to the back, when she'd supported my father through thick and thin. How could I do such a thing? So much that they didn't, and probably would never know.

"I will do no such thing." Her voice raised a little more. "Do you know they tried to ban me from coming?" she said to the person nearest us, who looked from her to us, aghast. "If you'll excuse me." She sneered at us both and spun around. She stalked towards the edge to look at the photos around the room. For the sake of peace, we allowed it, thinking that that would be the end, that she just wanted to be there. But suddenly, her voice tore through the room and a lamp crashed to the ground, smashing into pieces. I jumped out of my skin.

"THIEVES! You are thieves! You have been into my house, without my permission, and stolen these items from me... you two are THIEVES! I should never have trusted you."

"Oh my God," I said under my breath, and tried to catch the sob in my throat. Jack was immediately next to Evelyn.

"Get off," she said loudly, as he tried to take her arm in order to lead her out.

"Time to go, Evelyn. Time to GO!"

She had begun gathering up the photographs and was hugging them to her body. She tried to avoid dropping them, as Jack took hold of her.

"I will fight you two for everything. Everything I said."

"Put the pictures down, Evelyn." Jack's grip was vice-like now, and in one swift movement, he pulled her arm out so she dropped them all. They smashed to the ground loudly but thankfully, didn't break.

Tears were coursing thickly down my face, and Ali had run to my side – I felt her arm around my waist – supporting me. I spotted Laura watching, mouth open. I felt a glimmer of sympathy as Jack was brawling with Evelyn. Could she be truly mourning? Was all of this sending her mad with grief? But I still couldn't allow it to happen. Not in front of my father – he would not tolerate this. Wouldn't want this scene playing out, destructing his funeral.

"Not in front of Dad," I said aloud. "Not in front of his coffin, not here, NOT HERE." The room went silent. Evelyn gazed directly into my eyes. She seemed almost regretful. Frightened even. Like a spooked cat before it darted away.

"Please go," I said, just once.

Jack took Evelyn's elbow again and she finally allowed him to escort her from the room. I followed. As we stepped through the short corridor towards the door, he leant close to her ear and I saw his lips moving, but I couldn't hear what he said. A secretary appeared.

"Is everything alright?"

"Fine, thank you," responded Jack. We reached the door and he led Evelyn through it. "You'd better be careful, Evelyn," he said, and released her. She turned to look at him with pure hatred. A black limousine was waiting outside and we watched her get in. The car sped her away, heading for the Long Island Expressway, back towards the city. That would be the last time we would ever see her.

CHAPTER 31 (JACK)

Six months later.

Most things seemed to have gone according to plan after the funeral of Amelia's father. The will was read and almost everything had come to her. Including the violin, which was a relief – it was a family heirloom and Amelia had cherished it since she was a child, despite it being locked away in the attic. A trust was set up, so there were rules and regulations about how she could use the assets, but the cottage was hers. There had been enough cash to settle the majority of the loans that had mounted up whilst they were away in America. Now, they were almost debt-free – but for one last loan. Amelia had been so exhausted after everything that happened that Jack had paid to upgrade their seats on the flight back home. In order to afford it, he had secretly borrowed money with high interest, and used his company assets as collateral. He had not told Amelia because he knew she'd refuse if he suggested it. The deadline for the final payment of this loan was looming.

After Roger's death, Amelia had struggled at first, and once home, had gone to bed for days with a fever and depression. She seemingly began to accept things after the incident with the violin. Roger's UK neighbour, Gwen, who had lived in the cottage next door to his all her life, (which was a "very long time", according to Amelia), had written to her. The old lady struggled with getting about these days, but insisted on always preparing Roger's cottage for him when he came. It was clear she had put her all into the letter, as it was not just a show of sympathy. Her old-fashioned script curled across the thick writing paper.

I'm so sorry, dear Amelia, because there is something else I must tell you. I have the violin. And the lock to your father's cottage has been changed, but I have a key for you. Your father's lady-friend, Evelyn, telephoned me to say that Roger was poorly and that he wanted the violin sent to him. I was to retrieve it from the attic as soon as possible, and then change the locks. I didn't know why the locks needed changing, and it seemed wrong to ask. But she wanted proof and suggested I put the receipt in with the violin. It just didn't feel right, which is why I am telling you now. I thought it should be your father that asked for it himself, though she said he was incapacitated. And she was very insistent – I didn't know how to say no. The long and short of it, Amelia, is that I didn't. I never sent the violin. I have it here with me in my home. After I saw "Stradivarius" inside the violin, I checked and I couldn't afford the insurance to send it, so I wrote to Ms Evelyn and enclosed the new key and the receipt, but told her it was impossible to send the instrument, and that I was sure Mr Roger would understand. Just let me know when you want to collect it, dear. I will keep it safe for you.

"It's the proof we've been looking for. She thinks the cottage will be left to her. And she wants the violin because she thinks it's worth a fortune."

"Well, we've beaten her to it, thank goodness," said Amelia, and she actually smiled.

***

Over the next few weeks, the house in Oyster Bay was sold and the proceeds added to the estate. There were shocking amounts paid to lawyers and for taxes.

As the summer came, the weather was promising, and Amelia's mood was too. The leaves were full on the trees, and fine, sunny days stretched into long, balmy evenings. Jack and Amelia returned to work and things got back to normal.

They had visited Roger's cottage a few times and were cheerfully planning their move. Amelia worked with an architect on drawings for an extension of the kitchen, and another room over the garage. They wanted to make the changes before they moved in. Re-decorate. Re-plant the garden. Make it theirs. They planned to move in in October, which would coincide with Amelia's office move to Baker Street in September. She would work at home for three days and travel to London on the train for two. They were both looking forward to their new life in the country, with its quiet country roads, wildflower meadows and pretty walks. Long summers in the garden and winters by the roaring fire. Beyond the grief, there was hope.

"Let's have a barbecue," said Jack, "before we leave London forever – nothing too big, just a few friends, some good food and great wine – whad'ya think?"

"We could have Pimms," Amelia said, smiling.

The forecast on the morning of the barbecue was bright. Guests were due to arrive around 3p.m. They pulled the cover from the barbecue and filled it with charcoal, ready to light an hour before everyone arrived. They had invited their neighbours, a few friends and a couple of Amelia's work colleagues. John and Tricia came early to help them prepare, and even brought a gazebo in case of rain, which seemed likely as the day went on.

"Thought we might not be able to trust the weathermen. They usually get it wrong, but always when you entertain al fresco," John said, with a laugh.

Luckily, everyone was just enjoying the last of the spare ribs and Amelia's homemade potato salad when the heavens opened. A few people huddled under the green gazebo, including John and Jack; others went inside.

"Things settled down now for you, mate?" John asked Jack, as he poked at the still glowing charcoal with a rod.

"It wasn't like you, mate, all those accusations. It can't have been as bad as all that. What was in your head?" he'd asked, as if he was concerned that maybe Jack was ill.

"Ah. You weren't there, John. You didn't see Amelia through it all. That woman in America was evil. Corrupt." He was hurt his friend was doubting him. "We weren't the only ones. She tried to ban others from the hospital too. One of them told us that she had put a chair up inside the door to stop people coming in, until a security guard demanded that it be removed, and they took it away so she couldn't do it again. She was sick in the head, John – you needed to see it to believe it."

"Yeah, but to accuse her of poisoning? I know you were sure at the time, but as it turned out, wasn't one of your better ideas, eh?" he said. "I bet Amelia's father went ballistic. Then chucking her out of the funeral. I know it was stressful, mate, but I mean, the woman's only human."

Jack looked at his friend with disbelief and shook his head slowly. No one but no one would ever understand. Desperate to change the subject, he said, "Yeah, we're all only human, I suppose. Another beer? How's work?"

The barbecue was a success and having everyone around helped them both, but especially Amelia, emerge from their grief. During the summer, they had heard nothing from Evelyn or her lawyers, although Jack believed that the silence would be short-lived. Even Laura was quiet. Amelia had told him she'd heard from her once, to check they had returned home safely. As far as he knew, she had completed her training in-house, finished her trial period with the law firm, and was now working there full-time. His wife was pleased she'd been able to help the girl – he thought they'd be in touch more often.

"I guess she's just too busy being a hot-shot, young lawyer," he'd suggested.

"Mm," replied Amelia.

***

One afternoon, in early August, several weeks after the barbecue, Jack's mobile had buzzed on his desk. Amelia's name showed up on the screen.

"She's suing!"

"What?"

"As if she didn't put us through enough. She's suing the estate. I'll send you a copy of the email now. Make sure you're sitting down. It's an outrage, I'm furious. I'm coming home early, we need to plan a good response."

Her indignation at not being included in Roger's will must have been eating away at Evelyn all this time. She'd not only come in between Amelia and her father, she'd caused arguments between the two of them, left Roger's friends bemused and uncertain, and even affected the way his own friends felt about him. Again, he felt the hate begin to move inside of him.

The email was from Henry Attfield, the executor. There were two attachments. A letter from Matthew Lapinsky and a spreadsheet.

Enclosed for your review and payment, by the estate of Roger Kavanagh, is a verified claim against the estate, being presented by Evelyn DeGrawe. Also attached is a copy of Ms DeGrawe's affidavit, in support of said verified claim, attached to which are various exhibits, which further summarize and document the details and amounts claimed.

Jack scanned the spreadsheet. His eyes ran down one column and onto the next. The list included various foods bills and grocery costs, haircuts, personal assistance, food supplements, taxis, other travel expenses, annual gifts (including one to herself for $8,000), photo processing, courier fees, postage fees, cleaning costs, pool guy tips, telephone engineer tips, packers' tips, reimbursement for stolen property, reimbursement for damaged property, and personal time in putting together the actual claim itself. On the next page was a list of medicines and hospital costs, which, actually, had already been paid for by Roger's insurance policy. The total amount of the claim was highlighted, in yellow, at the bottom – $586,289.06.

Half a million bloody dollars! This had to be a joke. But no, he looked at the letter again. It was there in black and white. They would need money to defend themselves. But the loan – that last loan. He needed to pay before the end of the month – his business depended on it.

CHAPTER 32 (AMELIA)

It was nice being alone in the cottage. Jack was busy with work – had some sort of big meeting on – so I'd suggested coming up here on my own. "I could do with a night away, and I'll get a lot done," I'd said, when he told me he'd be late back.

Earlier in the summer, we'd been here to change the lock once more and sort out Dad's clothes and other things. I'd chosen a good charity shop in the village to take them to, but we had the antique items valued. After we retrieved the violin from Gwen, I'd told her the story behind it over a slice of her delicious homemade fruitcake.

"Dad told me it could be a Stradivarius years ago, but he was always sure it was copy. Though he kept it secretly in the attic, just in case. But it doesn't matter to me if it's a copy or not. My great-great-grandfather was a bookie. He went to racetracks all over the country and worked hard to make a good living. There was one high-rolling punter who was often at the same venues. They got to know each other and my great-great-granddad would accept bets from him with credit – in the 1840s, the only gambling allowed was at racetracks, so he was confident he'd make it good. But eventually, the punter died, owing him thousands, and his family gave him the violin to settle the dues. It belongs here with us – nowhere else – it's a legacy."

The fiddle was on the table, inside its shabby and broken case. All its strings were broken and curling everywhere like a bad perm. A musty, dusty aroma emanated from it. The valuer had told us it was a fake. Just like Evelyn, I thought.

At first, the cottage was empty without my father's essence. Lifeless. Like the very soul of it was waiting faithfully for him to come home to it, so it could embrace him and remind him of his life here in England. Now I'd come in and torn that away. He was never coming back, I felt like telling it. It would have to make do with us from now on. It should be grateful not to be empty so much of the year. The cottage soon began to take on a new look, a fresh life, and became more like home to us. The main changes were in the gradual redecorating, but also, I'd brightened it up – some floral plates for the dresser, new pots and pans, colourful cushions on the new sofa, new linen and a throw on the bed, garden accessories, and a bench for the lawn. I'd mowed it that day. I thought of the time my father and I had picnicked here with my favourite doll. We'd lain a green and blue checked blanket on the lawn and had boiled eggs and sandwiches. Then we'd lay on our backs (I'd positioned the doll so that she could do the same) and Dad had shown me how to see shapes in the moving white clouds... a dragon's head, a hand pointing north, a flying bird. I'd made a daisy chain and dangled it in his sleeping face, before putting around his neck. He'd worn it all afternoon.

His ashes I had scattered, as he wished, with Helen's, in a place on the magnificent hill nearby, where we once flew a kite. We had picked a quiet evening when no one was around. First Helen and then my father. I had let the mild wind take them far and wide, across the heather and the grassland, through the wood, onto the sky and down the valley to the stream. I imagined them there together, at last. The image was so vivid that my stomach had leaped and my heart had hurt, as I watched their dust settle at sundown. They really were just memories now, the two of them.

After I'd received Attfield's email, a week ago, I had felt resentful for hours, but then suddenly, the muddy waters cleared, and I became organised. As if my brain had sorted something out, on its own, without telling me.

"We can deal with this," I had said to Jack, as I entered the kitchen, feeling almost brilliant. "It only looks frightening because we're reading it all wrong. These are just words on a page. We can break it down, item by item, and strike off each one with a reason to reject it."

It would be fine, I thought to myself, as I relaxed in the deep bath. Anyone could see that she was just a deranged, old lady. She wouldn't get her way. She didn't even have support from Laura, who refused to side with her – especially after she witnessed how the old woman treated us when my father passed away. Laura and I had become quite close over the summer. I told her about the lock and the violin. It helped. I wanted to keep our friendship to myself for the moment, so I didn't tell Jack how much we'd been in touch. I lied and told him I hadn't even heard from her. I somehow felt that the relationship could be more... useful, that way.

As I dried myself, with one of the new pink, and exceedingly fluffy, towels, I flicked the radio on. The tune playing reminded me of my mother. I thought about how jealous she would have been if she'd known he'd left me the cottage. It had been many years since she'd died – maybe 20 by now, could be more. In my teenage years, she'd been so bitter about her break-up, and so jealous of Dad's new wife, she'd begun to drink. "A coping mechanism," she'd say. "How could I attract a man when I've got a horrible, ignorant, tarty teenager in tow," she once said to me, in the middle of a dark night. I'd woken to find her pacing up and down the living room, swigging whisky straight from the bottle. I'd walked towards her to try to help her go back to bed. Quite a grown-up thing for a 14-year-old, I always thought. But I stopped dead in my tracks as her hand came up. The stinging sensation on my face brought tears to my eyes and blood from my nose. That was the first time.

The disease had already pinned itself to her by then. It sought her out, found her, weak and susceptible, caught her, trained her, owned her for years to come.

Some people said she'd probably deliberately timed her collapse to coincide with one of my visits. But I was never sure of that. She was unconscious when I arrived. Even though I knew what to do, something in me stopped panic rising and brought calm. It also stopped me calling for help. I sat down and chatted to her sleeping face for an hour. By the time the ambulance did come, she was not quite dead. I went with her to A&E. She lay, still as a millpond, for hours and hours, her skin clammy and pale, a machine keeping her alive. I knew she wouldn't make it. Later, it comforted me that I had been there because she didn't die alone. I'd never told anyone about finding her. It was a minute detail I felt didn't need attention. People would only ask why I didn't call the ambulance sooner, and I didn't know the answer to that.

In the bedroom, my mobile rang. It was Jack.

"Hello gorgeous," he said, lovingly.

"Hi, darling, how was your meeting?"

"Yeah it was fine, thanks. What about you? Are you ok?"

"I've been busy here all day – the weather's been great. I've done the garden and the cleaning. Knackered now."

"You'll sleep well then."

"Yes, but I'm still planning on leaving early, so be home before lunch."

"Great – I miss you when you're not here."

"I miss you too, honey. Only a night though."

"Night-night, darling. You know I love you, don't you?"

"I love you too, Jack."

In my slippers and dressing gown, I padded downstairs, past the cheaply-framed, childish painting of a clown's face that I'd created for my father in primary school. It was brown now. I poured a glass of red wine, switched on the TV and slumped in front of it. Tomorrow, I'd register myself on that American Bar Association conference in New York. Laura had already confirmed her place. It would be a fantastic networking opportunity. Especially with the deal we'd just won for the new American law firm. We were growing this part of the business fast – trending a new way forward. In actual fact, it was probably essential that I was there. I could try to get a couple of other appointments, and maybe a speaking opportunity. All for the sake of the business, of course.

***

As I parked outside our house, I was baffled when I saw Jack sweeping out the empty garage.

"Where's the Porsche?" I asked.

"Sold it."

"What?"

"It needed two new tyres, a radiator fan, new struts, a control arm and brake pads. I just thought, until this saga is completely over, we shouldn't spend the money. We may need to it pay her off."

"How much did you get?"

"Half what it was worth – 6k. A pittance really – it won't be enough but it could be a start. It's just a car. I'll get another next year, after we've moved. We have more important things to worry about just now."

"Oh, I'm sorry, darling. She was your pride and joy, I know you'll miss her. We won't lose to that woman though," I said, as I put my bag down and embraced him. "We'll beat her in every way possible, just you watch."

"Yes, my love. We will – I know we will."

CHAPTER 33 (JACK)

Jack walked up to the payphone confidently. It was a while since he'd used one. Everyone had mobiles these days.

He opened the red, window-paned door and stepped in. Stale urine offended his nostrils. His fingers dabbed at the silver buttons in front of him and he held the heavy, old-style receiver to his ear.

"Yes? 'Ello?"

"Bill! It's Jack Jones. How are you?"

"Eh, mate, it's been ages. I'm good, you old fucker, what are you doing? 'Ow's it goin'?"

Jack could hear Bill smiling and smiled too.

"Yeah, yeah, I'm alright. Listen, I know it's out of the blue, but I might have some work for you... Fancy catching up over a pint?"

"Yeah mate. Could do with some dosh. Where? As long as it's not at the old manor." Jack already knew Bill wouldn't want to be spotted around his former dealing area.

"Can you handle a short train journey to Motspur Park? There's a pub there, right by the station. Tomorrow. Lunch on me. 12.30, or 1p.m. in the other pub, across the road and to the left, 200 yards down, if it's not cool."

"Gotya"

He experienced a buzz and felt nostalgia for old times. It had surprised him how easily he'd slipped back into planning mode, with all the right procedures. He didn't even have to name the pubs. Bill knew the script. They had both read it many times. They had always been careful where they met, and caution was still needed – even though Bill was clean, he was still an armed robber, a murderer and a grass.

***

He arrived at the first pub deliberately early to check it out. If the first location wasn't good, if he looked out of place or if there was any other police business going on (and he could spot that a mile away), then he would move to the second location immediately, without acknowledging his guest. "Field craft", it was called. Very important if you didn't want to get spotted.

The pub seemed fine. Fairly quiet. He got a pint from the barman and picked a table so he could sit with his back against the wall and see the door. At 12.30 on the dot, he spotted Bill arrive and watched him get a pint. He knew Bill had clocked him on entering, even though their eyes hadn't met. Bill picked up his drink and walked over to the table, where he sat down opposite Jack. No handshakes or back patting – a softly, softly approach. The aim was to attract as little attention as possible.

"So," said Jack to Bill, "what you doing these days?"

"This and that. You know, ducking and diving."

"Bobbing and weaving, eh?" Jack laughed, and Bill chuckled. It was clear they were both happy to see each other. But they moved straight to the point. There was no more small-talk. If the plan was to work, the less time spent together, the better. If they weren't seen, they couldn't be connected.

"So, what's this work you've got for me then? I 'ope it's a good earner?"

"Depends on what you call a good earner." He wanted to make an impact. "You remember David Luk, don't you?" Jack paused. It was all he needed.

"'Course," said Bill. "Yeah, I know. I owe you – what do you need?"

"What I need is someone in the States for a while. I'll pay for your flights, room and board, and give you a small fee. If this goes well, we can call it quits, and that will be your remaining payment. You won't owe me nothing anymore."

Bill's eyes lit up slightly. His eyebrows raised and he lowered his chin.

"Never been to the States. How long will you need me there?"

"However long it takes – could be a few days, could be a month. I checked your status – you're off the international watch list now, so you can travel with no issues and a visa will be easy. You'll need answers for why you are there and where you are staying. You'll say you're writing a book – researching it – something to do with social development, or human rights... you'll see why later."

"Interesting. When do you need me to go?"

"The sooner the better."

They both checked their surroundings. Everyone was quiet and minding their own business. A few more people had arrived and were milling at the bar. Jack continued.

"Ok. Here it is. My father-in-law lived in America. Really nice guy – you know, I liked him a lot. Amelia adored him – they were very close. The man was a widower. He met this Yankee bitch a few years ago and took up with her. Trouble is, she's been a fuckin' gold-digger from scratch. Rumour has it she managed to kill off her other husbands - two of them. Looks loaded but probably isn't. Full of fancy pants ideas – mutton dressed up, you know, fur coats an' all. Swans around as if she owns everything and everyone..." Over the next 20 minutes, Jack told Bill everything that had happened.

"Evelyn her name is – Evelyn DeGrawe. Amelia lost her zest for life, Bill – it nearly killed me to see it. But the woman didn't stop there. After we came home, Amelia had tried to find a new home for the cat – Benson – the bitch had dumped the poor thing at the vets." He looked closely at Bill and saw a flicker in his eyes. Bill was an avid cat lover – it had always amused Jack. "But when she heard about it, she accused Amelia of contesting. There was this big tornado of lawyer's letters back and forth. Thankfully, it was short lived. The cat died at the vets during all the arguing and the lawyers agreed not to pursue it – it seemed so petty. Anyway, it doesn't stop there. Now she's suing his estate for half a mill. It's like she's obsessed. If she can't get it one way, she's going to try another. It's got to stop. I want her out of our lives before she destroys us."

"Shit man, I can see you're really fucked off."

"You couldn't even start to guess. Are you in?"

"You sure about calling it quits – slate clean?"

Jack nodded.

"All expenses?"

"Flights, food and board, and the fee. Do you good to get away – laying low, somewhere where you haven't been. And you can stay a while after it's done. Have a holiday."

"It sounds doable. And I trust you. Ok. I'm in."

This time, they shake hands – just once, over the table.

"Good job," said Jack. They leant towards each other over the table and began to plan.

They arranged another rendezvous, downed the remainder of their pints and left, first Jack then Bill. Outside, they ensured they walked in opposite directions. They weren't together for even 45 minutes.

Jack only spent a few hours putting together the vital information that Bill would need, being careful not to raise any suspicion from Amelia. He used all the research he'd done when he thought she was poisoning Roger, and added stuff he had found at the house in Connecticut. But he was careful to keep it to a minimum. Essential stuff only – the less Bill knew, the better. He stacked the information into a green folder and put it into a holdall. He added an old GSM listening device that he had used on surveillance, and handwritten instructions on how to use it. He inserted them into a brown A5 envelope and wrote a five-figure number on the front. Bill already owned a set of binoculars and a long-lens camera. Finally, he took £5,000 in cash from the sale of the Porsche and stuffed it in the green bag too.

He'd got twenty for the car. He'd put the six he'd told Amelia about in their joint account. The rest was for the start of Bill's new life.

Their second meeting was in a multi-storey car park in Croydon. He arrived by train and walked to the meeting place. He walked up the stairs, like a shopper, to Level 4, where Bill had parked. He found Bill's car, got in the front seat, and hauled the bag onto the back seat, as if it was full of dirty washing.

"Alright?"

"Ready to go, boss"

"You should have everything you need in there, including half the money. The rest is in a locker at the airport, in dollars – the code is on the envelope, which you should destroy when you arrive in the States."

Bill nodded. "I'll be in touch when it's done. You can trust me, Jack, you know that."

"Good luck." Jack patted Bill's shoulder. The slam of the car door echoed loudly.

CHAPTER 34 (BILL)

Bill Skilling surprisingly had no criminal record. It wasn't just down to the meticulously-planned execution of his drug deals. No, diligence had gone out the window in Australia (somehow, he became hooked and desperate). It was only luck that allowed him to escape the armed robbery there. He'd reached home turf, thanks to Jack, who had also protected him after he killed David Luk, so he would inform. He most definitely owed his life to Jack.

People in his old manor thought he was dead. But he was still recognisable, and this was always unnerving. He'd moved to a different area north of London and laid low for three years, under another name, living off his proceeds. He'd made a lot of money before he left. He put himself through rehab, and still had change. He was low-key. He didn't live a rich life. He was almost reclusive. He didn't have dependents, nor friends, nor a woman. He was too paranoid his past would catch up with him.

In America, he could start a new life. No one would recognise him there. Once he'd done this job for Jack, he could be a free man. He could disappear into the great big US of A – get a job, a girlfriend, maybe even a house. Live a normal, guilt-free life. Of course, he jumped at the opportunity.

He was tall and thin, his face pock-marked from teenage acne, a shallow scar on his left cheek from a stab wound in his dealing days. His hair was shoulder-length and dark grey. He always wore an army-print baseball cap and dark glasses. His grey goatee beard gave him a South American look. He would only ever wear jeans, trainers and t-shirts. He owned only one jacket, a parka, which he wore in winter. Everything he did was slow and careful. He walked as if each step mattered and took thought to perform. He never ran anywhere because people would notice a man running.

He spoke as if his listener may not quite understand, and he laughed like he was stoned.

Buying the airline ticket, he had to remind himself that he was a free man and he could travel where he liked. The fact that he hadn't been abroad since Australia was the issue – he was out of practice and things had changed. He filled out the advance passenger information slowly and hit submit. The confirmation email pinged into his inbox. No one called him to say he couldn't go. No one doubted he was travelling for pleasure. No one would be looking for him. No one connected his name with a robbery on the other side of the planet, or the killing of a user.

When the day came, he took Jack's holdall and an old, battered suitcase with a few clothes to the airport. He'd learned the locker code and the cash was waiting, as Jack had promised. He stuffed it into a body belt, put the empty carrier bag back in the locker and left the door open, ready for the next person. The belt made him hot and he was sweating when he went through security. But once on the plane, he relaxed, and began to enjoy the morning flight. About an hour in, he looked at the immigration cards that the stewardess had handed him. He laughed quietly to himself at the irony of a question on the green one.

Have you ever been arrested or convicted for an offence or crime involving moral turpitude, or a violation related to a controlled substance; or been arrested or convicted for two or more offences for which the aggregate sentence to confinement was five years or more; or been a controlled substance trafficker; or are seeking entry to engage in criminal or immoral activities?

He ticked the box next to "No" confidently, and didn't once think about the word "liar", because someone might read his mind or it might show in his face.

After breakfast, he flicked through the *Daily Mail*, and then watched a film that had not long been released – a weak thriller about a murdered family. He was still hot from the dollars wrapped around his body. He visited the toilet four times to cool off. He ordered rum and coke at every opportunity. The deliciousness of the dry, sour drink helped him relax enormously. No drugs these days, not even cigarettes. But booze – he could never quit that.

He had been through the folder several times. There wasn't much there – the name and address of the apart-hotel where Jack recommend he stay. It was opposite the woman's block on the Upper East Side. A vague plan of her apartment layout, as well as a photo of the building, which Jack had printed on a sheet of A4, with the windows of her floor marked in a red circle, and the office floors at the bottom in a blue one. Evelyn's address and telephone numbers, cell phone and landline were all printed clearly on the sheet, and there were two maps of New York, offering bus and subway routes.

His head ached when he finally arrived at JFK and joined the queue for immigration, carrying the holdall and the camera equipment in a separate, silver-coloured case. He stepped from one foot to another, as the line snaked up and down the taped-off walkway. He was behind a group of Japanese tourists, all different heights, already messing with their cameras, and in front of a middle-aged, Scottish couple. His heart beat hard in his chest.

"Good morning sir," the officer said, pleasantly, when he finally arrived at the desk. The man looked him directly in his face and then down at his passport picture. His face was round and black and his afro hair was cut short and neat. His black shirt was tieless, with a white vest showing at the neck. He looked serious, but still offered a smile. Bill thought it was smarmy and was not really in the mood to reciprocate. He badly needed a shower. But he was well prepared. He had done his homework and knew the answers.

"Welcome to the US."

"Thank you," Bill responded, politely. The officer nodded and flicked the pages of the passport.

"Which other countries have you been to recently, sir?"

"Only Europe in the last few years."

"Have you ever been to Australia?"

Bill felt an unpleasant pull in his groin, as if he needed to pass wind. The Australian stamp would be in his old passport, not in this one.

"Well, yes... why do you ask?"

"Just thought I could detect a hint of an accent, sir."

"I see," said Bill, relieved. "Well, I lived there for a while many years ago, but I'm English through and through."

He was still sweating.

"I see. What is the purpose of the visit?" asked the smart black man.

"Research," said Bill. "I'm a writer. I'm researching for a book. On humanitarian affairs."

"Interesting."

"Yes."

"I wish you good luck with that," said the officer, who was still looking down at the documentation. "Where are you staying?"

"At the Keepman Tower Hotel, Manhattan, East 52nd Street. I've written the address there."

"I see that, sir. Good area for the UN."

Next, his fingerprint was scanned, his photo was taken, and the officer stamped a single page before bidding him a great trip. He was in. The relief flooded through him and he suddenly felt the most coherent and alert since he had left London. His luggage, the old, dusty, brown suitcase, came round quickly, and he found himself outside in another queue for a cab. It was already lunchtime. He donned his dark glasses and his baseball cap. A pull at his goatee and he was ready.

***

"I'd like a room with a kitchen please, facing south, if that's at all possible – I'm suspicious like that and I will sleep better." He winked at the pretty receptionist, but then, he nearly ruined it. "Do you have anything on the 17th floor – 17 is my lucky number, and I could really do with some luck with this book." He flashed her a smile. "I know it sounds mad but it would make my day." He tried to sound friendly, but worried that it was actually sinister.

"Well, sir, you're in luck," sang the receptionist, almost brightly. "We can offer you a room with a kitchen on the 18th floor – only one floor up – there is a partial view of the river... it's facing the building opposite."

"I'll take it." Bill was overjoyed. "Can I have it for a week, maybe longer?"

"Certainly, sir. The room is ready for you to check in. I'm so happy we've been able to help you. We need the first night's payment as a deposit – the rest you pay on check out."

Bill paid for the whole week with his sweaty dollars, and the receptionist was grateful for her tip.

The room was perfect. It housed a big double bed, tidily made up with crisp, white sheets, big, fluffed-up pillows and a golden-coloured bedspread. There was a phone on the bedside table and a big, brown, leather armchair next to it. Opposite the bed was a widescreen TV, and next to that, two cheap-looking dining chairs, set at a small, square, wooden table. Two would be a squash, he thought, but he wouldn't be entertaining. Behind the table was a long, narrow window, adorned by floor-length curtains and a stained blind. The dimension of the window offered him the advantage of being able to sit at the table and point his binoculars. He walked up to it, moved a chair out of the way and pulled up the blind. And there it was. Huffington Plaza, right in front of him. He craned his neck and managed to spot a small section of the river, glinting behind the railings of FDR Drive. He quickly identified which windows belonged to the woman. His eyes were gritty from travelling, but his excitement at the perfect location of the room spurred him awake.

The kitchenette was in the corridor, which led through to a small bathroom. A wardrobe with a few hangers offered space for his modest selection of clothes. He unpacked the battered suitcase into it, replacing his t-shirt, and adding a layer of deodorant. He put the remaining cash in the safe, along with his passport. Then, from the holdall, he took out a pair of high-powered binoculars with an extendable, folding tripod, and the GSM listening device. It was a small, sturdy, black unit, the size of a matchbox. It would be very easy to conceal.

He looked at the building opposite and then down at the scratchy floor plan. He started with the window in the middle of the 17th floor, which the drawing told him was the main bedroom. A quick check with the binoculars confirmed this – mirrored wardrobes, a bright, purple bedspread, and a large print on the wall. He moved right – this room was smaller, but he could see a desk on the far wall, and a wide, brown, leather sofa adjacent. Next to this was the kitchen – tall, grey cupboards, and a space where he thought there could be a table. The dining room – he made out a black, oval-shaped table with six chairs. The final window was on the corner of the building. It was so well-lit that he could see right through this room – blue sofas, a big, square table, a couple of non-matching chairs, and he could just about make out a chaise longue in the furthest corner. The apartment was empty.

Right, he thought, as he suddenly felt a pang of hunger. He took out one of the maps from the folder and checked the address of the AT&T store. He needed to get his bearings quickly, before he caught up on sleep. Down in the lobby, he changed a few notes to smaller ones and walked out of the building. He turned right towards First Avenue. The late summer sun had scorched the air all season. There was an on-going cacophony of car horns, diesel engines, multiple languages, whistles, people yelling, men drilling. He took in the yellow hanging traffic lights and the white lines crossing the frantic one-way street. He waited with some other sticky pedestrians, whilst the sign glared "Don't Walk" in orange. He heard a snippet of a conversation of two women with broad, loud accents. The sharp tone struck annoyance in him.

"Yeah, she lives in Brooklyn, he doesn't... I don't know why..."

"Well I haven't heard anything at all from her about that, you know, he doesn't seem to do a thing."

A man in a white shirt and loosened tie was in front of him, shouting into a mobile phone. "He needs to wind his neck in... I'll be back in 20 minutes..."

"Walk" was suddenly flashing and they all crossed together like a gaggle of geese, while the cars lined up to their left.

Opposite was a tall, brick building with a low, green awning, advertising coffee. The aroma engulfed him as he entered. Inside, he ordered a takeaway cappuccino and two SIM cards, paid in cash, and emerged onto the pavement, smiling – the girl who had served him had "absolutely loved" his accent – "*Are you really from Engerrland?*"

He walked south for one block, stopping at a Duane Reade convenience store to pick up a cell phone handset, and crossed back to the other side again. Now, he could see Evelyn's building. It was clear that the first few floors were a hive of business activity – there was even a bank on the ground level. Someone had taken the time to plant spindly trees on the edge of the sidewalk – nice touch, he thought. He walked past the front of the building, noticing the big, glass door, the driveway where a couple of taxis were waiting, and the doormen. There was an underground car park. He walked on the opposite side of the road, as he knew it was a dead end – he didn't want anyone to notice him turning around and coming back. On the other side of the block, he was relieved to discover a small corner-type shop, with a selection of prepared food. He bought bread, milk, cheese, butter, chocolate chip cookies, coffee and tea, a bar of Hershey chocolate, coke (for the duty-free rum), some cold meats, a jar of pickles, an odd-shaped cucumber and two microwaveable meals.

Back in the room, he inserted one SIM into the phone and one into the listening device, then emptied the contents of the brown paper bag into the fridge. He quickly made and hungrily devoured a tasty sandwich. After the last bite, he sighed contentedly and suddenly, felt his exhaustion. He took a quick look into Evelyn's apartment and saw no movement. He lay on his back on the bed and found it to be very comfortable indeed. He noticed his headache had gone and fell into a deep and dreamless sleep.

CHAPTER 35 (AMELIA)

It felt different to be flying to New York for a reason other than to visit my father. It surprised me to feel excited. There was also an unfamiliar sense of adventure brewing in me. The conference was a great opportunity. I knew a few other people who were going, including Laura. The networking chances were endless, and there were plenty of excellent workshops on offer. I embraced this small chance to grow my business, plan future strategies, and I believed good things were just around the corner.

It was late when I checked into the conference hotel in Midtown. I unpacked and, despite it being the middle of the night at home, sent a text to Jack so he knew I had arrived safely. The bright lights of the city and the throngs of hyperactive people milled outside. I showered. As I regarded my body in the mirror, I wished I was at least one size smaller, as I did a thousand times a day. But I blow-dried my dark-blonde hair, put on a bit make-up, including lipstick, a pair of jeans with a white shirt, and took myself to the bar for a glass of wine.

I watched the people and their worlds go by in my dark, quiet corner, and talked to no one except the expert waiter. I read a paper, ate some nuts, and actually managed to relax. Back in the room, I lay there in the dark for some time. I didn't have to wake up early – registration for the event didn't start until the afternoon. So I'd have time to adjust my body clock. Maybe I could allow a trip to Saks. It wasn't too far. I remembered it was one of Laura's favourite shopping spots – she had bought her luggage there, only to have the customs official stick labels on it when she came to London. That was funny. It was hard to believe that was over two years ago. If I had time, I considered walking to Ground Zero, to see how it had changed since the last time I saw it – Dad's 75th. Memories of that night came flooding back and I cringed at the thought of Evelyn, the venue, the food. My father was so embarrassed that night, he had to get drunk. It still amazed me. He would have been 78 this year. I missed him, and a tear popped out quietly, rolled down the side of my temple to the pillow. Why would anyone want to make life that difficult? She had brought all that hatred upon herself. And Jack had been wonderful through it all – how he stood up for me, calmed me, helped me see sense. And I pictured us in the newly-decorated cottage. My musings became random and erratic and, as sleep came, I began to dream about my mother.

***

I saw Laura at the registration desk before she spotted me, and walked boldly towards her.

"Hi, hi hi!" she said, as she turned, sounding every bit as thrilled as she looked. "Oh my Gawd, how *are* you? It's so *good* to see you."

She was wearing a light-grey, impeccably-tailored designer suit, and her shiny, blonde hair sat perfectly on her shoulders. But for my deeper shade of blonde, the style was almost exactly a copy of my own. I also noticed that her nails were salon-perfect too. She was careful to air-kiss, so as not to smudge her red lipstick, but she embraced me warmly. If there was something different about her, it was in her eyes – they met mine with a confidence I hadn't seen before. It was success. It was happiness. And it was catching. I beamed back.

"And you, Laura – look at you – you look quite the professional. So smart. I love your hair."

We attended the workshops that afternoon together, and met many other associates from many other companies. We didn't have time to gossip. We worked the room, together and apart. I collected dozens of business cards, and gave away twice as many. A drinks reception began at six in the evening, where I saw Catriona Lewis and her US partner, David Green.

"So, our little plan a couple of years back worked out ok then?" I said to her, indicating Laura, who was deep in conversation with a group of three smartly-dressed legal specialists, and reminding her of the introduction in London.

"It certainly did, Amelia. That girl of yours is working out a treat apparently – she's really going places. They love her to bits here, don't you, David?"

"Oh lordy, yes. She has a very bright future ahead of her, that young lady. Talk of the devil, here she is," and, right on cue, Laura strode over, looking sassy, confident, and sporting a smile so big, it threatened to dislocate her jaw. "Were your ears burning, my dear?"

"Oh my, were you talking about little, old me, my lovely colleagues?" and she giggled, as she touched Catriona fondly on the elbow, being careful not to spill the champagne in her other hand. She beamed at David. "Darling Amelia – you are the one I thank my lucky stars for. I wouldn't be here without you. I'm loving everything about this job." She glanced at David again, who smiled back. "Obviously, I'm still a junior, but they're giving me so much, it's incredible. Now, let me introduce you to some people..."

We talked recruitment, candidates and law. Change, the future and forecasts. Cases, witnesses and defendants. Fashion, tourists and cars. We met professors, attorneys and graduates. Publishers, suppliers and bankers. Not once, despite Laura knowing about the claim, did we mention Evelyn. That subject could wait.

Before I knew it, I was feeling exhausted, and decided to leave. Dinner wasn't necessary – the canapés had been coming all night, and I could always order room service if need be. I hugged Laura fondly in the foyer of the hotel.

"It's been great doing this with you – we should go into business together," she smiled, and I saw her younger features emerge.

"Maybe one day," I laughed.

"I'm so looking forward to tomorrow, there are some great speakers," she said, her genuine excitement clear.

"Yes, it's a really good event. And well done, Laura. You're clearly excelling and will make an extremely good attorney. So, see you tomorrow."

"Thank you. Yes, 9.30? Here?"

"Perfect. And I've booked a great steakhouse for the evening. You will love it."

"Sounds great. I can't wait. See you in the morning."

***

The following Monday, I was back at work in Wimbledon by 7.30a.m. Sarah arrived at 8.30a.m. As she looked in, she placed a freshly-made cup of coffee in front of me. "How was it?"

"Brilliant," I said, beaming at her. "I made some really good contacts, a lot of good introductions – lots to follow up on. I took a number of openings from a mid-sized firm based in Washington. It may be a good idea to plan another trip, to meet some of these people face to face. Anyway, I'm going to shut myself away for the day and really get my head around it... don't think I'm ignoring you – let's get together at the end of the day, yeah?"

"Right you are, boss," she said, and winked.

"Thanks for the coffee, boss," I replied.

The momentum stayed with me all day. I started planning all sorts of events and focusing on how best we could take these new US partnerships to new strengths. I started forecasting like mad, and even outlined the benefit of a new office in New York. I began a business plan.

At 6p.m., Sarah knocked quietly on the door of my office. I looked up at the clock and gasped.

"I can't believe the time – where's the day gone?"

"Glass of wine?" she said, with a smile, as she chinked a couple of glasses in her left hand and held up a bottle of Sauvignon blanc in her right.

"You star," I said. "Shall we have a catch-up?"

"Yes, because I haven't seen you all day. What have you been up to, hiding away in here?"

"Writing a business plan. The conference was excellent. I have some great ideas and I'm dying to share them with you."

"Great – well, let's hear them."

"Why don't we go into town and catch up over dinner? I've just realised, I'm absolutely famished."

"Oh, you're reading my mind – let's go to that new place on the corner. It's so great to see you smiling again, and I'm loving your enthusiasm – looks like the old Amelia is back," and Sarah gave me a quick hug.

"Ok – I'll just call Jack and let him know."

I felt elated. When I realised how long it had been since I experienced such happiness, I almost felt guilty. Only a few months since Dad's passing... when was I allowed to feel this; when was it ok to feel better?

I hauled my bag onto my shoulder – sunglasses, keys, money, phone. Sarah led the way out of the door and I closed it gently behind me and locked it.

CHAPTER 36 (BILL)

Bill woke with a start and looked at his watch. It was 7.17a.m., and the sun was angling in so brightly, he squinted and shaded his face with his hand. He got up to draw down the blind, but his eyes had adjusted before he got there. He looked out – people were sprinkled down on the pavement below, moving in all directions, like ants evicted from a kicked nest. He looked through the binoculars into the apartment. No movement at all anywhere. After eating a slice of toast, he showered and dressed, took some cash from the safe, and left the room.

In the lobby, he waved and smiled at the pretty, blonde receptionist.

"How's the book going, Will?" He was now considered one of their long-term residents, having been there just over ten days.

"It's all good, Amy, all good."

"That's great. Well, you have a good day now," she smiled, as he walked purposefully out of the door, crossed the busy street and entered Huffington Plaza. It was a large entrance, with three sets of tall, glass double doors. The two doormen, Sam and Hal, were doing a fine job, meeting and greeting, ushering taxis, opening and closing doors, and directing and helping everyone that came and went, in their matching dark jackets, trousers and caps. They smiled at everyone.

Bill's own look had experienced an overhaul in the past few days, and he now wore tan chinos, a smart, short-sleeved shirt, tucked in, and a pair of aviator sunglasses. He'd cut his hair very short and put his baseball cap away in a drawer in his room.

"Hey Mr Killen, how are you today?" Hal asked him, politely.

"Good, thanks Hal" he responded to his alias quickly, "and you?"

"Cool, thank you. I think Mike is ready – I'll let him know you are here – you can go right up", and he signalled with his thumb to the elevator.

They all knew him now. He had befriended Mike, whose organisation was based on the third floor, which was the highest of the office levels. They helped mainly African countries to improve and expand their global trade. He had agreed to help Bill with an important section of his book. It would be good PR for them. This involved meeting and discussing each chapter, in detail, of which there was eight. Because of his regular visits, he had come to know the building inside out. He had secured his initial meeting with Mike on the first day. He'd done the research before leaving home. He'd simply called and asked for an appointment. It had been that simple. They had got along so well that afternoon that Mike invited Bill (or Will) along to drinks at the bar with the team. By the end of the evening, he was on first-name terms with all of them.

On his first visit to Huffington Plaza, Bill had waited as the elevator doors opened, and walked in. Before he touched a button though, the old man he had been watching entered the building and walked as fast as he could toward the doors that Bill held open, waving his walking stick feebly. Bill took off his sunglasses and cap, pushed a hand through his scruffy hair, and smiled pleasantly at him, whilst he stood back, allowing the older gentleman to enter.

"Thank you, sir," the old man said.

"No problem," said Bill, in an American accent. The old man tapped in a code on the panel next to the floor numbers. Bill pushed another number, and travelled with his lift buddy to the 17th floor.

"Have a nice day," he said to the man.

"Likewise," was the reply, and his aged hand waved again.

The number the old man had tapped in was three-zero-four-one. It wasn't rocket science.

Bill took a deep breath in and held it. He listened for any sound. Nothing. He let the breath out. His heart beat faster, as he reached for his back pocket. Inside the well-used leather wallet, among his new membership and loyalty cards, his UK driving licence was a blank, laminated card, a bit bigger and more flexible than a credit card. He had made this himself years ago, when was regularly gaining access to homes of users that owed him. It worked much better that credit cards – didn't break so easily. He noticed with joy that the lock was a simple Yale type. He inserted the card into the vertical crack between the door and the jamb. He tilted it so it bent around in front of him, nearly touching the doorknob, and then pushed it until it slid in a little more, forcing the bolt down. Then he bent the card the opposite way. It slipped easily and quickly under the end of the bolt, forcing it back into its chamber and freeing the door from its lock.

He took the plastic shoe covers out of his other pocket and flipped them quickly over his soft soles. He was in. The apartment was in darkness, but the glow from the corridor flooded in and illuminated a small table with a lamp just inside the door. He flicked it on and walked through the corridor, passing the dining room and the kitchen. He knew his way from studying the plan. All he needed was to find somewhere to put the device. Where would she spend the most time – where was the telephone? His torch focused on the fake fireplace and a table to its left. He opened the drawer to find it empty, but for a small, silver pocket watch that was in a box without a lid. He pulled it out and put it on the carpet. He peeled off the adhesive label on the device, pulled the drawer all the way out, and stuck the box to the inside back panel. His hands were shaking, and he found it difficult to return the drawer to its place, but he managed on the third attempt, and then returned the watch to its dark home. He was back in the corridor in seconds, having flicked off the lamp and quietly closed the door. To his relief, there was still no one around. He took the covers off his shoes, returned them to his pocket and walked calmly back to the elevator.

"See you tomorrow, Will," Mike said jovially after the meeting, as he slapped Bill gently on the shoulder.

"That you will," said Bill, and whistled a tune as he walked out into the sunshine. What he'd learned about aiding refugees that morning was fascinating. He really could write a book about it. He went straight to his favourite diner and enjoyed a steak for lunch, before heading back to his room for more data logging. This took up the majority of the afternoon – Evelyn's comings and goings were carefully recorded and he even followed her to a hair salon near Central Park. After a short stroll around the lake, he saw Evelyn home, watched her settle in front of the TV and then put his equipment away. He felt peckish and realised he hadn't eaten anything since lunch, so he took a bus ride south to Midtown, found a deli and ordered a pastrami sandwich. Then, he was in need of refreshment by way of a few beers.

As the evening grew late, and the alcohol took effect, he contemplated how much he was enjoying this project, and this city. When night came, he was outside the bar on the pavement and was astounded at the rate the city was still moving. Lights blazed from every building and there were people everywhere. He was reminded of Piccadilly Circus at closing time. He wanted to inhale the atmosphere, and wandered down Lexington Avenue, then west across Park and Madison Avenue, onto 5th, where he turned left. He passed St Patrick's Cathedral, the New York Public Library, Grand Central Station, and then he spotted the Empire State Building. He was at the top within 20 minutes – it was gone 11p.m. now, and he shared the view with just a few. He took in the sights, the lights, the smells – he saw the Chrysler Building, the blacked-out Central Park, the bridges. Beautiful, he thought, as he drew breath. What a world. Anything is possible for me now... anything. He felt calm and peaceful. He had stalked Evelyn, silently and incessantly, gathering vital information all the while. All he needed now was patience for the right moment. He looked down and wondered how long it would take her to reach the ground if he pushed her off.

CHAPTER 37 (BILL)

Evelyn came home. Bill saw a tiny movement through the binoculars and immediately dialled into the listening device. He could hear motion, maybe some pots and pans in the kitchen, but nothing clearer. He focused on the bedroom and saw her unpacking a bag. She walked up to the window and seemed to look directly at him, her gaze scorching through the early-afternoon sunshine. He lowered the binoculars and shivered, but watched still. He saw the curtains close, took a breath and put the glass back to his eyes. She entered the lounge, picked up the phone and sat down on one of the blue sofas facing the window.

"Hello darling, I'm home."

Pause.

"Oh good."

Pause.

"Oh yes, I've had a super time and very productive. Helga helped me with the last of the garden things. But, you know, no matter how wonderful it is there, you can't beat coming back to the city."

Long pause.

"Ok, yes, that would be fine. We could go for cocktails if you like. Come a little earlier... That sounds divine. Ok darling, see you at six. I will take a nap now. Bye-bye."

From watching a delivery to Hal, he knew that Evelyn had tickets to a gala dinner at the Waldorf Astoria. And he had heard her book a limousine for 7.30. Tonight's the night, he thought, and felt a rush of energy. Tonight, she would be tired, and hopefully intoxicated. The apartment would be dark and she would be unsuspecting. Evelyn disappeared out of the room again and he saw her next in the kitchen. She took a bottle from the fridge, poured some of the liquid into a glass and drank it. Then, she disappeared out of sight and Bill assumed she was napping. But he didn't relax and he never took his focus off the apartment.

The hours ticked by. At 5p.m., she walked into the lounge in a robe, picked something up from the sideboard and strode out again. All the while, the bedroom curtains remained closed.

At 5.30p.m., Bill attempted to dial into the bug, ready to watch her receive her guest at 6p.m. Yesterday, it had crackled a few times annoyingly, and even switched itself off once. But today, it seemed fine. Right on time, at six exactly, Evelyn walked into the living room with a blonde-haired girl. She was still in a bathrobe, her thin, grey hair straggling down around her shoulders. The girl was wearing blue jeans, with a white t-shirt under a navy jacket. They were already engrossed in a disagreement, but he could only hear Evelyn. The girl was too quiet.

"It's a matter of diplomacy, sweetie."

The girl responded with something angry.

"Well, I think it's up to me to decide that, and none of your business."

The girl threw her arms up in the air and her voice raised, but her speech was still muffled. The woman became rigid in anger.

"Because he wrote it in the will; that's just the way it is..." She turned away and the rest of the sentence was muffled. Suddenly, there was a loud crackle and a high-pitched whistle in his earpiece, causing him to wince. He took it out and shook it. When he replaced it, there was nothing – the conversation was blocked out altogether.

"No, not now," he said aloud. Again, he shook it violently and replaced it. CLACK. BEEP. The thing shut itself down and refused to restart. He threw it across the room in frustration.

The sun was getting low in the sky and was glinting off the windows. It made watching difficult, but he could just see the two women animatedly shouting at each other, their bodies angled forward to each other in aggression. Evelyn was next to the fake fireplace. A single cloud blew overhead, and for a moment, he could see them both quite clearly. It was like watching a silent movie. The young girl was still shouting, the older woman looked stunned. Their body language was screaming malevolence. Then, the girl was in front of Evelyn, hiding her from Bill's view. Her right hand came up over her head behind her then came sailing down, straight into the side of Evelyn's face. He saw the woman fall to the floor, her head colliding with the mantle on the way down. He held his breath, waited. She didn't get up. The girl stood, as if rooted to the spot.

He lowered the binoculars slowly. That wasn't supposed to happen. That wasn't part of his plan.

He looked again – the girl was gone. He grabbed his key, a small, polythene bag from wardrobe, and flew out of the room. On the pavement outside, he spotted her run out of the lobby and up the street towards First Avenue. He watched her for a few seconds, before she melted into the crowds.

"Hey Sam, how you doing? I left a document in the office last week and realise I need it urgently... mind if go and get it?"

"Sure thing, Mr Killen, go right ahead."

Once in the empty corridor, Bill took the shoe covers out of the bag, along with a covered, typed report. His shoes protected, he walked softly through the hall to the living room, with the paper rolled up and shoved in his back pocket. Evelyn was lying there, her legs bent under her, the blood from her head seeped over the hearth and soaked into the fawn carpet. It had spattered the sides of the mantlepiece and part of the wall above. A high-heeled shoe was wedged under the edge of the rug. He put two fingers to the pulse of the woman's neck, but not before putting on his gloves. She was dead.

A police siren screamed outside. He froze as it sped past. Without pausing again, he went quickly to the table next to the fireplace and flung open the drawer. He ripped out the device and placed it in the bag. Then, he hastily exited the apartment, leaving everything as he found it. As he moved quickly down the hall, he removed both shoe covers and gloves and stuffed them in his pocket. In the elevator, he calmed his breathing. As the door opened, he almost walked into Sam.

"Got it!" he said, loudly, waving the rolled-up paper above his head.

"Great," replied Sam, smiling. "Have nice evening, Mr Killen."

CHAPTER 38 (AMELIA)

It had been a great week at work. Several of the leads that I had followed up from the New York conference had resulted in valuable contracts, and I was now head-hunting for some of the biggest firms in the US. Sarah and I were being quoted often in the industry press, and the company was moving from strength to strength.

It was the late summer bank holiday weekend. Jack and I were in the car, heading for the cottage. We were making some final touches before our big move in just two weeks. Amazingly, the builders had finished the extension on time, and we were both delighted with their work, despite the whole thing costing much more than they quoted.

Jack was eager to get there. "I love it there," he said, enthusiastically. "It's like the place has a new lease of life. Not just the extension and the garden, but all our new stuff – it's like a brand new start – time to start making fresh memories, baby. Put the old ones away and move on."

I took his hand, which was on my lap, and held it gently. "I don't know how I could have got through this year without you," I sighed. I watched his handsome face, as he concentrated on the road ahead. He'd also worked hard this year, but his marketplace was very specialised. Still, he was making ends meet and we didn't need to worry about a mortgage anymore. He was content and knew that he, we, had achieved something. He had a happy glow about him. He'd even begun to talk about Christmas – when the summer wasn't even over.

"We can put the tree up in the living room, in that space under the stairs – it will be lovely in there with the new fireplace. It's going to be so fantastic, baby." He gave her hand a squeeze and threw her a quick sideways smile.

***

On Monday morning, we both indulged in an unusual lie-in. We had planned to leave early to beat the traffic – but that didn't happen. As we were enjoying a fry-up, my phone rang. I didn't feel like speaking to anyone. We'd had such a nice weekend, and I wanted to savour the final few hours.

"It won't be anything important," I said, with a yawn. "They'll leave a message." I smiled at Jack and got back to the Sunday magazine I hadn't finished the day before.

"Wow – look at you, all relaxed. I don't think I've ever witnessed you ignore a call. Here's to taking it easy," my husband said, as he raised his mug. I raised mine too and we clinked them together like wine glasses. Giggled.

At around 11a.m., we had finished packing the car and were just preparing to lock up before beginning the journey back to London. As I was leaving the kitchen, I finally picked up my mobile to check the message.

"Oh – it's Attfield's office," I exclaimed, coming out of the front door, my keys hanging from my pocket. Jack leant out of the driver's seat. "Not a holiday there, I suppose. But it must be the middle of the night still. He says to call immediately."

Henry Attfield picked up straightaway.

"Thank you, Amelia, for returning my call – I have big news." It struck me how professional he was. His delivery was slow and carefully worded, without appearing patronising.

"And what news would that be, Mr Attfield?" I asked, with a smile. I had always addressed him the same way, out of pure respect for him, as my father's lawyer and my trustee.

"I hope you're sitting down, Amelia." I got into the front seat. Jack looked across at me.

"I am now," I said.

"I am afraid that Mrs DeGrawe, Evelyn, has passed away. She died in her apartment on Saturday. In the early evening, to be precise. It looks as though she tripped and fell. She had hit her head on the mantlepiece, in the living room. The force of the blow caused a massive bleed in her brain and she suffered a terrible haemorrhage, which was fatal. I'm sorry to be the one to bring you the bad news."

"Oh," I said. I couldn't think of anything else to say, and I stumbled over my words, knowing I should say something else so Mr Attfield knew I had heard him. "Well, um, gosh – I'm, I'm not really entirely sure what to say, or how to respond, Mr Attfield. What does this mean exactly?"

"Well, firstly, we have a duty to inform both the clerk of the court and yourself of the death, and this has now been done. Then we will affirmatively take such steps as are required to foreclose the claim. The first step will be to file a motion to the court..."

I had stopped listening and stared at Jack. "She's dead," I mouthed. "She's dead."

"What?" he mouthed back.

I took a deep breath and nodded, before I realised Attfield was no longer speaking.

"Ok. Thank you. Thank you for letting me know. Thank you, Mr Attfield. I may not have taken everything in. Can you give me some time for the news to sink in? I will call you later this week, if that's ok?"

"Yes, of course, Amelia. I know this will have come as a shock. I hope you have a good day, despite the news, and I look forward to speaking with you later in the week."

"Oh. Yes. Thank you." She put down the phone and looked, open-mouthed, at Jack.

"What?" he said.

"She's dead!"

"Who's dead? Evelyn? Is Evelyn dead?" he asked, urgently.

"Yes. Evelyn. She's actually dead."

"Hallelujah!" he said, not smiling.

"Jack!"

"Sorry. But I'm not sorry she's dead." He reached over the handbrake and encircled me in his arms.

"You know this is good news, don't you?" he said, trying to reassure me.

"Well yes, we can get on with our lives." I knew what I said was true, but I suddenly felt a tinge of guilt.

"Yes. We can finally get on with our lives, baby. At last. See?" I noticed him hug me slightly more tightly, as he asked, "How... how did she die?"

"She was found in her apartment – she'd smashed her head on the fireplace – caused a terrible bleed in her brain – a terrible accident."

"Oh," was all he said.

We looked at each other. He started to laugh. I thumped him playfully on the shoulder. Then laughed myself. Suddenly, we were both laughing uncontrollably, loudly.

"Stop," I said, to no avail – Jack was holding his stomach, but couldn't stop. I was reacting to that and felt tears on my cheeks. And then there seemed to be an implosion in my head, and my laughter turned into a weep. An incredible feeling of loss, for my father, grabbed me. Suddenly, I was crying hard, sobbing, gasping for air. I realised that I was finally grieving. Finally letting go. Not once, in all these months, had I cried properly for my father's loss, his departure, his death. In that moment, I missed him more than ever, and silently promised I would never let a day go by when I didn't thank him for what he had achieved for me.

CHAPTER 39 (JACK)

Jack cuddled his wife and felt the most satisfying sense of fulfilment. It was going to be a fantastic Christmas. Not difficult, considering the last. Life was idyllic in the country. No noise, no distractions. Peace. With his beautiful, clever wife.

The news about Evelyn, at the end of August, was not a shock. Amelia hadn't known whether to laugh or cry, but he felt a joyous relief. The woman, who had somehow entered their lives, and caused so much damage, unthinkable havoc, who came between Amelia and her beloved father, and almost between them, had now exited. She was out of their lives for good.

Jack had received an anonymous text, in the middle of the night. The night before Amelia had come home from her conference. He read just two words. "Job done", it had said. He knew who it was from; and he was never to hear from Bill again.

A part of him wished he could tell Amelia what he'd done for her. How he'd planned and executed what had happened so perfectly. But he knew he couldn't. She would never forgive him.

They were warm in front of the fire, the Christmas tree twinkling behind them, the smell of pine occasionally mingling with the scented candles. They laughed, as they watched another repeat of *Morecambe & Wise*, and relished the delicious cake that Amelia had baked weeks ago, with its hard, white icing and marzipan covering. This is happiness, he thought. I'm right where I want to be.

Amelia had sent flowers to Evelyn's funeral. She'd said that no matter what happened, Evelyn was in her father's life, and it was only respectful. Roger would have wanted her to do that.

She and Laura had become close friends. It had surprised him – but it was nice that something good had come out of the awful experience. They talked regularly on the telephone and emailed almost weekly. He was glad that Amelia still had a connection with New York.

"Are you happy, sweetheart?" he asked her.

"Yes, of course. Very." She leant over and kissed his cheek. "I almost wish we could have taken Laura up on her offer of New Year at the apartment, but it's just a bit too soon. Next year will be ok, I'm sure. The office will be open by then – won't it be great to be able to stay in Manhattan? Right in the heart of everything. I can just see us, having cocktail parties, overlooking that skyline. It's just such a perfect outcome."

"Yes, it is," he said, with no remorse. "Here's to next year." And they smiled at one another and toasted their future.

EPILOGUE

Righteousness? What is righteousness, really? A state of mind? A quality? A knowledge that one is morally correct? What she'd done was morally correct, even though it could be termed bad. So it was righteous. She stood a little straighter. A small movement. Yes, it was righteous. She was righteous.

"May the love of God and the peace of the Lord Jesus Christ console you and gently wipe every tear from your eyes. Amen."

"Amen," she repeated. Amen indeed.

"Mother!" she said, as they left the graveside, walking towards the gates. "Leave your hat off, for God's sake. You've lost it once already and you don't need it anymore."

"Don't be so rude, Laura!" the mother said to her daughter, under her breath, ignoring the request, as she struggled putting it back on.

Big, fat rain droplets began to splash on the tarmac as they walked. Umbrellas popped up. The black cars were waiting at the gate. The angels watched them, as the evergreen trees arced and bowed with the breeze. The clouds moved quickly, darkening the day and mocking the shadows of the tombstones.

Back in the apartment, she nodded at each person who gave condolences. "Thank you. Thank you. Yes, we will surely miss her."

She blinked. Evelyn deserved it. She had turned her grandfather against her. Made him hate her. Almost ruined her career before it even began.

She was by the fireplace, where it happened. Looking down, she noticed the stain in the carpet. She bristled. She hadn't realised it would be so... bloody. She thought it would just be bruising, or if there was blood, just a little. Oh, but it *gushed. It was horrifying. She had arrived deliberately early to pick a fight, as she and Amelia had planned.*

"Remember, get her angry," Amelia had whispered, before she went through to departures. "Make sure she hits her head. It's her weak spot."

Amelia had told her about the aneurism Evelyn had years ago that had weakened her. Told her how she'd stayed with her, stroking her hair, knowing it wasn't just alcohol. But anyway, it had been so easy. Easier than she could ever had imagined. She just lured her close to the fireplace, and when she was close enough for her head to hit the mantle, far away enough not to be able to save herself with an outstretched arm, a sharp, heavy punch across the face, before she knew what was happening, and wham! Her head struck the corner and made a cracking noise – she knew later that this was probably the moment her skull had fractured. Evelyn had uttered a gurgling whimper. The blood came straightaway, even out of her mouth, her ears. Before she left, she took of one of Evelyn's shoes, and wedged the toe under the corner of the Persian rug. It would look like she tripped. It wouldn't matter if her fingerprints were on the shoe, she had borrowed them lately. She and Evelyn were the same size and she often borrowed her things. She had left immediately after checking the woman had no pulse, but not without asking the doorman to check on her later that afternoon – "she looked a little pale..." she had told him.

"Thank you. Yes, we'll all miss her."

She bid farewell to the doorman, as she climbed in the limo.

"I'm going to the event alone because she's not well enough – I won't be coming back tonight."

"Thank you for coming. Help yourself to sandwiches, and there is tea and coffee in the kitchen."

It was very difficult to act so sad, when all she could do was look at the apartment and know it was finally hers. She looked at the skyline. It was raining hard now. It was beautiful. It made her feel lucky. She was so lucky. She could always claim self-defence – the woman had a history of violence – she hit Jack hard that time when the couple were visiting. Amelia had told her. She would vouch for her.

"Thank you, Mr Brown. Yes, she used to love this place. It's so beautiful, don't you think, even when it's raining?"

And now, it was to be her home. Amelia had promised to help her run the place financially, as long as she could have the use of it when she visited, which, by all accounts, was to be often. She was very thankful to Amelia. Owed her a lot. It would be fun when she visited – she was already looking forward to it.

"Poor you, losing your step-grandmother like that," said one of the guests, a man she didn't know. "I bet you're going to miss her real bad."

"Yes," she replied, "I will." She looked at the skyline, through the magnificent floor to ceiling windows. A pretty bunch of lily of the valley stood in a jug on the table, just in front. She sighed.

Amen, she said to herself. Amen indeed.

THE END